IMPOSSIBLE VIEWS
OF THE WORLD

This Large Print Book carries the
Seal of Approval of N.A.V.H.

IMPOSSIBLE VIEWS OF THE WORLD

LUCY IVES

THORNDIKE PRESS
A part of Gale, a Cengage Company

GALE
A Cengage Company

Farmington Hills, Mich • San Francisco • New York • Waterville, Maine
Meriden, Conn • Mason, Ohio • Chicago

LIBRARY OF CONGRESS CATALOGING-IN-PUBLICATION DATA

Names: Ives, Lucy, 1980– author.
Title: Impossible views of the world / by Lucy Ives.
Description: Waterville, Maine : Thorndike Press, a part of Gale, a Cengage
    Company 2017. | Series: Thorndike Press large print peer picks
Identifiers: LCCN 2017031179| ISBN 9781432844301 (hardback) | ISBN 143284430X
    (hardcover)
Subjects: LCSH: Large type books. | BISAC: FICTION / General. | FICTION / Literary. |
    FICTION / Contemporary Women.
Classification: LCC PS3609.V48 I48 2017b | DDC 813/.6—dc23
LC record available at https://lccn.loc.gov/2017031179

Published in 2017 by arrangement with Penguin Press, an imprint of Penguin Publishing, a division of Penguin Random House LLC

Printed in the United States of America
1 2 3 4 5 6 7 21 20 19 18 17

For my friends

■ ■ ■ ■

MONDAY

■ ■ ■ ■

1

The day Paul Coral vanished, it snowed.

It being week one of April, the sky supplied a slush of frozen gobs, pea-size hail.

I make it sound worse than it was, but in fact it was shitty. Emergency signage diverted me from the ground-floor staff entry up the museum's palatial front steps, for once not because of the perennial construction, but on account of a strike by security guards. It was a Monday, and this was the Central Museum's way of keeping costs down with whichever firm was temping. Limited permeability, etc. Probably unrelated, but no one had thought to put out any salt.

The guards had a fierce and litigious union. Their strike was of the French variety and likely to meet with results. They had stayed pointedly home, but other dissenters were present. A couple of diehards swaddled in tarps still protested WANSEE's plans for the Nevada aquifer. At week five, their foam board was deteriorating, but the gist was the shame of privatizing a natural good. I hiked by with a nod.

WANSEE was a Belgian corporation poised, if my Facebook feed was not entirely alarmist, to control a significant portion of the planet's groundwater. WANSEE was also supplying CeMArt with vital special exhibitions funding, a fact that would probably have kept me up at night had I not long ago abandoned all hope of an oligarch-free cultural landscape. As matters stood, I was indifferent to sleep, though for more personal reasons.

Above billowed a claret banner three stories high advertising the newest show bolstered by the Belgians' largesse, "Land of the Limner," with WANSEE'S sponsorship tagged in nice italics along the bottom. Stabilizing poles clanked like mad.

I breached the neoclassical façade and had my totes searched. I wore my museum ID at my collar for optimum motility, re: hands, burdens. A scab shined her penlight into my eyes.

I am not tall. In fact I am short, with highly regular features. I despise makeup, though I wear lipstick, and, to further frustrate my appearance, I smoke.

The security worker switched her light off and waved me through. I stepped into the cavernous atrium, enjoying the familiar rush of silence that meets Monday's ears and, more particularly, a whiff of senescent freesia, as stems were methodically plucked from a moribund display by a man in a yellow smock.

I would have just made my way to the department, but Marco Jensen, who worked the central desk, was already present, stocking pamphlets, from which labor he recused himself in order to wave me vividly over.

I swerved obediently, arranging my face into a pattern of delight.

Marco was like, "I want you to remain calm."

This was a signal. I did a discreet sweep of as much of the cathedral as possible. Marco appeared to do likewise, for that area which was behind my head. I leaned in.

Marco was vibrating in place, actually.

"What?"

Marco is at least eight years younger than me. He is from Malibu by way of Yale and is very easy to look at. "You know *Paul?*" Everyone in the museum knows Paul, but this was beside the point. "So, like, apparently" — Marco nudged the words out with care, in the process presenting me with

11

multiple views of his meticulously razed chin — "he's *missing.*"

"What?"

"Yup. Since late last week. Didn't show up for a certain meeting and isn't returning calls. Forget email."

"That's bizarre."

Marco smoothed back an errant slice of hair. "I take it you haven't heard from him?"

"Hey," I was saying, "I have to run." I paused. "I feel like we should really talk, I mean, that's so *intense.*"

"Completely." Marco was nonplussed.

"OK," I said. "Ciao."

I have modes of being that are less than elegant, and I have frequently used these to my advantage. On this particular morning, I assumed the demeanor of a roach on its way back to its nest through a lighted kitchen. By this I mean I kept my head down and shot up the main stairs, affecting I could perceive nothing that was not placed directly in front of my face.

You cannot help respecting a person who looks busy as fuck; at least, as long as you don't talk to them, you can't help respecting them. Being as extremely — relatively speaking, I mean, to most adults — petite as I am, I have found that others need little persuading that they either cannot see me or that I am not worth the effort.

At any rate, I did not encounter anyone before I gained the department's rear door, which is built into the wall paneling of one of the minor European galleries and looks more like another decorative aspect of the molding than it does actual ingress.

Paul Coral was almost a friend. Except I couldn't quite say that. He had worked at the museum for something like thirty years as the registrar of American Objects, and we had recently become kind of cordial or trusting or what have you. The odd thing about him, I should say, was that in all his time at CeMArt he seemed not to have *done* anything, by which I mean that it was extremely difficult to ascertain what exactly it was that he did. Most of his work, or the work that would have fallen to him by dint of his title, was accomplished by a parade of part-time minions and interns, with whom I had the dubious privilege of interacting by email. Paul's level of awareness of the work they did was difficult to gauge. He floated in and (mostly) out of his office, appearing to spend the lion's share of his working hours meditatively wandering the visible storage gallery and period rooms. One had the sense that he spent a great deal of

13

purposeless time in the museum's American sector. Perhaps he even slept there. I wondered, not very charitably, if anyone had checked the Dutch box-bed.

Anyway, I was feeling unnerved that I had lately begun to cultivate a modestly trusting relationship with this now "missing" person as I made my way to the study room, up the ramp that was at one point added to connect two poorly aligned but proximate floors, an error produced in hasty renovation, and then up the spiral stair, an improvement, legend has it, requested by a 1950s department head who resented any member of his staff's having to leave the warren in order to move between levels. I am currently unique among my colleagues in American Objects in that I am unable to slam my forehead against the upper treads, lacking requisite height.

It was now 8:05. This was a full seven minutes later than it should have been, for not only am I unfailingly punctual, I really do not like to make a big deal out of it, since I feel that this is not very comely in someone who holds what is for all intents and purposes an entry-level position, despite her doctorate, but this is simply the way things are at present, until the boomers disperse and perish, etc. I like to be early, is what I

14

am saying.

The lights in the study room were on. I thought an expletive.

"And *there* she is!" My arrival was heralded by a senior colleague, Bonnie Mangold, herself atypically on time. Bonnie was, in addition, the current "Miss Jean Brodie" of my existence, as my mother would have put it. I cringed, advanced.

I have, as people tend to do, known my mother all my life. However, my supposedly loving rapport with this parent rather too closely resembles my working relationship with Bonnie, in that it demands Herculean affective labor and produces Sisyphean rewards.

My mother's maiden name, which is also the name that she uses to conduct her day-to-day business, is Carolyn Wedgewood Basset. Her marriage to my father (who is deeply Polish and whose Philadelphian origins linger) is ongoing. I have his last name, Krakus, along with, what is less to be celebrated, his face.

I say this not because my father's face is so bad, but because my mother's face happens to be so unrelentingly good. She was born in the late 1940s but the face is still going strong. There is almost nothing about

15

her that you can separate from the face. Its great success is also hers.

I have seen pictures of her when she was in her early twenties, when she and my father first met, which seems, at any rate, like the historical moment at which the life of Caro, as she is commonly known to colleagues and other acquaintances (such as next of kin), begins. In these vintage images she is a fawn, a human Bambi. She is carrying a lunch tray in one splendid candid snap, and as she turns to the light both her eyes and mouth drop open. The face is heart shaped, the perfect mouth outlined in some lighter-than-natural mod lipstick, the eyes like two drawings of eyes and eyelashes, the balance between dark and milky white disturbing, exquisite. The corners of several accidentally bared teeth shine like Chiclets.

As a child, reared in the neurotic northern reaches of Manhattan's Upper East Side, I stared into an array of pictures like this one. These tokens of my mother's power were carelessly archived in a folder in a drawer, along with old invitations, postcards, pieces of wire and ribbon, washers, orphaned keys, and miscellaneous receipts related to maintenance of the household, which endeavor seemed to hinge mainly on furniture repair, dry cleaning of formal attire, and photo

16

processing.

My mother has not assiduously memorialized her astonishing youth. She is not so vain. At least, she isn't so vain in a predictable way, as someone with a face of this kind could probably be forgiven for being. My mother is a practitioner of a stealth vanity. And this means that she cultivates not herself but her environs. And these environs are understood to reflect, unfailingly and unceasingly, upon her.

Caro has been helped in her endeavor to create a loyal and unilaterally responsive local system and/or moatlike domestic economy by a certain commercial concern, by means of which she has related to, and profited from, the exterior world. This is her print dealership. It is named Basset's. It exists as a very taupe WordPress site as well as a narrow storefront on Madison near 79th Street, which also means that it is five minutes from my current place of employ. There is little I can do about this.

Basset's deals in late-eighteenth- and nineteenth-century prints and drawings, mostly northern European and Japanese. It has limited stock in: photographs, anything American, the twentieth century. Caro excuses Jasper Johns for some reason. Caro also walks to work. This is one of her stipulations. She travels four times a year. Her shoes are Ferragamo but her shirt-dresses Calvin Klein. She represents a mix of mutually inimical social philosophies whose ongoing roiling estuarial encounters are fairly well misted over by pretensions to aristocracy. Neither "Wedgewood" nor "Basset" is, as you may have already guessed, her real name. Far, far beneath, there once breathed someone named Mary Carol Lynch. As far as I can tell, no one currently living has ever met her.

"Mary" was the product of a single mother who was herself the product of a single mother. They lived near the naval base that makes up a significant part of San Diego. The difficulties of dating in the midst of unusual family circumstances in the decades after the Second World War led to alcoholism, anorexia, and psychopathy in my grandmother, if I have correctly interpreted Caro's koanlike sketches. Caro was therefore mostly raised by her grandmother, a chubby German mystic who had quickly survived her own much older husband, a minister. This grandmother, I have it fairly certainly even from limited photographic evidence, possessed the same preternaturally symmetrical facial features, eyes like velvet under glass, as Caro. My (thin, drunk, crazed) grandmother was merely interesting. At some point, in order to survive, my grandmother became her employer's mistress. Things were volatile, violent, and, again, from what I am able to ascertain, absurd.

Caro decamped and did not look back. She made no attempt to please. She had studied econ in college but, having learned of the existence of something called the history of art, somewhat haphazardly applied to Columbia for her master's and was, beginner's luck, accepted. She would have stayed the course for a doctorate had not, as she maintains, her dissertation advisor appropriated her topic (on the meaning of some of Degas's preparatory sketches) for his own hastily published article and eventual career-clinching book. Frowning upon theft and sloppy patriarchy, Caro determined to go into business for herself.

The corresponding name had a nearly simultaneous genesis: Caro was attempting to access some rare folio, perhaps in a halfhearted attempt to wreak intellectual revenge on the advisor, and had handed over her university ID and was slowly repeating her name to a male library employee, who was both caught in a challenging phone conversation and, as Caro puts it, "manically digging" through a stack of card-catalog drawers, one of which he managed to overturn on his desk, while (as I imagine) attempting to stare lasciviously at her. When her permission slip came back, the preoccupied librarian had erroneously recorded the borrowing party as one "Carolyn Wood Basset." Caro did not know what this appellation meant, but instead of hanging around for the folio, she added a "wedge" and called it a day. A few weeks later through a sensitive mutual acquaintance, a poet and vocalist named Arthur Garfunkel, whose corny advances Caro had neatly converted into friendship, she met my father.

Everything has been fine since. Caro had me accidentally a little late in life and treats me as a potentially pleasant extension of the juggernaut that she is. She does not know what to do about my face, which is squished if not totally unpleasant, sort of like the face of an affable cartoon pig. She does not know what to do with my mind, which is effective and undiscerning and very fast and sometimes given to drift. I am not so much like her.

When I was younger, there were a couple of different games it seemed to interest Caro to play. Of these, Caro's favorite was a kind of counterfeit adoption scenario. Caro would encourage me to befriend a certain attractive, poised girl who would be available to me by way of school. When this girl would come over to our house for some doll-related activity Caro would intervene, would speak to her, engage her. As time went on, Caro's interest would seem to deepen. I would see her alone with the girl, as I stood at some distance. I would look at Caro's smooth face, where inevitably there reigned an expression of magnificent satisfaction. As Caro came closer to me, usually to explain how the shared afternoon would now progress, now that *she* held the reins, her initial look of satisfaction would be replaced by a new enthusiasm, a desire to inform me of her own accomplishment. *Look how easy.* Look, Caro seemed to say, how easily I love.

2

In the study room, there were two people. There was of course my greeter and benefactor, Bonnie Mangold, illustrious departmental chair, celebrated by art historians on three continents. She was dressed, as usual, in layers and did not look angry. She looked, if anything, amused. She yawned and patted her mouth.

Bonnie had a habit of standing with her prosthetic left hand cradled in the nook of her right arm, by which I mean, with the hand tucked into the interior of her bent elbow. She gestured like a smoker with the right arm, tapping the tips of her fingers together for emphasis. She was imperious and overweight.

"Stella, honey," she said, because she is informal on all occasions, linguistically at least, "go have a look at the coffee."

I did not delay. I directed my steps toward the mini kitchen. The coffee, in its solitude, had exploded. It gasped forth its last quantities of steam. There was a long wretched drip of grounds and black water trailing from the machine's basket, and the counter was supporting a spreading puddle.

This was likely Bonnie's error. The Koffé-man was mechanically finicky as well as physically unbalanced and had to be propped up under one corner with a folded MetroCard I kept in our basket of orphan cutlery for this express purpose.

I walked slowly back to the study room. I wordlessly implored distance, against all odds, to maintain itself. The other person there was Fred.

At the moment, Fred was standing with his back to me. This afforded me a few seconds in which to make a catalog of his wardrobe. A perfectly pressed blue oxford, sharp as knives, was sheathed within an impeccable dove-gray merino V-neck. The wool slacks were charcoal, of a vaguely metrosexual but still classic enough cut and of such a quality material that though they sat rather revealingly across Fred's well set-up ass, the effect was of dissembled authority rather than promiscuity. I couldn't see much of his shoes, except that they were clean and black. He was imitating the way Bonnie held her arms, standing beside her, looking down

23

at something in front of them both, on the table.

I would not say that Fred, or Frederick, Lu was liked within the museum. Yet although he does not possess the Adonis good looks of someone like Marco, he was still widely considered the most handsome of our male associates. The strange thing, actually, was how little bearing his beauty had.

This is to say, Frederick Lu was not just aware of his own privilege; he had understood it, like, *aggressively.* Breeding sat about his person in the manner of an auratic glow, a protective coating. He was the unique product of a union between two of the wealthiest families in the city, the Lus (retail, imports, telecommunications) and the Weynmaarens (shipping, an array of "natural resources"), and truly one had to wonder what he was doing working at all. Indeed, in this sense Fred possessed quite a number of admirable qualities, especially from the point of view of that relatively plentiful museum-employee type, the eligible, educated girl.

I am drawing a certain distinction here. It's not that I myself was a total dog, as the expression goes, it's just that I had middling interest in sexual congress with any member [*sic*] of the institution. Though I know that

24

carefully placed flirtation is often essential to one's professional progress, I did not come to the Central Museum in order to escape the workforce. I liked having a job and wanted to continue having one for some time. At the moment, I didn't really have other plans, in fact. Which occurred to me as its own kind of problem, but more on this later.

The "girl" who works at the museum is very pretty and exceedingly neat. She is a fan of social networking in all its protean forms and not in an ironic way. She writes mildly dissimulated thank-you notes over email each morning, and on paper, more formally, probably a few times a week. She is creating a database that will be of use to her as she ages. Actually, she is so hypermotivated to create occasions for festive, conservative behavior that if this is the type of spouse you, cissexual male, seek, you really cannot go very far wrong with the genre you will encounter at the museum, as ours have exquisite taste, visually speaking, and your house will be an institution. I should also mention, in the case this was not sufficiently clear, that she is most traditional in that she will like you to support her, so please have (preferably), or have the ability to get, a lot of cash. You should enjoy shaving your face every day and be gone from your residence between the hours of 8:30 A.M. and 6:30 P.M. at a minimum of six days per week. Bonuses: your family is international; you own a ranch, farm, or series of cottages in a nonurban locale; you participate at an expert level in a sport that involves either the education of large animals or the execution of small ones; you are tall.

Usually she is in an internship and on her way to a master's. Occasionally, if she has not found a suitable mate within the window of two or three years that this method allows, she will begin her doctorate, but such cases, though tragic and actual, are happily quite rare. There is some overlap, I should note, between the museum and auction houses in this sense, though we like to believe we receive the choicer examples of this interesting, aspirational class.

And indeed the girls did like Fred. And Frederick Lu was not ashamed of liking them. But Fred was thirty-eight and unmarried, and he was already a full curator, holding an endowed post (the Thurston J. and Jeanne A. Prentiss Curator of American Decorative Arts) in American Objects, so apparently he had other stuff going on. I knew he was at least nominally unavailable on account of some other longstanding romantic allegiance. He had a fastidiously maintained patrician fade, a narrow white shock near his right ear, and his face looked a lot like Superman's, only more classically voluptuous. I now recall being told that once in Lu's earlier days he had dressed up as the Kryptonian American one Halloween. For a costume encourages comparison.

But Frederick Lu was known mostly for his early success. He must have been thirty-six or so when he got his current slot. This was before I began working at the museum. The rumor was that now he was being groomed for directorship of the entire place, the first promotion only a kind of necessary formality, as it were. I know this pissed Bonnie off, since she felt that if Nicola di Carboncino, the museum's long-suffering director, were to put his weight behind what she termed "a slightly more serious successor," the museum would have a real chance at keeping corporate inveighers at bay; in other words, we might stop serving as a kind of multipurpose banquet hall and conference center for our far too numerous J. Paul Gettys. Of course, the very fact of Frederick's heir apparency suggests that money was a consideration. I'm not sure if it hurt Bonnie's sense of her own importance, being so summarily passed over for the job, or if she disliked Fred for other, more personal reasons, since in any case it was well worth asking if the museum's director was not just a figurehead, a nominally empowered bureaucratic scapegoat onto whose shoulders blame might, as necessary, always be offloaded.

Bonnie appeared at the moment to be nodding.

I hazarded a cough.

Bonnie turned. "Stella, your coat."

Frederick Lu raised his face and acknowledged me without effecting eye contact.

I informed those assembled that coffee would be another two minutes.

"Great," said Bonnie. She made no move to integrate me into the on-going confab, so I left. I went and slung my coat around a hanger in the still mostly empty hall closet, carefully brushing any remaining wetness from it not so much out of concern for the garment but in order to distract myself. My hands were, as usual, trembling slightly. My pulse had quickened annoyingly and I could taste turmoil rising. But it would pass, I reminded myself. I took in several deep breaths through the nose then folded myself into the department's tiny bathroom and spent a few minutes patting down my hair and examining my face. My hair is cut short and, because it is thick and has waves, forms a triangular frame for my features. It's yellow, a dark blond without very much brunette in it. I tapped it at its edges, along the bottom, *tap tap tap.* I nudged it in hopes of additional volume.

I looked astonished. My eyebrows had migrated up my head and seemed unwilling to return to their normal place of pasture. My eyes were way too large. They appeared, if this is possible, *independently* scandalized. My mouth was crooked. It was always like this.

In the kitchenette, meanwhile, coffee had successfully precipitated. This at least was good. I transferred the beverage to an ancient beaker-shaped thermos. I procured a clean enough mug for myself and poured. I squatted and obtained milk from the mini-fridge. Then I made my way to my rightful domain, a closetlike office next to the miniature bathroom.

As I was setting my coffee down, the landline rang. I answered and Bonnie said, "Could you step into my office, please?" I asked did she want a coffee. She informed me that this was partly what she had meant, though not entirely unkindly.

I hung up and froze, wondering, for what was by then approaching the eight- or nine-hundredth time, whether or not Bonnie Mangold was aware that Frederick Lu and I had slept together.

3

"So," Bonnie said, "how goes it?"

It was as if she had just undergone some long cosmetic ordeal, a highly irritating but non-life-threatening procedure. She was lounging in the tall leather chair that abutted her marble-topped desk.

This office was always a cave. It faced out onto an airshaft, so despite its windows was ever dim, even on days of unmitigated sun. Bookshelves were recessed into all available wall space and contained leather-spined volumes and beribboned folios in varying states of decay. Bonnie's own prolific output was stacked and gathering dust at one end of a caged radiator that otherwise at all times supported several examples of her personal collection of bioephemera. On this particular day, two five-inch ivory anatomical Venuses were displayed beside their respective tiny wooden storage coffins. The figurines, probably of eighteenth-century origin and almost certainly valuable, lay with their bellies open. Removable stomachs and other detailed organic bits and pieces sat in a small white dish between them.

Bonnie's first love is anatomical drawings and engravings. She is good because although she really focuses on the Enlightenment, she has plenty to say concerning the transatlantic furniture trade and the importation of luxury goods into American interiors. She also knows an obscene amount about camerae obscurae and other mechanical drawing devices and their early employ in the British colonies.

She noted my wandering eye.

"They're copies," she noted, "of course. Plastic. One is for my niece. I ordered them from Munich a few months ago, but they took forever. I, actually" — she performed this lopsided smile — "well, I was looking for a birthday present for you. I hope you don't mind my playing with them." Bonnie laughed and reached down with her good hand to open a drawer in her desk not visible to me. "I did have the boxes around here somewhere."

I hastened to reassure her that she did not need to go to the trouble.

She sat up again, arranging herself. Her

prosthetic hand was visible, the color of Silly Putty.

I began to thank her.

She interrupted. "Coffee?" She meant, where was it.

I was still holding the teacup wrapped in both hands. I corrected my oversight.

Bonnie accepted with her right, immediately sipping. "It's warm."

I nodded.

"Sit," she said. She pointed with her prosthesis to a high-backed chair to my right. A needlepoint of a bald eagle, wings spread, was stretched across the seat, secured by brass tacks.

"Thank you, Bonnie," I repeated.

She blinked at me over the rim of the teacup. "Actually," she was saying, "I may be in need of your expertise."

I seated myself with legs crossed. I gazed covetously at Bonnie's coffee.

"Look," she said, "let me keep this brief. We may have a very small emergency. Or, we may have a small *need* at the moment." Here she had some more coffee. "I really don't know about Fred sometimes. He behaves so strangely it's difficult to ask him for advice. He's the most considerate being who ever walked the planet one moment, and then the next you're not sure whether

33

he remembers your name."

She studied me, and I nodded.

Bonnie smiled. "Forget what I just said! I think, at any rate, on this point he and I are finally agreed. You will drop what you are doing for the day today and complete the checklist for the show." She considered my face. "It's not done. I mean, I have no way of knowing where or in what state it is. It's practically comical. Paul . . ." she trailed off. "Paul would have attended to this, at least, I'm sure. I, well, I'd say go get on his computer and see what you can do. We need the text by four. Ozen should have sent you images by now."

It's not that I disliked Bonnie, by the way. I admired her. It was just, as with all relatively forceful individuals, one had to expend a certain amount of energy getting out of her way. I desperately wanted better intel regarding Paul, but I couldn't determine whether this was the time to bring up the matter of his personal fate, which here seemed to be regarded mainly as a logistical inconvenience.

The problem was that I didn't say anything.

The sparkle fled Bonnie's eye. "Unless, of course, this doesn't *interest* you." She blinked.

"No," I swore, unsure what "this" was. Though, for example, the anatomical Venus was not what I would have chosen for myself, a weird gift was still a gift, and I needed to make sure she knew that I understood that. Of course, the bigger problem at this point was digging up a plausible referent for her incredibly brief disquisition on the fortunes of Paul. In other words, how to appear enthusiastic but also completely and very politely disinterested.

"Good," Bonnie was already saying. She set her cup down.

"Oh, good," I repeated.

Bonnie leaned across her desk to pass me a violet Post-it. "I had the techie people reset his password first thing. You should have access to anything associated with his account. I don't know how forensic this is going to get, but again" — here implementing strong eye contact — "it's an emergency."

"Right," I said.

"We're attempting to be respectful. It's been a very long road."

"Of course," I told her.

"You already know what I mean. And I think you, Stella, with your strong sense for spatial, uh, discontinuities, with your knack for research, can just kind of plow through this pronto, if my instincts are correct, and it will be behind us."

"Sure," I said.

"Great."

I took the note.

At this moment there was a knock on the door. Bonnie rose and for some reason silently made motions indicating I should dissimulate the paper displaying Paul's Ce-MID and brand-new password, "PASS-WORD."

"Come in," Bonnie trilled.

The door was nudged a crack.

It was Ozen, the conservator, with a tale of sorrow. "I'm so sorry to bother you, Bonnie, but I think I'm having some trouble with those pictures you so kindly sent? Because I am not sure what you mean by D-I-M-S, which I had looked up online, and though I know it's certainly related, we are of course short on time, and so I wanted to check in with you as soon as possible."

"Uh, how soon is soon?" Bonnie said/asked, attempting to gauge remotely the level of Ozen's distress and/or incompetence.

I smiled at Ozen. Ozen did not smile in turn.

"I think by, like, middle of the day?"

"Well, all right!" Bonnie was making a sort

of hand-washing gesture in midair above the surface of her desk.

Ozen nodded. Her features slackened into an expression of fealty and obvious relief. Ozen is Turkish and willowy, a specialist in the restoration of tempera, mixed oil and tempera, as well as strategies around natural resin and glair glazing. She was originally a student of the Byzantine icon, and her international status seems like someone's muffled admission of American Objects' baleful inability to staff itself at all diversely — specializing, as it does, in the possessions of very dead and very rich white individuals of mostly British descent. I don't entirely dislike Ozen, but neither am I an avid fan. When she nods, her head moves fully down and then up again, so that the crown of her hair is visible. I find this freakishly inefficient. She is beautiful and thirty-two, engaged to the tune of what appear to be four carats, earnest in the extreme.

Bonnie rewarded Ozen's acquiescence with a brilliant grin that migrated alchemically across the space between them and reappeared on the girl's own face.

Showing signs of elation, Ozen bid us adieu and went off to reapply herself to Preview.

"She's so lovely," Bonnie told me.

"I really don't know her," I replied.

Our mutual derision pleased Bonnie, and she chuckled, shaking her head. She had opened a drawer in her desk and was now ignoring me, indicating that it was time for me to leave.

I should note that I am what is termed a cartographic specialist in the art history world — and a dilettante in the world of cartographers. In truth, I should probably describe myself as a "nineteenth-century generalist." My dissertation was on late-eighteenth- and early-nineteenth-century political cartoons in America and France, and I therefore have some familiarity with contemporary maps, because of their frequent use to satirical ends. However, this is not to say that I understand either geography or schematics in any deep or intuitive way. I've done a few analyses of cartographic personifications (e.g., an obese nincompoop covered in leeches who is supposed to symbolize the empire of Britannia), but here my expertise begins or ends.

All the effort I put in during the course of my doctorate is mostly of avail to me these days in that it has made me hyperliterate in Microsoft Office and empowered me to compose a reasonably polite email in under three minutes. Every month or so I'll go back and reread my one published article, "Importing 'The Curious Zebra': Some Notes on Meaning and Ambiguity in Satiric Depictions of America, 1780–1800," hoping to revive some of my former critical rigor.

This was, at any rate, what Bonnie had been referring to, re: "spatial" skillz, re: what it was I was meant to be doing, re: patching up "Land of the Limner" 's nonexistent checklist of works to be exhibited. Her vague language points up not just my junior status but a more general uncertainty regarding what it is that can be done with me professionally, not to mention what it is that I should be leaning in, or whatever, *toward*. For due to funding constraints as well as certain conventions of departmental hierarchy, it will be impossible for me to obtain a promotion at my current place of employ for at least another eight years, barring (in)voluntary exoduses or unforeseen tragedy.

And here is the other thing one must be aware of, as far as the institution is concerned. Persons with authority are always looking for ways to increase the utility of their own command: What they would most like you to do at all times is to be an additional and, what is more important, ideally obedient pair of hands. Along with this nonoptional fealty comes the demand that your passivity in relation to them be a display that, while heartfelt, is at base just that. Once they are safely retired, you are expected to come into your own as an intransigent and scruple-free beast, at which point you may select your own toadies.

For Bonnie, there is a kind of extra truth to the hands metaphor, which point I won't belabor, except to say that her need of others was probably, in the end, what made her such a star. You have to be like this, somehow. You simply cannot be self-sufficient and have this job. It does not work like that.

From what I understand, Bonnie lost her hand when she was an adolescent, maybe eleven years of age. She is not the one who told me this story, so it is possibly apocryphal, certainly part of the lore that surrounds her. It was a hunting accident. She was somewhere remote with her father, northern California or Washington State. He was some kind of heir/environmentalist. I had never heard of him, Konrad Mangold, but I guess he had written an early essay on pop ecology that showed up in *Playboy* and was a big deal at the time. It was the late fifties. The legend is that he would take

Bonnie out with him into the country, and they would live off the land. You're supposed to imagine that they had a Land Rover and a smartly kitted cabin that used to belong to a senator, that Konrad took field notes in watercolor, killed and cured his own venison, read the stars. But, to make a long story short, Konrad shot off four of the fingers on Bonnie's left hand one blazing July noon, and because they were at such a remove from modern medicine, Konrad decided on a genre of field dressing he claimed had been engineered in the Black Forest in the first weeks of spring 1945, a glorified tourniquet no doubt, since when they were at last able to access a professional, the whole hand had to go.

It is from this strange event, as I have perhaps already suggested, that all of Bonnie's power comes. The guilt of a wealthy, virile dad was subsequently manipulated by young Bonnie, and I do not think that she has stopped getting what she wants since. It is not worth nothing to have had an early loss like this, to have thought unflinchingly through it.

4

Fred's latest show title, "Land of the Limner," dredged up an anachronistic term and broadcast it worldwide, pretty much sans context. I was not sure how much I admired this plan. I was in possession of a pretty carefully cultivated fear of the public's uncooperativeness, but my trepidation was not always shared by the more entitled of my colleagues. It was, at any rate, Fred's baby and therefore inviolable.

The word limner has a weird pre-American history: Derived from Middle English *limnur,* indicating in the fourteenth century an illuminator of manuscripts, it came, in the sixteenth century, to be associated with the production of watercolor-on-vellum miniatures, which was strictly a leisure activity and nobody's job. By the 1570s, limnings were a popular form of recreational portraiture in England, exempt from the control of the guild of the Painter-

Stainers Company because of their association with nonprofessional image making, i.e., rich people's fun. Limnings, as miniature portraits, showed up in the colonies of New England before the invention of the mezzotint engraving technique and so were one of the only formats for the transatlantic transmission of portraiture for imitation and reproduction by incompetent Americans. Limnings were obsessive little things. They emphasized particulars of costume and facial features, contributing to the development of early New England's cramped portrait styles and a sense of what painted faces should look like, i.e., heinous.

When the word came at last to refer to an actual American painter, a limner, it indicated an itinerant artist who was self-taught. Limners produced works characterized by flatness and fields of bright or otherwise unmixed color. The appearance of flatness was not solely due to an inability on the part of the artist to employ perspective and modeling but also to the origin of the image, in part or in sum, as a preexisting print, usually an engraving of some kind, or, later, a photograph. The limner moved from town to town, making portraits of adults, children, and sometimes pets. The work was commercial and not always strictly defined.

Limners were aligned with (and sometimes did the same things as) decorative painters, engravers, carriage painters, sign painters, cabinetmakers, glazers, brush makers, painters of floor cloths, and inventors, among other freelancers. Limners necessarily advertised in local newspapers, therefore, offering their varied services, sometimes along with a promise to refund clients not entirely satisfied with the likeness produced.

Anyway, it was to the creation of a definitive list of paintings that would be exhibited in this show, of the limner and his "Land," that I had been dispatched. Already out with respect to the window were concerns about Paul Coral's privacy, professional and otherwise, plus any consideration regarding how he might feel about me doing what was, for all intents and purposes, still his job. I wanted to laugh a little. Additionally, no one seemed to care whether or not I understood *why* I was doing what I was about to be doing, which was sort of priceless. Evidently, it was assumed that my fealty to the department was such that I either already knew what was up due to grapevine machinations (true) or was not concerned, thanks to unconditional devotion. I arrived at the door to Paul Coral's office. It was unlocked.

I proceeded to do my job. I ensconced myself in Paul's peeling midcentury Naugahyde lounger. I fired up his PC. I collected pertinent dimensions, materials, and provenance for a list of some forty works, beginning with the stiffly blushing maidens favored by patroon limners who sold their services to Dutch ranchers of New York in the eighteenth century, passing through the paradisiacal imaginings of photographer and full-time Christian fantasist Erastus Salisbury Field, and concluding with the advent of modernism. I threw this shit together in Word, resized Ozen's images for her, dropped them in, then printed to PDF. I composed a measured email to Bonnie and scheduled it, document attached, to be delivered at 3:16 P.M.

Then I did a lot of other things. Upon entry to the office I had promptly locked the door. Though it was the case that this gesture on my part was likely to arouse suspicion in anyone attempting to enter the space suddenly, I could always chalk up my gesture to accident, claim ignorance of the way in which Paul's doorknob functioned, burst into tears. I could present myself as harried and visibly shaken by the intrusion. I could express annoyance and behave in a distracted manner. I was meanwhile copying the contents of Paul's account onto a thumb drive.

And not only this: I knew that I did not have time to go through Paul's filing cabinets. But to tell the truth I was not overly concerned with the deep history of Paul Coral's career. What I wanted to understand was the contemporary era. I wanted to understand why Paul was, so obviously and very nearly loudly, doing nothing at all, all the time. Because what this indicated to me was that Paul Coral was in fact doing something else, and that he was doing *a lot* of something else, and that all of his efforts to appear un- or underoccupied were actually a way of hiding in plain sight, as it were, his real business.

I did allow myself to go through the top drawers in his desk. There was not so much here: a dried sprig of lilac, a nickel, and a yellow pebble. Well, and there was also a plastic lanyard to which was attached a ring of three keys. I might have pondered this act, but for some reason history and the laws of physics conspired to render events such that I did not ponder this act. I simply removed the keys from the back of the metal drawer and placed them in my pocket. This was how it happened.

And there was something else. There was

a piece of paper floating loose in the shallow central top drawer of the desk, the space normally reserved for pens. This piece of paper had been folded into a smaller square and then unfolded and refolded multiple times, as if someone had been in the habit of carrying it around in the breast pocket of his shirt. It was an image, on a legal-size sheet of paper. It was in the drawer facedown and so I extracted it, turned it over. In an eerie echo of Bonnie's earlier citation of my so-called skills, it was a xeroxed reproduction of an image of a map.

It was also one of the more astonishing images I have ever seen.

This map, titled "ELYSIA" in an intricately linked script, showed a township near a river. I studied it. It had not been drawn up by someone whose exclusive business was the making of maps, as evidenced by the extreme, one might say exquisite, detail of the forest areas outlining the town. These wilds were portrayed not from overhead but from the side, seen as by someone on the ground, trunks beneath a full canopy. Birds no bigger than the heads of pins flitted here and there, and quadrupeds cavorted amiably.

But the author's true skill was revealed in the image of the town itself. Its buildings were small, hutlike, and precious. The structures were all similar, but each was exquisitely unique, with peaked roofs and elaborately carved, domed doorways, frilled window frames fitted with leaded glass. What appeared to be glittering mirrors, crystals, diamonds, or some other type of decorative article were fixed in numerous surfaces and dangled from the buildings' winsome eaves. A select number of arteries, passing between and among the varied lots, had minute names in a fine script I could just make out: *Metzotinto In., Landskip In., Frieze strt., Fret-Work brdr., Stair way.* In the adjacent waters the words *The River Hudson* had been inscribed in curling italic characters as supple as wet black hairs. Pointillist waves flexed decoratively alongside.

"It might be the work of a silversmith," I muttered, speaking aloud for the first time in several hours. I was squinting to read what looked to be a poem. This text was contained in a sort of ornamental lozenge bordered with pleated ribbons and tiny seashells, indicating the author's lingering interest in the rococo revival contemporary with the nation's secession from England.

I selected a rectangular magnifying glass from a coffee can containing pens, etc., on

48

Paul's desk and switched on its small recessed light.

> Where is this paradise you seek,
> A place where no one mourns,
> And nothing irreplaceable is lost,
> And nothing lost is irretrievable?
>
> Where is this paradise you seek,
> With tears dry and wrongs righted,
> Where nothing that occurs in dreams
> Knows human fear or cruelty?
>
> Where is this paradise you seek,
> Dear seeker, careful one, lover of the
>   world?
> Where is this paradise you seek?
> Where is this blessed Elysia?

I switched off the magnifier and gazed again
across the surface of the reproduction. The
town was an eerie item, a hermetic shape
hewn from the wilderness or perhaps simply
discovered there, once all the trees had been
razed, like a divine brand or promissory seal
set down on a bald patch of Eden.

I swallowed, blinked. I was, for some
reason, having a sort of feeling. I was
becoming supremely, lustrously psyched. I
didn't know what this thing was, or why

Paul had it, or what any of this meant. But the map was stirring and peculiar. It was abnormal and naïve. And it appeared to be very, very good. This meticulous image might even have been created for the sole purpose of visual seduction. Exhibit one: I, an expert in American graphics, was well in its thrall. And I thought through the poem again, tried to listen to the tinny, phantom music, muttering, "Dear seeker, careful one, lover of the world . . ." I shut my eyes. I wanted to walk around inside this picture.

As with all moments of intense temptation, I went rapidly on to be completely blind to both my own brazenness and my own wish. In a quick snatching movement, I had folded up the photocopy and slipped it, of all places, into my bra. Why dawdle? Anyway, it was something like four P.M. and I hadn't eaten anything plus I still had a whole day's worth of email to attend to.

By six P.M. it was clear that I was not going to succeed in getting my act together on this particular day. I was at my desk and the emails were piling up unattended. Letting certain recent major errors stand, I was now privately obsessing over a minor one, which is to say my seizure of the map. My initial pronouncement that the map might have been engraved by a silversmith was based on nothing more than the likeness of the overwrought script used for the map's title to a certain script one sees on hollowware of the period. Really there was no reason to assume that the individual who had engraved the plate that had produced the map of Elysia was a silversmith. Certainly he was not a mapmaker, that much was clear, but he (and I do regret the historical facts that force me to assure you that "he" was indubitably a *he*) knew his way around an etching after a fashion that made me think that he must have been academically trained, which is to say, in Europe.

Most works of this period are pretty predictable. And what was catching my eye here wasn't accuracy but rather detail. The delineation of shadow and the dappling of shadow on the miniature forest floor, which one could just perceive at the wood's fringe, were spectacular. Deer and rabbits surprised in the midst of their grazing looked up, tiny fringed ears erect. Leopards pranced behind narrow trunks — how they had arrived on the North American continent in time for the creation of this chart, I did not know. Grapes dangled invitingly. To be fair, the Dionysian park was not really very American at all, though there was the occasional pheasantlike fowl spreading its tail feathers, and beaver likewise shared the peaceable kingdom. There were beasts in excess and some that had never existed. In one hollow, a winged snake made its nest in an intricate basket of scavenged twigs.

I obsessed over the minuscule scenes, caressed the xerox, smelled and very nearly licked it. There was one grotto, dim and even more difficult to make out than the rest, in which I thought one could spy two human forms, pale and entangled in embrace, but this might just have been an error of the stylus, toying with my curious eye.

I would likely have continued in this vein for several hours more had there not been a blunt banging sound indicating that Bonnie was employing her left hand to knock at my door and that I therefore had approximately three seconds to slap my MacBook down over the map, no doubt jeopardizing its vulnerable hard drive.

Bonnie let herself in and announced that she was not displeased with my work. Evidently, she had received my email. She informed me that if I had meaningful research to do this week, then she hoped I'd cut myself some slack and get to it.

I think, by the way, that this is what many people long for, generally speaking, in a boss. Or a mentor. I guess "long" is probably too strong a verb, but, then, I was quite happy. I even did a little affective jig, beamed up at her, such was the collegial mood.

"And this is what you'll be wearing tonight for the gala?" She was looking me up and down where I sat. I should note, too, that the longer she remained in my office, the freer Bonnie seemed to feel to forget our not entirely unfriendly moments of yore. She was hovering, now scanning the stacks of maniacally annotated academic articles on my shelves.

"Oh shoot!" I said. I tried to laugh it off. "I've been so *blindsided* by these developments . . ." I made no effort to complete the sentence.

Bonnie let this outburst lie where it had ignominiously fallen. "Well, I hope you have a date."

There was something else pissing Bonnie off, but it wasn't going to be possible to know what that was, that much was written on the wall.

"Sure," I informed her.

Bonnie performed a curt smile for my benefit. If I hadn't known her better, I would have said that she was privately enduring some sort of mental torment. "See you downstairs."

She disappeared, leaving in her wake an open door, which I rose to softly close.

Sometimes it is best to assume that one is not the unique cause of others' anger and/or unease. I will not say that it is always best to make such assumptions, but under normal circumstances one can generally decide that the unhappiness of others is due to effects independent of, and likely unknowable to, oneself.

With this in mind, I distracted myself by researching the underwriter of the gala I was about to attend, ready or not. In the bathroom, I consulted Wikipedia on my phone while I changed into something less comfortable. I had time for two numbing grafs:

GDF WANSEE is a leading Belgian-based multinational corporation headquartered near Brussels,[1] with operations in water, water treatment and desalination, and waste management. In the early 2000s WANSEE also encompassed American telecommunications assets, but has since divested these.[2]

History[edit]

WANSEE is one of the world's oldest continuously operated multinational corporations. Traceable to the 1822 founding of the <u>Algemeene Nederlandsche Maatschappij ter begunstiging van de volksvlijt</u> (literally: General Dutch Company for the privileging of people's industry) by <u>King William I</u>, WANSEE emerged when, in 1859, a branch of the Dutch consortium joined the French- and Egyptian-controlled <u>Canal Company</u>, or Compagnie universelle du canal maritime égyptienne.[3] Its current name comes from involvement of the shipping corporation <u>Van Der See BV</u>.[4] It is thought that GDF WANSEE's long service is due to its remarkable prescience with respect to international <u>water crises</u>.

" 'Prescience with respect to,' " I said to no one in particular. "Ha!" *Engineering of* was more likely. But WANSEE's success was also apparently due to its ability to distract detractors with social occasions and I was (a) talking to myself and (b) about to be late to this evening's circus.

I privately, to myself, called the look I had on my "late sixties look." It wasn't a particularly inspired choice of meme, but there's something about dressing slightly conservatively when you're actually not that made me think it worked for me. I had been told that the garment I had on was a sheath dress. The neckline did a certain thing. I was also wearing a pair of low YSL heels from about 1991 and was carrying a black envelope clutch (basically unidentifiable, designer-wise) from Forever 21. I descended, *sola,* to the lobby.

And I was more than ready, in spite of what I had said to Bonnie, to attend this evening's event alone. Which was why I was rather confused by the sight of a formerly close acquaintance, who was now no longer such a friend, and who, upon espying me, became not so much happy as nearly frenzied with weird delight. This person was my husband, Whitaker.

And when Whit saw me, he did this thing he does where he shows the bottoms of his top teeth and, like, instinctively reaches up to loosen his tie. I staved off unreserved rage by imagining insipid notions that might occur to him, like "the milky hemispheres of her bosom," as I approached. He wasn't, I should explain, supposed to be here. According to the separation agreement, my soon-to-be former husband wasn't supposed to be anywhere near me, but legally we were still hitched and so I couldn't pretend that I did not know who he was, particularly since he had lately fucked with me more violently and absurdly than I had previously believed humanly possible.

"Hey, babe," he actually said. In this moment, I realized that he was not here by accident nor was he on some unfathomable networking mission. His suit was navy and Italian, his tie red. He is not ugly, exactly, but has this slightly gerbil-y face. Our ten-year wedding anniversary was just five weeks off and I was praying that Whit would be merciful enough to sign divorce papers before that day.

"What," I said, by way of preemption, "are you doing here?" I may have included "the fuck" in this phrase. It was very difficult for me to determine what exactly I was saying at all, so loudly was the blood clanging in my ears.

"You look fantastic," Whit told me, psychotically unfazed. He added, ambiguous creep that he was, "And *so* young."

The lobby was filling with swells, and a string quartet struck up some Mozart. I had not explained a great deal about my separation from Whitaker A. Ghiscolmb, to whom I had basically been wed since childhood, around the museum. My reticence was due less to anger or shame than to a sense that these events were beyond trivial. His unbid-

57

den appearance tonight was, on this count as well as many others, incredibly inconvenient. I had lied to Bonnie, I now recalled in horror, because I did not in fact have a date, and if she were to see me tonight in the crowd with my present interlocutor there would be hell to pay. As, additionally and even more depressingly, just because I hadn't talked about the breakup at length didn't mean that everyone in the museum did not know, in documentary detail, what had happened.

I squirmed. Fur coats were being flung down on a folding table to my right. I was beginning to hope that one of them might possibly be enchanted and, if I were to crawl inside it, would helpfully transport me to an alternate dimension.

"What are you doing here?" I repeated.

Whit shrugged. "You think no one invites me to parties? You should have seen the invite for this one. Pretty snazzy!"

"I'm serious," I told him. "I think you should leave."

"Well, I want to talk. It hasn't exactly been easy to reach you."

I had blocked Whit's electronically communicated self on every device, platform, and service I made use of. I said, "True!"

"Ouch."

I pondered the possibility that some aspect of "Whitaker A. Ghiscolmb, Esq." 's personality had come unstuck from his legal name and/or professional identity and considered itself freshly at liberty and available to evil this evening, what I believe the experts like to call a "psychic break." I squinted at him, trying to remember when last it was this legal eagle and I had been pals. He seemed cold to me and somehow drowsy at the same time. He kept pursing his lips and then smiling. He was contemplative, that was the word for it, and really it was odd.

Whit said, "What, you're going to turn down an evening with one of 2014's most versatile tort litigators under forty-five, according to fidigest dot com?"

Because I had no idea what to reply, and because it felt like part of my brain had just caught fire, I turned and started walking briskly away from him into the Egyptian wing. I knew he was coming after me, but at least I was putting multiple meters of marble tiling between us and other humans.

"Look" — Whit suddenly had my elbow from behind and was directing me into an alcove behind a fragmentary Hatshepsut — "if this is about *her,* then I'm sorry. OK? I really can't help it if I have a type! I'm still attracted to you, Stella. You know?" He had placed his body, screen-wise, between me and the as yet light parade of perfumed and well-combed invitees, and now he yanked my dress expertly up and placed his hand on my inner thigh.

The novel sensation of his erection against my hip bone distracted me, it's true.

5

When Whit makes reference to *"her,"* he is referring to a woman named Estelle Dooskin. And when I say he and I were married as children, I mean that I got married to him the summer when we were twenty-five, two months before I started my doctorate. As is traditional in my family, this took place under the aegis if not auspices of Columbia University, where Whit and I had met as freshmen. And I was in love with Whit Ghiscolmb in a way that made me feel I was doing a logical thing, because when you are in love with someone in this way you are going to spend the rest of your life loving them, which proposition still holds some unfortunate veracity for me.

Whit once prank-called a professor I felt had slighted me during my orals and pretended to be a concerned museum-going dermatologist, detaining the scholar on the phone for two hours one night discussing the finer details of rosacea in Titian and the more general biology of blushing on and around the human ass. He picked me daisies from store window boxes and stole carnations from diners. He drew me cards in crayon and ballpoint on my birthdays and holidays, inscribed with promises to love me all my life. (These cards usually sported likenesses of hilariously deformed walruses and kittens.) Our couch had multiple, unnoticeable pee stains on it, he made me laugh so hard.

But somewhere in the midst of what seemed to me a literally incredible store of good fortune, Whit was secretly pondering my disinterest in bearing children and finding that it disagreed with him. He wanted, as he began informing me just before he passed out from yet another survival-agnostic drinking bout, something he called "a wife," someone who would "be supportive."

Because it was then my custom to work as many as sixty hours a week outside the domestic sphere, and because we were already married, I ignored him. And I ignored him because I in fact knew, when he said such things, exactly what he meant: that he was privately envisioning his parents' hallowed suburban partnership, their teenage wedding in the early seventies, his father's extrovert career first in litigation then in local politics, his mother's charmed trajectory from high school coed to home-maker to part-time librarian, the manor outside Stamford and their Maine escape, his four identically gerbiloid siblings. I ignored him because I could not believe that he wanted any of these so-called comforts — what I as a child of outsider Yuppies perceived as the wages of white privilege and cronyism — for himself, even as he was obsessively wanting them, pining after them, numbing his pain at the lack of them with tallboys and processed meat. I ignored him because Whit had read his Zinn and listened to his de la Rocha and for a while wrote ac-complished opinion pieces denouncing American historical amnesia for an under-grad review. I ignored Whit because Whit loved complexity and tolerated identity politics; because he loved me for my mind, which was complex, and I believed he wanted this complex mind to flourish in the cutthroat milieu into which I, Stella Krakus, had been, for better or worse, launched.

But Whit no longer gave a damn about complexity, and the only way he was capable of caring for me or my identity was by leav-ing me in as slow and humiliating a fashion as his pickled brain could devise. It's also possible that I ignored him because I simply did not care enough, at this point, what he thought or wanted, living with him sucked so hard.

And there was something else. It was year 7.5 of our marriage, and I had been at CeMArt for about six months. A group of previously unseen early Fraktur bookplates had come up at auction, and though German folk drawings are not my specialty, I felt that these represented a body of work the department's collection might usefully absorb. Anyhow, if I were eventually going to be recognized as an authority in Early American works on paper, this was kind of *the* acquisition it was going to make sense for me to make as junior staff. Frederick Lu agreed with me, at least as far as the drawings were concerned (who knows how he felt about me personally at this stage) and negotiated the necessary funds. We had lunch a couple of times, met with a few patrons together, and I got to know his face, how the corners of his eyes tensed during mental processing, how he sometimes liked to laugh in a natural, almost human manner once he was done with business. It was clear to me, too, that even if it might be going too far to say that he "saw something" in me, as the expression goes, he was relieved or refreshed or mildly enlivened to know that I was the hire made. I did not bore him as a possible future head of the Department of American Objects, and that deficit of boredom was the kind of deficit into which it did not entirely displease him to gaze.

And gaze he did. At length. And our discussions began to encompass more general departmental operations, not just the Fraktur acquisition. Fred sometimes sought my advice. One afternoon we found ourselves feeding ducks together. It was odd. I began thinking about him on the weekends. I wrote him a note whenever he shared a point of view in a larger meeting to let him know what I thought of what he'd said. He expressed gratitude. He started coming to see me very briefly each day. He'd hover just beyond my open door. He smiled.

I had simultaneously started seeing less and less of Whit although I lived and slept and ate with him. Around Whit I sometimes felt as if I were wrapped in invisible cotton batting, a body condom of some psychic sort. And though I believed that Whit was the partner of my life and though I was gainfully employed and though I had every material comfort, I was having difficulty seeing my future. One night, at the close of a particularly bitter tussle over the lack of groceries in the house, Whit had exclaimed, "We're not even having kids!" and went on to smash a container of cottage cheese with his fist. I do not remember what this was apropos of, but the phrase stuck with me. It was very odd, not the sort of observation Whit had previously leveled, since, as I noted, it was not so much a criticism of me, in particular, as of the both of us, together. And this — if not the dried cheese flecks, lingering in local crevices over the months — made it seem like it had come out of someone else's mouth. Not that it wasn't Whit who was saying this line, but that he had heard it somewhere else first and was relaying the sentiment to me, who was here a mere secondary interlocutor as far as my husband was concerned, another item of furniture in a residence he'd ceased to cherish.

I was lonely. I was also a little ashamed, if I am honest, of Whit, who as far as I knew had not read a book that was not a work of sports history in more than thirty-six months. He was taciturn at receptions and parties, frowning, flushed, impatient. He seemed at times exceedingly reluctant to spend time with me.

I watched Frederick Lu. A server at a restaurant one afternoon leaned over, after Fred had excused himself, and told me, unasked, "You know, that man really likes you." Others elsewhere also seemed to indicate that this was indeed the case. And it felt plentiful, this liking, but also totally useless, because I was partnered for life and that was what I wanted, to be partnered for life. Not to mention that Fred had presumably had experiences of this nature before and was now having one of these experiences again and that was the long and the short of it, that it was cyclical, it happened to him. Fred had trends, and this was the extent of his meaning.

At least, this was what I fervently believed until one Friday Fred asked me out for a drink. And I went, knowing in my gut what I was doing, and had this drink with him. And I went and had additional drinks with him on subsequent occasions, all the while knowing what I was doing, and we fed more ducks, now explicitly feeding ducks together, and then one early September when American Objects had decamped en masse to a rural Delaware location for a workshop in furniture appraisal and was residing in a series of brick huts at a former-foundry-turned-B&B, I replied to a late-night email of Fred's bemoaning his lack of phone charger by appearing in person at the door of his hut, phone charger in hand, and he in turn responded by inviting me into his hut, and so I entered, and we were in his hut together. And had extremely sweet and pleasurable sex. Which we repeated on the subsequent evening. After this, all fucking hell broke loose.

It was mostly in my mind, the hell. I dealt with it by precipitously taking a week's vacation. I read five or six books on meditation and spent a lot of time sitting on the floor, breathing. Whit was made vaguely curious about this behavior on my part and showed the first spontaneous interest in me he had managed to muster in more than a year, telling me that this new practice might really be a good way for me to at last confront some of the intractable personality issues that had for so long plagued me. I even agreed with him. Meanwhile, it fell to me that not fifteen minutes could pass without some memory of Frederick's body in hot proximity to mine overtaking all other mental activity. Not only was I betrayed by my vagina, but the rest of my body seemed helpless to prevent me from becoming an adulteress. This was, I told myself, a somewhat challenging period in the lifetime I was spending with my true love, Whit.

Months went by. Fred and I felt each other up in a couple of taxis. We did not have sex again. I begged Fred to help me understand what was going on. He asked me to be gentle with him. He told me that there was someone else in his life, too, a woman with whom he maintained a tacitly nonmonogamous partnership, who worked as much as he did. Fred did not tell me her name, but thanks to my burgeoning online stalking habit, he did not need to. I cursed myself in front of him. I told him that I wanted to walk into traffic. He told me to be gentle. I said that I was hoping a bus would run me down. I said that I wanted to move to Nevada and find work as an accountant and forget my own name. I told him that we could not do this anymore. I pleaded with him to see me. I told him that I was going to leave the museum. He told me that he loved me. I told him that I could not tell him that I loved him. He told me that he could not see me anymore. I told him that the only thing in the world I wanted was to be with him. He told me that I could not see him anymore. I told him that I was planning to leave the museum. I told him that I could not be with him. He said that he did not know what to tell me.

He said that it was possible that he loved a lot of people, that he was happiest this way.

I was nursing very immediate memories of what were to me bizarre and painful events, when this past summer, postliaison with Fred and just after my ninth wedding anniversary with Whit, I went away with my husband to his parents' island enclave in Maine. I was keeping to myself during a time of chaotic family encounters, which was how I found out that Whit's phone was full of pictures of Estelle Dooskin's crotch.

Quickly: Estelle's name was actually already tattooed on Whit's arm. He had met her in high school. She was the child of professional Doberman breeders, a petite pretty woman who, hitchhiking one June with an older boyfriend, had, through no fault, other than bad luck, of her own, been involved in an interstate police chase that ended when the pursued Jeep, the backseat of which she was asleep in, rolled three times. Her boyfriend died. She suffered severe head trauma, brain injury. So she was an eighteen-year-old sophomore when she met Whit. It had taken her a little while to get back to school.

From what I knew, most things were on Whit's side. One of the effects of the injury had been to lower Estelle's sexual inhibitions, a fact Whit had more than once described to me in graphic detail. But she was mercurial, and broke things off with Whit senior year for the much older owner of a local bowling alley. Then she absconded to New Zealand, where for many years she apparently made a living from online sales of humorously altered sock-monkey dolls. You will be unsurprised to learn that in spite of the tattoo, I did not find this person even nominally threatening, as far as Whit's affections were concerned. However, when Estelle returned to the States and took up residence in Queens and waitressing in Park Slope, I might, had I known of her presence, have given Whit's absence more thought. Estelle had, unbeknownst to me, been back in Whit's life for more than two and a half years by the time her pussy, adroitly accommodating a hefty rubber dildo, appeared to me among Whit's text messages. And though her face was nowhere in sight in this lurid image, nor in numerous other photos, some of which divertingly demonstrated novel and unforeseen uses for socks, not to mention clothespins, spatulas, and oven mitts, I was able to determine that this impressively taxed anatomy was Estelle's own on account of Whit's blithe association of her full, real name with her contact info.

Naïvely, I assumed it was a brief flirtation. I had spent most of a year suffering through my attachment to Fred, which I was coming to see mainly as a kind of character test I had failed — and then failed to get over failing. I expected Whit, when confronted, to tell me the relationship had gone on a matter of days, at most a few weeks, and beg my forgiveness. He did not.

I countered by moving out of the house and requesting a divorce. Whit informed me that I would never be happy until I gave up the false consciousness I'd acquired in the professional world. I needed to have children or get a simpler, more honest and authentic job as a waitress or elementary school librarian, preferably some combination of the above. As things stood, my way of living was ruining other people's lives, by which Whit meant his. I thanked him for the advice. He called me a cold unnatural bitch and said that I had never loved him. I hung up on him and blocked his number for all time. A month later, with the grudging assistance of my dad, the other attorney in my life, I had him served with papers.

Thus, when it came to removing Whit's hand from my inner thigh, this was done fast. It took a nontrifling quantity of self-control not to scratch out his beady gray eyes, but I opted instead for a firm *"Stop."*

Whit stared me intently down. "Nice to see you, babe," was what he said.

"This is scaring me."

He grinned idiotically. "Really? Am I?"

"This," I repeated.

"Well, in that case, I'm sorry." Whit turned to the wall and readjusted discreetly as an antique bachelor limped by.

When he showed himself again, his face was difficult to read. He just stood there, totally patient and obedient. Was part of him hoping that I would chastise him, granting him the public dressing-down he unmistakably craved and humiliating myself in the bargain, perhaps even losing my job, depending on how colorful things got? Or was he here to dig something up, sniff a smell? Probably he wanted to perceive what, in organic detail, he was sacrificing on the altar of his parents' way of life, palpitate the goods one last time, obtain some sense of what those goods had been up to while he'd been out to sea on the SS *Dooskin.*

It's an understatement to say that I desperately wanted Whit to leave, but I also knew that *he* knew that this was the very thing I wanted. And so, on account of the problem of mutual knowledge, I elected to engage in behavior I knew would throw Whit off. I'd get, I reasoned, the restraining order later.

I said, "Can we please just go in?" I was strict but quietly so. I pretended to be fed up.

Whit replied by amiably offering me his arm as if it were 2005, and we strode past the long Plexi case containing the museum's mostly decomposed copy of the *Book of the Dead.*

Whit, meanwhile, had discovered something amusing in his silence and was chuckling to himself. "It's funny," he said, "I actually feel like I understand you *so well.* You know? You just make so much sense to me!"

We were wending our way around the remains of a temple that had once belonged to the Egyptian government, and before that to the Egyptian people. I let Whit's comment settle. Then: "That's nice, Whit. I'm glad you feel like you understand me." I was outwardly cool, accommodating, but inwardly I imagined a god playing this conversation back on her all-knowing iPhone and uttering a thunderous pronouncement that would condemn Whit to an eternity scrubbing toilets and stripping motel beds: "STELLA: 1; WHITAKER: 0."

"No, I mean, I really get it. I get *you.*" He was shaking his head. He took my hand in his and squeezed it, stopping and making a point of gazing soulfully into my eyes. "Your problem is that you just don't know how to be around other people!" He sighed. "It's going to be OK," he reassured me, needlessly, I might add, unless he was referring to his own sanity. He swung open one of the heavy glass doors that separate the grounds of the transplanted temple from a hallway display of rare baseball cards. Whit gallantly held this door ajar.

"Wow," I started to say.

But he was like, *Hush now.* He put a finger to his lips, skin at the edge of his eyes crinkling.

6

The scene into which we stepped bears description.

The American Wing is built around a sizable architectural piece, a customs house harvested from Salem, Massachusetts. Its marble front steps descend into an ivy- and fern-filled sculpture courtyard, where it's all greens, gold, and ivory and pert adolescent breasts. The grandchildren of the tormentors of witches and warlocks swished up and down these sloped gray treads and passed beneath the snowy tetra-columned portico into a place of gossip and taxation; now you pass through into a total of five floors of period rooms, a mismatch with the 2.5 stories delineated on the building's front, but whatever. It's an impressive layout, and I don't think the idea is that you are supposed to imagine what it was like so much as you are supposed to like how it is now, all pressure-cleaned and lit with recessed halogen. There is this fragrance, by the way, pertaining to all large open spaces in the museum, that makes me think that it is the exclusive task of some member of staff to think about how cleaning products smell when combined with high levels of western European and American midwestern BO plus CO_2. It's this comforting, vaguely herbal scent, with just the smallest touch of canned air or airplane, just the slightest industrial indication that you are not at home. I mean, it's immaculate but not at all impersonal, which is a difficult atmosphere to pull off.

However, tonight our corporate sponsor, WANSEE, had seen fit to make a small adjustment. No more were the marble blocks of the Salem customs house visible to the inquiring eye. Instead, someone had glued what appeared to be a ginormous plastic map to the spotlit edifice. It was a map, as far as one could tell, in other words, barring some Californian and Mexican sections that had been cut away to make space for the portico, of the North American continent. It was illustrated in imitation of a style contemporary with the French and Indian or Seven Years' War, judging from the rococo frame of conches and scrolling vines, the slightly eccentric shaping of the

Great Lakes, the zipperlike indication of the Rockies, the mushy sketch of the West Coast. It was obviously a Photoshop Frankenstein accomplished by an individual with limited knowledge of the aesthetics and cartographic progress of the era. WANSEE's instantly recognizable trademark icon of three blue waves appeared in five locations. Were these current water holdings, or was the map an elaborate expression of ambition? In what I supposed was the neighborhood of Nevada, there was indeed such an icon, supporting a reading of this cartographic stunt as more victory dance than mere yen. We were gazing at WANSEE's America.

A person dressed as a pilgrim and bearing a silver tray hove in sight and hung a left. He offered an array of twenty-five instances of the identical micro-tizer: an egg of caviar on a die of cheese on a stamp of rye.

"Nice," said Whit and tossed four of these specimens onto a napkin.

"Cool ruff," I told the pilgrim. The pilgrim wore a paper version of the starched collar of Thanksgiving lore and some sort of black velveteen doublet that looked to have been lately discarded by a regional theater company.

The pilgrim smiled obsequiously and spun away.

Whit was chewing. "They didn't hold back on this one."

"No," I concurred.

Whoever had "designed" the party, WANSEE's first at CeMArt, had made the interesting choice of leaving be the anachronistic late-nineteenth-century marble nudes (who disported themselves here and there among the vegetation), having added only a number of six-foot free-standing candle sconces, presumably of appropriate period style. With the lights dimmed, the effect was of some unholy Sabbath feted by Puritan patriarchs and frenzied naked Goodies Prim. It was kind of fantastic.

Whit was feeling up my right hip. He made some sounds of satisfaction as he masticated his Jarlsberg treat. "Nice," he was repeating. It was disgusting.

I accidentally caught the eye of Marco Jensen, who was absorbing the conversation of a pair of female interns harnessed with matching J.Crew costume necklaces, the garish rhinestones of which evidently symbolized the wearer's wealth, modesty, and intelligence. I watched Marco excuse himself.

I told Whit that maybe some white wine

would be good, silently muttering a prayer that (1) Marco's social existence was somehow post-Facebook and (2) even if it wasn't, he had not, thorough being that he was, friended my soon-to-be former husband shortly after friending me last year. I also knew there was no way in hell either of these things could possibly be true.

"Right, white," said Whit, eyes brightening. He winked, and went tamely, mercifully away.

Marco glided up. In fact, he seemed a new man (boy). "I didn't see you today." He was casual, agitating his wine by its stem.

"Sorry," I said. I tried to shrug with my face. I mean, I tried this slightly pathetic-looking thing where I furrowed my brow. It was supposed to demonstrate a refined balance of confusion and regret.

"Oh, it's OK." Marco indicated he had intended only that his remark be interpreted literally. There might even have been a touch of concern. Then: "Isn't this crazy? I mean, what *is* that?" He tipped his shapely head in the direction of the shell of the customs house. "Product placement?"

I smiled. "I do not know."

"I'm over it." Marco frowned. "Who do you think is here from corporate? Paris was saying she thought she already saw the entire board." He took a careful sip, searching my face.

"Oh."

"That's a big deal."

"No kidding," I told him. My right calf muscle had gone to sleep. I attempted to remove my foot halfway from my shoe and flex it surreptitiously.

"But anyway" — Marco took a step closer — "what I really wanted to say is that I talked to Irina, you know, in HR? I mean, about Paul, his situation."

"Right."

"All I know is they aren't saying anything."

"Is that what she told you?" I glanced in the general direction of Whit's unfolding mission. He was now second in line.

"He's just gone. When I was like, Oh my goodness, all shocked, she was like, I *know.*"

"What does that even mean?" This came out a little franker than I had intended. I had my eye on Whit, who was engaging the barkeep, a female in a hot-, as in heavy-, looking full-length corseted dress and matching Pilgrimess wimple.

"So it *means*" — Marco lowered his voice — "Irina was like, we don't really have much of a read on this thing. Meaning this is beyond the museum's purview."

"That's pretty specific."

"I mean, not really."

"But, you're saying, something happened?"

"Look, Stella, I have no clue."

Marco and I were both glancing over each other's shoulders to make sure there was no one in range. I felt the stirrings of what was sure to eventuate as a vicelike ache just above my brows, along the hairline, with a 20 percent possibility of a full-on crown of thorns by the time ten P.M. rolled around.

"So, basically, no one knows anything?"

"From what I know? No." Marco finished his wine. He tipped the glass fully up. Lowering the vessel, he added, "It's obviously serious."

I might have had something more to say regarding the issue of seriousness, but it was at this moment that Whit and Chardonnay returned in triumph, and Marco raised an eyebrow and vanished.

There was nobody who knew as much as Paul Coral knew about the museum. Paul also knew a lot more about my personal life than most people do. We'd have a conversation, I mean, it would be possibly fifteen minutes at lunch, and by the end he would have gotten more out of me than someone with whom I had been acquainted for years would have in, say, a year, not that I'm much on quantifying my own indiscretion.

Paul was from upstate and, judging from his cultural references, had lived through some portion of the seventies. He was of medium height, slim with a potbelly, white, had droopy blue eyes set in an oversized, gourdlike cranium to the rear of which adhered the remains of a head of theoretically blond hair, and was extremely refined in his speech, with an aristocratic accent I was not quite able to place, which fact suggested, to me at least, that he had made it up. The only thing I knew about his life outside the museum was that he was a Catholic, since he had at one time shown me a gold medallion he wore for St. Anthony, recoverer of lost things.

Paul was also the only person I knew at the museum, aside from some *very* senior curators, who referred to the museum's harried, aristocratic director, Nicola Di Carboncino, by first name and using the correct Milanese pronunciation. It was rumored that they made it a point to have lunch together once a month. I have no idea whether this is entirely true, but you would have thought that this might have given Paul some sort of protected status, at least within the institution.

83

Paul was also reputedly a poet. This last detail I picked up by chance at some point when I was up near Columbia. I was surprised to see a poster for an academic conference at which Paul appeared to be opening the proceedings with some sort of homily. There was a Q&A period scheduled. Which is to say, with him. There was even a little author photo, which was really what caught my attention to begin with, since there he was in a pantheon of people one would genuinely have heard of, for example, Judith Butler and Cornel West. The theme of the conference was simple enough. This was a little less than a year ago. The poster advertised, in elaborate script, ironic against a background of a pale graphic of the Dow or some other index, "On Debt." This, by the way, is the kind of thing you can get away with in the humanities, this sort of juxtaposition-as-argument kind of thing. I should have gone to hear him speak, this is what I should have done, but I can assume only that I thought I was busy that weekend. From what I gathered, Paul Coral was, I mean, *is* — or, perhaps, the other way around — relatively famous. By which I mean, for a poet in America.

The garden courtyard of the American Wing

was now filled to capacity with white-collar museum staff and wealthy New York persons of taste and various allies off of WANSEE's no doubt strategic list. It was WANSEE's party, and this meant they could do what they wanted. (Which they *ex facie* had, see freshly affixed map.) Were we all supposed to be ecstatic at the prospect of privatization of the earth's water? Merely impressed that such things could be accomplished, and legally? Relieved? The inclusion of so many employees of the museum itself was by no means a standard thing, but was likely intended to demonstrate WANSEE's bounty, stimulate institution-wide compliance, etc.

Bonnie was present, sporting an ankle-length caftan of dark green silk that would not have appeared out of place in any episode of the *Star Wars* franchise, and actually she looked quite good. If there is something unusual about your physique, I think you have to be careful with formal attire, but the caftan had full sleeves and was distractingly, elaborately belted. This is like how I am short. Regardless of whether I would in fact wish to, I simply cannot rock a miniskirt. Additionally, it was now only a matter of time until my nonsensical choice of escort came to the attention of Bonnie

— as well as, what was even more unpleasant as a probable eventuality, Fred.

7

I was saved by electronic chimes.

The lights dimmed twice then stayed down for good. Silence dropped into the crowd and was at once universally assumed. A cone of brightness grew from a spot originating on the second-floor balcony, and the gaunt figure of Nicola di Carboncino stepped stiffly into its center.

Di Carboncino's cordless mic was already live. After looking down into it for several long seconds, he commenced.

"Good evening."

Polite applause partly covered the labored breath that followed this salute.

Di Carboncino smiled wanly. He was a reptile, spotted, white haired, red lipped. Hot light agreed with him, and he seemed to ken to his task. "I should like to take this opportunity to welcome all of those who have elected to honor the inauguration of this museum's newest exhibit with their presence. Thank you all so very much for your support."

The temperature of the *salle* jumped two or three degrees as numerous monied do-gooders felt themselves acknowledged. The initial affective reaction was shortly matched by continued careful clapping.

"Thank you, thank you." Di Carboncino's eyes grew noticeably larger, rounder. He appeared very much to look out at us, his public; to absorb the fact of the audience. "Now I am pleased to welcome to this, shall I say, *stage,* the coordinator of this very same extraordinarily enticing exposition, the extremely distinguished curator of our department of the *arts décoratifs* of North America."

There came some patter as glasses and snacks were shifted to make unabashed appreciation possible at the next opportunity.

"I hope you all shall welcome him." Di Carboncino, smiling, revealed his flawless and certainly false upper teeth. "I look forward to his continued leadership at this institution, as I believe he may set the very highest standard for curatorship, even" — di Carboncino's perennially black brows flew up — "*internationally.* I give you, Dr. Frederick Lu."

The assembly gave in to unrestrained applause. Di Carboncino, quivering, handed the mic over to Fred like it was a long-stemmed rose.

I studied Bonnie's expression across the crowd. Her mouth had become small, from what I could tell, but it was not at all obvious that/if she objected to the theater transpiring before her.

Frederick Lu was now holding the microphone with three fingers. He made it look light, easy. His left hand was fitted palm side in into the corresponding pocket of an insanely well-cut blazer. He was the consummate impresario and wore, otherwise, this unclassifiable expression of mildness, his face strangely smooth, free of any tell.

Fred blinked. "Thank you so much, Nicola." He inclined his head in the direction of the Italian's exit. "And let me reiterate how pleased we are to have everyone here with us this evening." The informality of his fluent American English was, I hated to admit it, a significant relief. The throng settled. It lapped its drinks.

Things were set up nicely.

"As you all know, the title of this show is 'Land of the Limner.' It tells the incredible story of painting in early America, as well as in later, more modern America, and in just a few moments I am going to invite you all to preview the galleries. Tomorrow we open to the public, and I can't tell you, though it may be slightly immodest of me, how thrilled I am to be bringing some of these works to a wider audience for the first time in the history of their conservation and exhibition."

"Well, well, well, if it isn't Dr. Sexnerd III!" Whit stage-whispered rather more audibly than not, patting the ball of my right elbow. "Here's who was keeping you so late at the office, eh? Yum yum!"

I didn't look at him, just shrugged, fighting off the desire to slap him in the face.

Fred pedaled magisterially forward. "As scholarship and curation have brought us new syntheses of facts and artifacts from the historical record, it has become ever clearer that we may need to reevaluate the way we understand the confluence of art making and daily life in Colonial and earlier industrial times. To put it simply, this is just a very exciting time in our department at the museum and for studies of American art objects more generally. It's an honor and a joy to be able to participate."

Whit was again moved to speak. "I take it you two used to finger-bang during budgetary meetings?"

I kicked Whit's ankle, but lightly, a warning.

"Ow," Whit breathed. Then, bringing his mouth distastefully close to my ear, he hissed, "No, I get it. He's had his fun. After all, Stella, let's not forget: You're a rough seven who's going through a messy divorce, making you a temporary six and a half. Not that anyone's keeping score." Whit paused. "But I bet you're *still* fucking in love with him."

I pretended to be deaf. Fred meanwhile lingered on his theme of thrilling newness for several additional phrases. You got the impression that it was of the utmost professional importance to him to designate whatever work he did as a potential innovation, fresh and necessary though not precisely creative, just the natural result of tapping into whatever were the finest mores of his time. This is what he was, basically gratis, bringing to all of us. I mean, at the rate of roughly $200K per annum. All we had to do was like the museum that was fortunate enough to house this receptive, synthetic juggernaut (i.e., Fred) and choose its needs for our write-offs. Anyway, how many of us didn't know how ridiculously wealthy Frederick Lu was? Zero? Except that of course his reputation alone was worth more than any of this.

I was feeling like a bitch, actually and genuinely, as if I were just about to get hit with my three days a month of uterine distress, except that this wasn't the time. I was forcing myself not to think about what Whit had said, instead looking at Fred's face, just studying it, no longer hearing his words, when for some reason something shifted, his eyes moved, became fixed, and I had the distinct impression, nearly impossible though this was, that though he was at least twenty feet away on the other side of the courtyard, he was looking right at me. Fred was staring at me as if, and not just *as if,* he could make me out. Part of the reason this was apparent was because — certainly only for someone who really knew his face, but still — he looked, under the mask of magnanimity, distressed, *cut,* even. My heart tightened. It wasn't that I was waiting to feel something for him. There was just this opening for a second, and I saw him see, which is to say, I saw him see something, which is to say, me, his unfortunate former fling — apparently relapsing with a man both he and I knew to be beneath her.

I am not proud of it but I panicked. I turned and mouthed, *Bathroom,* handing Whit my glass.

My turd of a husband, satisfied with the insults he had managed to land thus far, made no comment. He accepted the object and did not attempt to follow as I slipped out of the clutch of enchanted auditors.

I was thinking I was pretty smart.

"This exhibition is a great reward, the culmination of years of progress in our field, and it is for this reason that I am more than simply grateful, I am indebted, and this is not a word I use often, *indebted* to our colleagues at WANSEE Holdings, whose generous support makes it possible for thousands of visitors to come into contact with remarkable works of art. I am so proud . . ." Fred was saying as I walked out of range of his voice, a feather that mysteriously touched me, and through the glass doors that led to the center of the museum, the European collection.

The wound was open again. Even in spite of the donor-directed filler that Fred talked. It had been disturbed. I thought again of his eyes. It was entirely possible that I was inventing their indications.

The wound moved a little, was touched by air. What did he feel, I wondered. Did he also sometimes have thoughts, visions even, of hours in the day in days that did not exist, during the course of which he and I spoke to each other and explained this to ourselves? What did he think of, when or if he thought of me? How elaborate and important was his life, really — with what kind of ease was he granted the ability not to think of me at all, and when he did not think of me, how did he smile when he recognized, somewhere at some slight distance from him in the ether of proximate human minds, my own unceasing thoughts of him? How great was his surprise that I could find nothing better to do with my affection? Did this stupidity on my part further convince him of the sagacity of his decision to turn away from me? What if I were something other than what I was? What if I had successfully recognized my soon-to-be nonhusband's long-term philandering at a point in time at which I still had a heart that was whole? When could this have been, what was the last possible day, hour, and/or minute on which I could have looked Whit in the eye and said, *You're wrong about the choices I am making with my life. I am not making the wrong choices. I am simply living with the wrong person.* And walked away and forgiven myself for this, even without knowing that he was not honest with me, for I should have known that he was not honest with me, not because he lied to me about what he was doing with his dick, but because he informed me daily that I was a tragic fool as well as a person who did not really love him, and it was only later that I became either of these things.

I grew calmer, as I passed among musty wood Madonnae et Christi and the reclining dead in effigy, their pointed shoes. I had no intention of going, directly or specifically, to the bathroom. I took out my phone. I went into SETTINGS > PHONE > BLOCKED and scrolled down and temporarily made Whit into a contact named "Shitty Shitface" so as to send him a text to the effect that he was now on his own recognizance for the rest of the evening and if he had further communiqués for yours truly please to be sure to address them to her BY WAY OF HER LAWYER, with whom she would also be discussing the meaning of his behavior tonight. As we no longer shared an apartment, making use of gala invitations mistakenly directed to my former permanent address was not just scummy — an abuse of the publicity department's buggy database — but calculated injury. And don't forget to sign the papers! And then I blocked him again, having succeeded in not refreshing my memory of his digits, though it was entirely possible that I could still recite them on cue.

I felt all right, pretty nearly good. I was unlocking the side door to the department when I recognized that I was now also ravenously hungry. I fairly busted into our chambers, fell up the stairs. I threw everything I needed workwise into one canvas bag, shoved my work clothes into the other. I popped momentarily into the bathroom to check on my face. The lighting gave my skin a greenish cast, as if the face were made of some very fine metal, my features limned with a flat enamel.

I retraced my steps, bared my totes to a lone guard in the lobby. It was a very young guy, ginger. He just nodded me through. Then I was out on the street with my umbrella, jogging in heels to 86th.

I was born and raised in Manhattan, but the adult version of me, now under duress of an impending (I very ardently hoped) divorce, had relocated to Greenpoint, Brooklyn. The commute from the UES demands the collaboration of three trains, but it really isn't that harrowing and costs something like thirty minutes all told.

Tonight I was thinking a little, just sitting in my seat. There was a lot of new narrative to wrap one's head around and I wanted to avoid the fantasy space to which I occasionally liked to retire to consider what it would be like if Fred and I were to reconcile in exactly the way I most enjoyed to imagine, if you can imagine. The problem of being, and/or totally not being, in love with someone you work with is that there is not very much wiggle room in which to figure this irksome dialectic out. The workspace in question had, however, lately been slightly enlarged by a certain vacancy in personnel. And I seemed to be more intrigued by the causes and results of the subtraction of Paul Coral from the Department of American Objects than almost anyone else I knew. When something big happens and everyone acts as if they do not care, then this is the time at which you absolutely must begin paying close attention.

I had learned the significance of this truism by way of a heart that had not so much broken as become irrelevant to the various affective economies in which it made its living. I had ignored Whit's episodes, choosing instead to understand this as some phase through which he was, as loudly and as drunkenly as possible, passing on his way to middle age, and I had amiably enough elected to interpret my own short-lived romantic venture with a senior coworker as some kind of proof that I really was as wrong and malignant as my wildly critical partner portrayed me, to myself, to be. I had let the ends justify the means, and not even in my own self-interest.

■ ■ ■ ■

TUESDAY

■ ■ ■ ■

8

The next morning I lit a cigarette, ambled to the G.

The weather had settled into the hectic but snow-free spring for which the city is known. Clouds dodged in and out. I mean, the sun beat very briefly down, until cover made the temperature drop more than a decade. This was all in the course of twenty seconds.

I was affecting a sense of well-being, and basically it was working for me. At the close of the previous evening, I had let myself into my railroad, consumed half a block of yellow cheese over the sink, and proceeded to pass out in my clothing. At 4:45 A.M., heart pounding, I bolted from a dream in which I found myself standing on an intensely green lawn in front of some sort of castle, observing the misty wedding of a pair of tall individuals who bore plausible resemblance to my friends Reihan and Cate, even as I was incongruously yelling, "YOU DON'T EVEN KNOW WHAT A MARRIAGE IS!" to Whit, who was slouched against some neoclassical decorative element nursing a drink.

I just lay there on my back for a few minutes, panting, trembling. I reached over and checked my phone. It was the same dream. I mean, the setting was variable, the supporting cast, season, time of day, etc., but the basic events were intact and succinctly, cruelly repeated. Meanwhile, my phone told me nothing. There was a noteworthy sample sale coming up and a female friend I hadn't spoken to in several years because of geographical distance missed me. I sat up in bed, switched the light on.

The night before I had unfolded Paul's xeroxed map and laid it out on my bedside table. It was possible that my dairy-drugged self was under the impression that through some process of osmosis I would absorb the import of the document while unconscious. The desired transmission had not occurred.

I studied the page. I Googled, on the phone's miniature browser, "Elysia," turning up a genus of sea slug that feeds on green algae, an elegiac Wikipedia entry for a short-lived Tucson deathcore band that had broken up before releasing its first full-length album, and references to the Elysian fields of myth, the afterworld of the blessed. *Enelysios* means "one struck by lightning" in ancient Greek, and it is thought that the name for paradise might have come from a conflation of good fortune with that rare event of being hit by a bolt from Zeus, though this seems a bit overwrought to be a true etymology. Elysia is also apparently a woman's first name, which was news. In a pathetic last touch, I tried adding "town." No dice.

It wasn't until I went after the poem's strange line of questioning, "Where is this paradise you seek, / Dear seeker, careful one, lover of the world?" that I got something: G. G. Hennicott's *Lorelei of Millbury,* a novel from 1843. After this victory I was basically up, showered, and out the door, with a brief interlude to wing a message to Bonnie to say I might be perceptibly tardy, the dentist and so forth, how sorry I was.

If you have ever been inside one of the New York Public Library's Manhattan branches then you know it is a total crapshoot as to whether the book you want will in fact be present in its shelving slot as advertised in the online "AVAILABILITY STATUS." There are usually a certain number of funny smells in the building as well.

But I was happy, because I did find what I was looking for. A man in a lumpy blazer making a stack of photocopies of a 2012 issue of something called the *New York Psychic* saluted me wordlessly as I exited via the north stairs.

G. G. Hennicott's first and only literary production was a slim volume. The edition was not the premier, but pretty close. The binding had been accomplished without too much ceremony in blackish-green cardboard. The endpapers were black and white, with a netlike design and elegantly drawn examples of the *Simulium yahense,* or blackfly.

The frontispiece gave the full title of the book, *Lorelei of Millbury, or Impossible Views of the World, a Romance.* The accompanying illustration, described below its lower border as being "Engraved from the Daguerreotype by Paul, Giles & Co.," showed an angelic young girl in a lacy series of crinolines staring up at a cloud of disembodied faces that steadily returned her gaze.

The date of publication appeared in Roman numerals, and the publisher styled himself "Apud Gilbertium Lacunam Felicem," with the "Apud" being Latin for "At the house of," and the rest of it presumably indicating his name.

I was on the train back uptown at this point, and even though I was slightly concerned about upsetting fellow commuters with the moldy reek and disintegrating pages of my reading material, I had to dip in.

I turned to the first chapter:

Chapter I: One Midsummer's Outing and Its Unexpected Consequence

"Oh Father, it is simply too cunning for words!"

So went the enthusiastic speech of a smiling young miss, Miss Lorelei Pleasant, as she rushed to embrace her beaming parent, the kindly Dr. Pleasant.

It was a temperate afternoon in late July, when all of creation benefited from the redness of a setting sun, and weary wasps and damselflies skated and trembled upon a thousand emerald blades in every verdant lawn and blooming meadow. One heard the soft jubilation of the dove and scented dreaming lilies!

Alas, for the Pleasant household, the beauty of this gentle season came not without remorse, for the arrival of that very date and hour at which we espy them here marked the memory of a tragic loss within their home, insoluble even to the medic's art, alack! That of Lorelei's beloved mother and Dr. Pleasant's cherished wife, Mrs. Pleasant, whose passing was now grown a complete year old.

Yet, rather than mark their mutual tragedy with further sighs and bootless lamentations, Dr. Pleasant, rendered the unique and doting protector of his lovely daughter, had devised a cheering diversion for the evening, that they two might at last conclude the period of mourning with some renewed fellowship and joy . . .

I read on for a few more pages before glancing up. I was at my stop.

Walking to the museum, I pondered the rest of the first chapter, in which Dr. Pleasant, a leading man of the town, gives his daughter Lorelei an elegant picnic basket. This makes sense because the two of them are about to head out to some Protestant social event ostensibly organized by Dr. Pleasant to help clear the air, re: the mother's death. They've invited all the correct persons of the area, and they're going to drink spicy cordials and eat tiny cakes and listen to people recite poems and other wholesome business.

But, the reader must bear in mind, all this is going on out of doors, meaning that the limitations of polite society, with its damask shackles, are about to disappear. I thought back to one moment of sublime development:

The dulcet tones of Patience's song, along with the mellow accompaniment of the notes rising from Sigismund's lute, lulled Lorelei, but only momentarily. For while all the company seemed joined as one in the enjoyment of this guileless country melody, Lorelei felt herself waken within herself, for she thought she heard another song more lovely and more true than the one to which she had first lent her ears. This other tune seemed a kind of chant, more than a proper song, yet Lorelei could not wrest her attention from it. She felt she must hear more and immediately! Quietly, she slipped from the assembled group of dozing companions and crept away into a little copse of saplings from whence the gorgeous music emanated.

Back at my desk, I decided I might ignore my other work in favor of this unusual cultural document.

Guided by the haunting song, as well as a

dancing fairy light resembling a buzzing star, Lorelei passes through a vegetable barrier into another world. The prose offers "vivacious lengths of vital arabesque vine," for example, or "the chortling, scent-drenched passage of a tree-bound breeze." The heroine comes upon a gleaming model settlement named Elysia. Here, as among the Houyhnhnms in *Gulliver's Travels,* all is order. This is a monoculture in which no one has a name, all citizens know no such thing as property, and, oh yes, all are expert practitioners of the séance. And, as I read with a jolt, *all Elysian persons are female.*

I inadvertently bit the inside of my cheek; tongued the spot, kept on.

Confusion arises at Lorelei's insistence that she "is Lorelei." Everyone speaks English, so it is not a problem of translation, rather a difficulty with what Lorelei means when she uses the verb "to be" in the sense of proper names. It's a little preposterous, but, then again, Elysia is not located within the bounds and/or limits of reality.

After a meal of imaginary fruits, a dance involving bells begins. Lorelei has a natural skill for the hopping steps. The utopians accord her the honorary title of "Expert in Movement," and she receives an amulet carved from a walnut shell. Then the utopians progress en masse underground. In a vast grotto divided by a great number of rivers, all ebbing and flowing around multiple islands, they participate in a ceremony best described as Plato's cave in reverse. Projected into the air are a bright host of mostly human figures. Occasionally they speak. One of the figures, a young girl, enlarged for the benefit of the audience, bears a striking resemblance to Lorelei. The doppelgänger maintains that the visitor is a long-awaited prophet and must be taught all the secrets of utopian society. A great hurrah goes up!

Here I paused, remembering with the same mix of apathy and pedantic satisfaction that attended the majority of my interactions at the museum an email I had meant to send regarding a wall label in the narrow drawings salon that abutted the German-American suite in the period rooms. Were we, I inquired of Bonnie and Fairfax Cleeg, the department's exhibition designer, employing the now-outmoded character *Eszett* (β) in our transliterations of text? I noted that I had reread the house style guide, that it was ambiguous. I attached a list of pros and cons, titling my bloodless message "Orthography q." Reflexively, I cc'ed Paul, a gesture that made the act of sending feel more than a little abstract.

I returned to the novel. The next sixty pages consisted of a Melvillean quantity of cultural explication. The utopians are artists. Their preferred media are light and glass. They pursue their livelihood and spiritual practices and craft at once, directing every effort toward the theater of the cave. Their most sacred belief is that no life is ever lost, and thus, perhaps, the lack of (reproductive) sex among the Elysian women, though no mention is made of this as a problem. All who die, the Elysians maintain, reenter the world as "clewes," spectral presences whose traces can be picked up by anyone with talent.

Those blessed with the ability to distinguish *clewes* convey themselves every afternoon to "the place of achievement." Here, in thatched huts, the gifted listen for the stirrings and voices of the dead. When someone has felt the approach of a spirit and, if she is very lucky and very competent, heard a voice, she trots back to the settlement, where the captured message is carefully transmitted to another member of the community responsible for disseminating the wisdom.

The utopians have no use for the written

word. They do, however, have a storehouse of technological wonders, having invented an early form of cinema. They have also created crystal dishes with holographic properties, musical automata that play by themselves for hours on end, a daisy-shaped mouthpiece that transforms human speech into noise interpretable by insects.

As in all literary paradises, learning occurs with a magic quickness. Lorelei's first sentence comes — she is meditating in her hut — from Dido, mythical founder of Carthage. *"Sunt lacrimae rerum,"* the queen explains, "yet in this place mortal things cannot touch you." Such an honor, the utopians inform Lorelei, rewarding her with use of the daisy-shaped mouthpiece for an afternoon, during which time Lorelei attends a congress of the ants. NB: The irony of the utopians' acquaintance with Dido's famous "name" is not noted by the narrator and, therefore, not explained. Henceforth Lorelei, whose communicative abilities have been tested and approved, is inundated with communications — from Marguerite Porete, Joan of Arc, Agnès Sorel, Margaret Cavendish (who insists on reciting a one-thousand-line poem praising the hardness of ice), Sor Juana Inés de la Cruz, Deborah Sampson Gannett, Sacagawea, and many,

many others, a pantheon of female artists and leaders.

In an echo of Dido's first mollifying pronouncement, the story offers a consolation: Lorelei hears the words of her mother. At first, these are only singular words or fragmentary phrases, but in time whole sentences slip into the world: "What does my daughter do? Who will my daughter be? How does my daughter love? Does she love truly?" Lorelei lingers for many days on a certain island in the cave, receiving such longed-for questions, insensible to hunger, thirst, or fatigue. But one day, the tender maternal queries stop and, in this silence, overcome with a sense of duty to her father, Lorelei informs the anonymous utopians that she must depart. Backtracking through the thicket, she recalls her initial impulsive escape, the song and guiding bubble of bluish light. Chastising herself ("How angry Father will be!"), she notes dusk coming on.

But as Lorelei regains the clover-rich knoll, the picnickers are still eerily present, "like figures in a painting," Hennicott writes. No time has passed in this world. Mortal things have indeed not touched Lorelei, with the odd effect that now her formerly familiar American life seems as if an eternal present one may exit and reenter at will, itself a mere partial reality, a projection. Time, for Lorelei, is now different! But the heroine's reflections are interrupted by a new song finding its crescendo on the singer's lips, and Lorelei insinuates herself among the formerly familiar horde, listening transfixed:

Where is this paradise you seek,
A place where no one mourns,
And nothing irreplaceable is lost,
And nothing lost is irretrievable?

Where is this paradise you seek,
With tears dry and wrongs righted,
Where nothing that occurs in dreams
Knows human fear or cruelty?

Where is this paradise you seek,
Dear seeker, careful one, lover of the
    world?
Where is this paradise you seek?
Where is this blessed Elysia?

9

I set the book down. This told me something. I felt haunted myself by the thought of that shadowy island, where Lorelei had remained for days, starving and thirsting for the sake of her mother's words. I doubted, for example, that I would find Caro's demise so inspiring, yet all the same I was, these days, far from free of persistent attachments. It was clear to me why one couldn't linger forever in a colorless place like Elysia, feeding off of the past; there was horror associated with that kind of indecision, and yet — couldn't one linger, just a little? Reality seemed, by contrast, rather limited, lacking in depth. It entailed picnics. Better not to hurry back.

I dipped into assorted databases, seeking some trace of G. G. Hennicott, as behind my chair Ozen marched up and down the hall, loudly in quest of a staple remover. Hennicott was, decidedly, a minor figure.

Of course there were no studies that took her/him as their sole object, but I did manage to find one heavily researched cultural studies work on "sentiment and inheritance in the early United States and beyond." *Finest Feeling: Debt and Fantasy in Nineteenth Century American Feminist Fiction* was by one Marina Gonzales Childe, assistant professor of English at Alabama State. I managed to get the page I wanted out of a sample chapter Princeton University Press had up on its website (in order to ingratiate the study with the eight or so scholars who would be into it enough to stomach the $78.95 hardcover price). I was almost annoyed with myself for having gone to the trouble, since really there wasn't that much being said:

Stylistic mimeticism — a diverging foliate line or metaphor that effloresces into meaning — displays these authors' interest in the lush liberties and ornamental value of nature. [. . .] This trend is also confirmed by less successful works, such as 1843's *Lorelei of Millbury,* by G. G. Hennicott, a romantic, science-fictive *fantaisie* which, if read in its historical context, might well be paired with a work like George Sand's *La petite Fadette* (1849), as it

115

demonstrates an interest in bucolic free-doms — an interest perhaps most gener-ously read as an allegory of social and political emancipation. This novel is the only known example of Hennicott's writing and no other archival or administrative trace of this individual exists, prompting some critics to dub the name a pseudo-nym. In the context of the period such scriptural obscurity was unremarkable, particularly for the probable author, an educated woman of means who had no intention of venturing into the professional limelight.

By the way, I have actually read Sand's *La petite Fadette,* a sort of limitedly optimistic Cinderella story set in the uncouth wilds of Napoleonic France. I also once saw a dress owned by George Sand at an exhibition in Paris. It was this amazing brownish-gold item, embroidered all over with tiny blades of wheat. I guess this is where my thinking on George Sand's "interest in bucolic freedoms" begins and ends.

I was trying to remember if there was anyone I knew who had done research on intentional communities in the U.S. Utopia is, generally speaking, a pretty popular topic in academia, probably because it allows those who study it to express in an allegorical manner their misgivings about the society, school, or corporation, as the case may be, to which they belong. Still, I couldn't remember there being anyone in particular I knew who was good on Protestant cults.

Premature though it probably was at this stage of my research, I was feeling a little dejected. Was the poem some sort of popular song? If so, why did it appear, as far as I could tell, only within the bounds of this novel and the map's cartouche? And what of the discrepancy of nearly half a century between the date on the map and the novel's appearance? Most pressingly, how could a place where people did not know what a proper noun was have a *name*? What was Elysia, if not a proper name?

I sort of wanted to wring G. G. Hennicott's no doubt long and exceptionally shapely neck, but more than this I felt unnerved. Elysia was a place where women lived together but did not have identities as we normally understand them. For reasons at once obvious and obscure, they processed messages from the beyond as their central cultural activity and economy, and also found the time to develop advanced audiovisual technologies in order to commune

117

with nature. They seemed not to experience the passage of time, as such, but did acknowledge the difference between the now in which they resided and the infinite expanse of the past. Their world resembled a manicured kingdom in a fairy tale, however it wasn't exactly that. I reflected on the nature of human memory, the ways in which it weirdly exceeds individual lifetimes, jumping from generation to generation. But what, in the present, *learns*? And does this learning actually take place anywhere save in utopia?

It was now midday and beyond having read this spooky piece of speculative fiction, I had not so far done enough with myself, workwise. Bonnie was nowhere in sight, which was one minor piece of luck. Having recognized my good fortune on this point, I suddenly remembered why I had been dreading this day since early on in the previous weekend: I was supposed to have lunch with Caro.

In addition to the normal miseries that attended our encounters, I was going to be twenty minutes late.

I texted to advise Caro as to my delay and true to form she did not reply. This is how you know she is a lady. She is aware of what you know, and she does not, therefore, need to confirm her knowledge by insisting on it with you. She lets you make your sad dash to her table at Orsay without comment. She will as usual be making notes in a minuscule linen-covered notebook, obtained during the course of her last trip to Florence, when you arrive.

"Hi, Mom," I said. For it is only within the confines of my brain that I refer to her by her first name.

"Hello, dear."

Caro was wearing a black silk blouse with a boat neck, gold earrings in the form of ancient medallions, Caligulas belaureled in profile. She accepted my kiss on the air near her cheek. "Well," she said, as I seated myself with a certain want of grace, causing the table to rock and her tea to chatter. "This is an interesting spring."

I nodded. "Did you order already?"

Caro smiled. "I can't believe it snowed only yesterday." Her hair is short, a puff, undyed, very white. "And, no, I did not."

I was panting a little, thumbing through the heavy menu, trying to convince the gloms of font affixed to its pages to resolve themselves into words.

"Have you been eating well, darling?"

"I'm still alive, aren't I?" I looked up. I

119

felt confident about an omelet.

Caro was unperturbed. "There is more to life than mere subsistence, of course."

A waiter appeared and accepted our orders, Caro's with a kind of shy joy and mine only on condition of my understanding that his libretto would soon be complete, at which point he would no longer need to come into contact with scumbags like myself at his place of work or anywhere else, for that matter.

"What an interesting young man," Caro observed, after our server's departure. She seemed to be asking me if I had ever known the joy of dating an artist.

I only nodded, attempting not to take the bait.

"You know," Caro said, consuming more of her tea with a relish that suggested it might in fact be a life-giving potion distilled from the comingled blood of virgins and Nobel laureates, "I realize that you don't know what it's like to have a parent who wants to have a say in who it is you are dating. You really have no idea! *I* just want you to be happy."

Now it was coming. There would be no way to avoid it.

"I remember, before I began going around with your father, the other men who would

120

approach me and, I mean, darling, I always thought, he is very nice, but what is *my mother* going to think? He's so impractical and what I really need is stability! I really *need* someone with a serious character, you know, not some jokester who likes to play fast and loose, because my all-knowing mother says I do, and that's why I feel so fortunate that things have worked out with your father, because truly it could have been a disaster, and that's what I admire about you, Stella, and I find so, you know, remarkable, because, where did you come from, Stella, whose child are you, because you, Stella, you think for yourself! I think I just really never even *knew* what the freedom to choose for myself was."

I was gulping down water, the better to slow my speech. What Caro meant was that she had never *liked* Whit, who had been bent on playing the buffoon from day one, and therefore my willingness to go through with and subsequently conclude a marriage that she had disagreed with from the start was a mark of my independence. Also included in her observations was the delectable datum that she, Caro, had been right all along. She was wondering what the time frame to my acknowledgment of this point might be.

My water glass was empty. There wasn't much I could do to hold myself back. "I saw him!" I blurted, choking.

"What?" Caro wanted to know. Her spine stiffened instantaneously. Clearly, I had her attention. "You are referring to Whitaker, and you are telling me that you have seen him? Has he still not signed? You aren't possibly *reconciling* with this person?"

"Yes," I said. "And no, he hasn't. And no, I am not."

"Oh my *God,*" Caro said. She was still stuck in her previous thought.

"Mom! You know I would never reconcile with him at this point!"

Caro was not listening. "After what he put you through — I mean, the *humiliation* you experienced. The thoughtlessness. The disrespect. The *deception.* To think that you were with him since you were, what, twenty-one?"

"Twenty." I recalled, not without a certain anguish, the winter our junior year when Whit and I had realized that we might be more than study buddies, the annotated letters we'd exchanged though we lived less than two blocks apart in Columbia housing, the first kiss in a park replete with snow, walks up and down Broadway, carrying disposable cameras because we liked the

122

quality of film, taking pictures of anything and nothing. Terrorism was all anyone talked about, but we were in love.

"Exactly. It's just unfathomable."

Caro's voice has a high edge, and it carries, particularly in environments including numerous hard surfaces. Other diners were beginning to take note of our interesting discussion.

"I *agree*, Mom," I hissed. "What I'm trying to tell you is that he showed up at the museum."

"What? You invited him to meet you at work? At the place where you are *employed*?" Caro wasn't exactly shrieking, because she is not capable of shrieking, but she might just as well have been doing so, judging from the looks of poorly disguised delight and prurient glee on the faces of the strangers around us. "Stella, dear, forgive me for saying this, but have you lost your ever-loving mind?"

"Mom," I said, "what I'm trying to tell you is that he showed up unannounced. They must have mailed me an invitation at our, I mean, his," I stuttered, "I mean *the old* address, and he ambushed me, basically. I couldn't get rid of him. It was very" — I paused — *"difficult."*

"Yes, I can well imagine it was difficult.

You probably haven't dealt with something of that nature before, poor thing. Men can be extremely persistent." Caro pursed her lips. "I mean, you have no idea what *hell* I used to go through." She sighed. "Well, now you've acquired a certain mature charm. I don't blame that idiot for wanting to hold on to you. The present challenge, of course, is to find someone on your level. But that's good, right? That's sort of fun?"

Caro was letting me know that she was not available for further discussion of these matters. When I had a new beau to run under her nose for potential rejection I was welcome to consult her, but Whit's case was, as they say, closed.

"Right," I told her.

A greasy grayish-yellow log that was the restaurant's rendition of an omelet was lowered before me. Caro received what I can describe only as the world's most vivid, most heartbreakingly crisp Caesar salad. "Bon appétit," the waiter sneered, flourishing a tiny bow in Caro's direction.

"Mmm," Caro said, craning her neck to get a good look at my plate. "What a yummy-looking omelet!"

I grimaced.

Caro tucked crunchily in, but then paused, midbite. "So," she said, "what else is new?

124

With work and all? I'm sure you're up to some extremely impressive things."

I reflected, not without melancholy, on my meager recent achievement with respect to a certain administrative PDF. I felt, for a moment, a little like I might start crying, but then something occurred to me.

"Mom," I said, "you know, actually something really strange happened?"

"Yes?" Caro answered, displaying her distinct ambivalence as regarded all that her daughter might deem out of the ordinary. "Yes."

Caro blinked.

I ignored her to the extent that this was ever possible. "On Monday, one of my colleagues in American Objects did not come into work." I was already out on a rather thin limb.

"So," Caro sighed, "you are saying that someone you work with was indisposed?" She turned a salad leaf over, absently stroking its curved spine with the tines of her fork. "I can imagine flu really gets around those cubbyholes where they like to stick you. How trying."

"I don't think it's the flu."

"You don't?"

"No, I do not."

"Then, did you *upset* this person? Is that

what you are trying to tell me?"

I contemplated this suggestion. It was interesting to me how much damage I managed to carelessly wreak in my environs from day to day, in Caro's mind. If you asked her, I had probably snatched a few purses, made multiple babies cry, and jaywalked repeatedly on my way to lunch, some of which was true.

"Yeah," I pronounced, feigning agreeability, "except I don't think it's that!"

"Oh no?"

I forced myself to smile. "But gosh," and here, via some nameless intuition, I saw an opening and went, breezily, right for it, "I must have mentioned him to you in passing before, no? Does the name Paul Coral ring any bells?"

Caro froze. She screwed her eyes shut, and for a moment I was concerned that she was about to expire on the spot.

Caro saw fit to open one eye. "Oh," was what she said.

I waited.

The other eye popped into view. Caro closed her mouth and smiled, simpered. "Ha," she said. Then, merrily stabbing the air in front of her face with her fork, "No!"

10

I bit my lip. Why not being acquainted with someone should be cause for this much joy I really couldn't speculate.

Caro munched her greens. Though she had made her way through no more than 5 percent of her salad, she appeared extremely full of something or other.

"Maybe," I suggested, "you've heard his name somewhere?"

Caro guffawed. "Unlikely, I'm afraid! As you know, dear, I've never really done well with institutional politics. Your colleagues at the museum would find it extremely amusing to think a lone gun like me kept tabs on them. I'd really *love*" — by which she meant that she would hate — "to give them that kind of satisfaction."

"Wait, really? Are you saying that you know Paul?"

Caro continued delicately chewing, as if I had not said anything.

"Mom?"

Caro swallowed whatever now extremely well-masticated bite she'd been working on. She made a show of deftly daubing the front and then the edges of her mouth with her napkin. She closed her eyes and sighed as if sated.

I waited.

"I cannot *believe* we're having this conversation."

"If," I let her know, "you were to explain to me what we are talking about right now" — I paused for effect — "I would consider it a real act of charity!"

"Oh" — said Caro — *"Stella."*

"I'm asking you, Mom!"

Caro shook her head. "I just hate to disappoint you."

A lifetime's worth of anecdotal evidence caused me to sincerely doubt that this was the case, but nevertheless I played along. "*Disappoint* me?"

"Yes. You're acting as if a mere manner of speaking *actually* meant something. I'm being quite general, you know."

"You're being general?"

"Indeed, I am."

"So, like" — I took a beat — "*use* my illusion?"

Caro was not familiar with this concept.

128

And when Caro is unfamiliar with a concept, it makes her more than a little peeved, vexed. "Please let's not insinuate that I am intentionally deceiving you! To be frank, I don't even know what we're talking about right now!"

"Right," I said. "Yes. That makes sense." The irony was thick, rubbery, and in its sudden, gelatinous entry into reality it had become modally indistinguishable from earnest and/or literal speech. This was the double-edged sword of working in the same industry as one's parent; as much as she might be a source of information, Caro could also withhold indefinitely, no matter how I squirmed. In other words, my mother also knew I knew she knew.

Caro squinted. She now appeared to be attempting to determine if my language mocked her, and therefore constituted a threat to her well-known superiority, or if I were merely acknowledging, in my own feeble and debased way, how great she was. When she at last put her fork down, I believed that I had struck a nerve.

Caro cocked her head. It was an action of unforced grace and indicated that she was about to make a pronouncement. I willed my own face not to register interest and/or need.

She began, "You know that your father and I are planning to leave town in a couple of weeks?" It was as if most of our preceding exchange simply had not taken place.

I let Caro know that, yes, I was aware of this.

"Well, darling, you know how sensitive the cat is. You know her attitude."

I blinked.

Caro was still talking to some piece of the air. "She's extremely sensitive! I so hate to move her. Such carefully developed expectations I have never seen in an animal! And she really *expects,* you know, your father to be there, right at eight A.M., with the wet food. She barely touches it, but it has to be there, otherwise things simply are not right, and then at six P.M., again. I just can't bear to think of what she'll do."

"What she'll *do*?"

"How disappointed she'll be! I can't just have the doormen leaving her dry food all week long!"

"No," I started to say.

"Yes, and we know that you are extremely diligent, Stella. I'm sure it's nothing for you to swing by on your way into the office. And, of course, you'll play with her for a little while, that's absolutely essential. And comb her two or three times? That really calms her down. And the litter box, she's *very* particular about that, as anyone would be, and it has to be cleaned at least once a day, otherwise you really don't know what she has in store. They thrive on structure and repetition, you know, and it's so hard for them to trust. It's a little known fact but, as I know you've heard me say before, cats are as motivated by loyalty as dogs, if not more so. It's only human inconstancy that masks this trait. Stella, dear, it really takes someone as on task as you, someone so dependable and so driven, I mean, someone who" — Caro apparently struggled to obtain the correct words — "who would understand that sometimes duty comes before love, and that, well, we could all be called upon to give up romantic love for our career! I'm just so impressed by how well you've done!"

Something was transpiring on my face that I hoped approximated a mild smile of pleasure and manifest delight. I wanted Caro to know that I eternally and forever meant business. That business was all my joy. And that I, a priori, condemned all fantasists, utopians, socialists, human rights activists, devoted liberals, kindergarten teachers, or anyone else for whom all aspects of life were not entirely up for grabs and/or résumé building. That I was extremely smart and therefore was likewise incapable of feeling whatever it was I was clearly meant to be feeling, based on the eminently reasonable kinds of things she said. And so I told my mother, "But of course!"

Back at my desk, I was meek. It is usual for my interactions with Caro to drain me heart and soul, but this was one for the books and/or archive.org.

In my inbox was a message from Bonnie, addressed to the entire department. It contained a link permitting me to direct my browser to a certain piece of coverage in the *Times,* an Arts feature. Although it was getting pushed out of first place online by a video about the size of logos on American sneakers, it was still a substantial bone.

The writer was a columnist named Glinda Corn. I'd seen some of her work before, and her favorite bugbear, then as now, was something she liked to call "connoisseurship," which was really just another word for being successful, which was to say, being known in your profession for having achieved success.

The piece ran:

A CURATOR OF AMERICAN ART AND DECORATIVE OBJECTS GETS CREATIVE

BY GLINDA CORN

Several years ago the curator Frederick Lu suffered a crisis of faith.

"I was feeling a certain lack of enthusiasm for what was then, approximately two years ago, the going thinking about how American works ought to be exhibited, what was modern, what was by contrast Colonial, antique," Mr. Lu said yesterday in an interview in his office at Manhattan's Central Museum of Art (CeMArt), where he is Thurston J. and Jeanne A. Prentiss Curator of American Decorative Arts of the Department of American Objects.

Mr. Lu, who sat at his desk beneath an early landscape of the U.S. Capitol, described meditative after-hours walks in the museum's storage area, during which he began to appreciate the breadth of the Central Museum's collection. He said, "I realized that these were things that were crucial to the present of this country, that came out of multiple, complex pasts — pasts that might not always be clear on first glance. There was something more here that Americans really needed to see."

Mr. Lu, 38, "exudes calm resolve and canny verve," said entrepreneurial chef and television personality Gordon Ramsay, who has become a passionate advocate of the museum and of Mr. Lu himself, inviting Lu to judge a segment of his reality cooking show, *MasterChef.* Lu, no stranger to pressure tests, was until recently nationally ranked in field archery and is one of the youngest senior curators ever appointed in the Central Museum's history. "I have always understood that our museum's mission will probably be forever married to the idea that there is a single artistic genius and this artist-genius has created certain indelible, irreplaceable works, cornerstones of culture," Mr. Lu noted. "But when it comes to the American collection, this sort of model for appreciation just isn't going to fly. Our problem was that we were in denial about that. We needed to get creative."

The decision to rehabilitate a collection of esoteric American paintings, of various time periods and styles, which had gone largely unseen by the public for the past hundred years, represents a definite change in museum policy. Lu fought hard to win support among his colleagues. As Nicola di Carboncino, CeMArt's director, explained, "One has to work to have space in an institution like ours, and, as with anywhere else in New York City, real estate comes at a premium."

Mr. Lu, a native New Yorker, is the son of Lulu Weynmaaren Lu, the interior designer and lifestyle author, and John Lu, the founder and owner of Recepro, the telecommunications firm. In between studies at Princeton and Yale, Lu took time off to work for his father, in order to become, he said, "a curator who knows his way around a boardroom as well as a gallery."

Mr. Lu believes that he has learned from the business world. "I just see the importance, the absolutely crucial importance, of communicating to people in terms they can understand," he said. "What I realized, too, is that we were taking the wrong approach in the way we were displaying crucially significant work."

Mr. Lu said that, based on his own observations and interviews he himself has conducted with the public during biweekly "strolls," many museum visitors seemed unaware of the incredible value of even "everyday items, like, to give an example somewhat at random, an eighteenth-century rococo dish for displaying pickles and salted nuts, a product of

135

the first porcelain factory in the United States." He said, "We want to invite visitors to imagine this eighteenth-century piece as somehow commensurate with an object they would have in their own homes, like from IKEA."

"Land of the Limner," his newest exhibition, is on view until August 31st of this year. The selections are of paintings made between the years 1620 and 1950, chosen specifically to illustrate a range of styles, from primitive familial scenes to stark modernist studies, in what he called "the changing nature of the American portrait."

"What I aim to do," Mr. Lu said, "is to rehabilitate our American imaginations. We aren't like other nations, that much is clear, but I think the problem is that we've forgotten *why*. We've lost that sense of wonder."

Though change happens slowly in a sprawling institution like CeMArt, Mr. Lu is determined to start the ball rolling in his own department.

"Part of my goal is to show the way in which America reentered Europe, at the same time as Europeans and people of other heritages were arriving in America," Mr. Lu said. "Americans have always been quite aspirational."

11

I hadn't brought my laptop in, and due to the vintage of the institutional desktop's operating system, the browser had long ago ceased to be updated, and images weren't loading properly, so though I was invited to "View the slideshow" accompanying Fred's profile, I elected instead to put the machine to sleep and check in with Bonnie before I called it a day.

Bonnie was present. "Hi there," I said.

After an encounter with my mother, Bonnie is cake. She is like an eccentric aunt who enjoys spoiling me and appreciates my impractical side. She presents herself as a plausible fantasy and/or replacement parent.

"Oh. Hi there." Bonnie wasn't precisely in the mood, but she was not entirely out of it, either. "The coverage is slowly trickling in."

"It is," I said.

"The world blunders on."

"It does," I agreed.

"Some people stick around for the ride."

I wasn't sure how many more mixed metaphors Bonnie would want to put me through before we could come at last to the possibility of literal speech. I decided to be direct. "How are you doing?"

"How am I doing?" Bonnie scratched her cheek with her prosthesis. "I'm fine, thank you. How are you doing?"

This was not going particularly well. "Good."

"That's good."

"Yesterday was quite the day!" I felt sure that this was the type of statement we could both agree on.

"And how!" Bonnie's face was a useless, placid sheet.

I forced myself to smile. "That was quite a party!"

"It was. I could not *believe* some of the guests." Bonnie raised an eyebrow and engaged my gaze.

"Yes," I said.

"Some real blasts from the past, if I do say so myself."

"There were," I muttered.

"Stella, is everything going, you know, *OK*?" The last word of her sentence was one of the most brutal euphemisms I have ever heard.

"Um, sure," I maintained. I may have followed this up with a cheerful "Ha ha!" I am not entirely certain. It had not been, as everyone increasingly seemed to understand, a particularly good six to twenty-four months.

"I'm very glad to hear that."

"Of course," I lied.

"Because the uncertainty of staff in this department being what it is, I really could not stand to have to *lose* someone else."

And there it was, acknowledgment and ultimatum rolled neatly into one, the Bonnie Mangold special. She was telling me a number of things: (1) that we were not yet speaking openly about whatever the situation with Paul was, and while she understood that it was only human of me to come into her office to inquire, it would be better if I were to assume a slightly more godly attitude and observe unfolding events from a dignified distance; (2) that Bonnie was aware that I was, at the moment, romantically fucked on several counts. As far as point two went, Bonnie was willing to let particulars slide, but she did not wish to see me rolling up to any additional CeMArt A-list events with the defendant in my nonamicable divorce absurdly in tow. (I willed myself not to consider the wide range of bizarre behavior in which Whit could have freely engaged after my exit.) The reasons for this stunt were not known to Bonnie, and she had little curiosity about them, but one thing she did know was that jealousy was the near-certain culprit. Reason told her that a triangle must have a third point, perhaps even a fourth, and she was doing her best not to look for candidates within the confines of our present working arrangement.

To the extent that I could smile, I smiled. "Thanks, Bonnie." For once, I really meant this. Overwhelmed by her candor, I removed myself from the premises.

I went home. I mean, I got on the 6 and missed my stop and ended up riding all the way to Union Square. After a struggle, I was ejected from the L at Bedford. It was buzzing with design girls in polyester and thin little bandmates whose tattoos appeared to outweigh them. I pushed through this candy-colored dream of taste, smarting some from my relative dowdiness, and found the street above similarly occupied: proofreaders dressed as majorettes, anorexics in suspenders, rich women in artisanal clogs propping up sobbing toddlers, languorous Swedes engrossed in lifestyle banter, recent escapees of Florida bearing a rickety kitchen table back to their six-person share, the occasional fleet of skaters outfitted like it was 1991, designers who were teenagers in 1991 with Swiss-made glasses and three-thousand-dollar attachés, twenty-three-year-old investment bankers looking to fuck something.

I don't care for Williamsburg, but I felt like I wanted the walk. I was unsure what, if anything, I understood about what I had lately experienced, my recent reading not really serving to help matters.

I walked. McCarren Park's floodlights were mystically dispersed by lambent, airborne moisture. Past the park I stopped in a bodega I frequent for coffee, The New Star, and visited very briefly with Idris, its middle-aged owner.

Idris observed, as he always did, "I notice you keep coming back."

"Thanks, Idris, see you tomorrow."

"By the way, my son is working then."

"OK, great!"

I don't really know what he said after that because I just ran out of the store. I get nervous about developing relationships these days, as much as I continue to seek them out. Everything has just been so unrelentingly bad. And I am sometimes a shy person, and this may be part of it. I was not looking for a new husband just yet, and, more than any of the above, it disturbed me that my singleton status, not to mention the accompanying loneliness, was so apparent to others.

I went into the twenty-four-hour organic market for wasabi peas and a couple of big bottles of lager. I was thinking about what I wanted to watch online, preferably something with women in outfits. It didn't really matter what it was as long as they were under the age of twenty-five and haunted by technology-induced memory loss and bad credit rather than the disembodied spirits of Western feminism.

I mean, this *was* what I was thinking about as I threw myself into the apartment and proceeded to crack into my exceptionally unhealthy provisions. Because it wasn't very long at all before I remembered that I happened to be in possession of materials that might explain recent events, were I to expend the modicum of effort necessary to interpret them.

I rooted around in my bags and picked out the flash drive, administered it to the relevant slot. An icon appeared, and I clicked on it. "Paul" I had named the folder. *"Paul,"* I prayed, "please explain to me what was going on in Elysia. And, if you can, please tell me where you are. I feel like I need you."

Then I read for several hours, eventually dragging the laptop into bed, in which location sleep and literature united, and I fell into the following dream:

I was following Whit Ghiscolmb up Broadway, vaguely in the upper eighties. Northern Broadway was a far wider boulevard than downtown, extending up an immense slope, an infinite Olympian hill of majestically low grade. Whit was wearing some sort of Amish reworking of the rollerblade, made of leather with rawhide laces, steel wheels. How I knew so much about the roller boots Whit had on I do not know, as he was some ten yards ahead of me, and the distance between us appeared, realistically enough, to be increasing.

As in so many of my dreams, I had already panicked. One never really knows where a dream begins, what its first scene is, or at least I do not. At any rate, Whit was already pumping away, skating easily. I struggled after him, but my knees were numb; it was impossible to command them to bend correctly, to propel my feet. I was ashamed. I felt a kind of sadness that would have resembled the kind of sadness one feels for a minor lost thing, the annoyance of a charm dropped off a bracelet at the beach, that is, if the sadness had not been so carefully mixed with dread.

I came to a campsite. I mean, I was suddenly elsewhere. There was a group of good-looking campers a little bit older than me, all searching around on their hands and knees, really giving the ground a good once-over. One or two appeared to be wearing the daisy-shaped mouthpieces last seen in Lorelei's excursion. These solicited advice from an assembly of evidently eloquent millipedes, grubs, and beetles. I was approached by a young man in shorts with a thick black beard. He took me aside. We stepped under a tent where there was a young woman in a purple T-shirt, her skin golden, lightly freckled. This woman began to question me, and I began to answer her in French. I had to use the most rudimentary words in order to make myself understood. Mostly loan words from the English.

I explained that I was the sister of the girl who had been killed. I had not seen her for several days, but during the night of the previous evening, I had dreamed a dream, and in the dream there was a serpent in my

144

stomach, and when I woke up it was gone.

The young woman, totally unfazed by either my unusual language or the tale of serpent-flavored continuity drift, politely asked what, never mind this sister, had happened to me.

I pointed, sniffling, to my knee. "I fell and cut myself, and then we put on this *bande d'aide.*"

■ ■ ■ ■

WEDNESDAY

■ ■ ■ ■

12

On Wednesday I was not just on time to work, I was a full hour early. I had slept like a log for approximately three hours and then arisen Lazarus style. I had floated through the subway.

I gained my desk, brought the computer to life. I intended to complete a few rudimentary email tasks before planning my day. I went into my inbox.

It was not to be so.

There was a pair of troubling messages. I decided to open the lesser of the two evils first. It was from Bonnie, timestamped 6:02 A.M. The subject line read "Call me when you get this." There was nothing in the body.

The second email was titled "Checking in." It was from Fred. It told me that Fred would like to have lunch around one P.M. today, please, if I was planning to be in the office (a curious conditional) and might be available. It didn't say anything else. It had been sent eight minutes after Bonnie's missive.

My heart was throttling itself like a mouse with its head caught under a trap. I sternly instructed myself that such a reaction was not just overkill but also premature. I took some deep breaths. I picked up the handset of my office phone, punched 9 for an outside line, and dialed Bonnie's cell, which is a number I have, not even inadvertently, memorized.

She picked up after two rings. "Hi."

"Good morning," I said. "I just saw your message."

"Yes."

I waited.

"Stella, are you sitting down right now?"

The subtext of this question totally escaped me. "At my desk, yes," very proud to be telling her that I was already in the office.

"OK," said Bonnie, "and your back is supported?"

I think I was at this point mainly relieved that Bonnie's interrogation had once again mercifully not turned to the matter of Frederick Lu. Although something in my brain chided me. This conversation was reminding me of a dialogue I had entertained with my friend Cate a week ago, our umpteenth rehearsal of the dissolution of my alliance with Whit. I had been describing the afternoon on which I came across Whit's sext collection. I was describing the feeling of that moment, of nothing being as it had seemed, which was a little like being in an earthquake, if this is something you have ever experienced. Whenever I took a step, to walk across the carpet, for example, to the window, with its pleasant view of August sky, it seemed like the carpet, the floor, felt either six inches higher than it should have been or six inches lower. Wherever I tried to put my foot, it came to rest in a place other than that which had been anticipated. I finally had to sit down, and while sitting I had an experience that I described to Cate as the feeling of "the unconscious rushing into my face, like a face-size river or waterfall."

Cate asked, "Did you faint?"

I thought about it for a second. It was difficult to remember everything. I told her no. But I said that it was possible that I had gone in and out of consciousness, that there had been these bright bursts, mental flares.

I briefly replayed this exchange in my mind now. To Bonnie I said, "The chair is doing its work."

"OK." She paused. "So I'm just going to

151

tell you this. Paul passed away. His sister found him."

I swallowed, probably audibly. I had the distinct sensation of having already known that Bonnie was going to tell me this.

"They're not sure yet if it was a suicide or an accident."

"Oh." Then for some reason I said, "What kind of accident would this be?"

"The kind," Bonnie told me, "where you overmedicate yourself."

"OK," I said. I wasn't crying or really doing anything. There was something weird in the air, like a thought. Someone somewhere seemed to be thinking the phrase *Things can get so unrelentingly bad.*

"Well, now you know. There's the end to that mystery."

Bonnie didn't say anything for a moment and neither did I.

"I'm sorry." This was Bonnie again. "I don't mean to be so callous. I'm actually pretty shaken. I've known Paul a long time. You work with someone and you think that's his life."

I didn't know if or how Bonnie expected me to respond to this. It seemed like what she was saying was accurate. It was additionally, I reflected, proof of how Bonnie herself lived, along with a symptomatic lack of imagination as far as the existences of others were concerned.

"Well, I guess I'll let you go, then."

"Right," I said.

"I'll be in on the late side."

"Yes."

"I'll see you?"

"Yes," I told her.

"Till then," she said, and hung up her phone.

It wasn't that I wasn't busy. It was just that the task of diverting myself with accomplishment seemed overwhelming on this particular day. I stared at Fred's email for a while and finally responded to the effect that I would gladly join him for a midday collocation, he should just name the time and place.

There was no more Paul, I thought to myself. No one to wonder over anymore, or to feel superior to, or to feel oddly touched and appreciated by. I considered getting up and going to gaze into his empty office as some sort of maudlin gesture of farewell. But just as I thought this thought, a strange spell came over me. My brain kept repeating the words "his empty office, his empty office." *Paul was no longer here.*

I, I recalled, had tampered with evidence.

I'd copied files from Paul's computer onto a portable drive and had begun to read them. Not that there was going to be a criminal investigation, necessarily. Then why was this the first thing that came to mind? I mean, it's possible that being told that Paul had addiction issues of some kind had something to do with it.

But could Paul not have just *died*? Could he have been — and how to put this with a minimum of drama — *encouraged* to do so?

I was really not particularly into contemplating these possibilities. I regretted immensely the fact that they were so persistently coming to mind. I wanted to stop this series of ideations and go back in time a couple of years, pausing for a moment at the Delaware retreat to elect *not* to pay a visit to the brick hut inhabited by Fred Lu, and I wanted go back into the somewhat deeper past to tell Whit that things weren't working for me, and that I loved him but this couldn't go on, that I needed to do what I was going to do in this life and if that bothered him so very much and gave him the impression that I was an uppity baby-hating snob so very much then we should not be living together or even speaking to each other, because it was really

154

fucking shitty and reactionary for a man with so much education and, basically, some nonnegligible supply of human decency to be telling the person he had, early on but still, verbally accepted as his life partner that she was not able to at once love him and be the person that she (indubitably) was.

But I could not go back into the past. At least, I could not go back into a personal past. And what that left me with was history.

I thought about this for a moment. It was not clear to me whether anything in my life was going to be OK ever again. I mean, this was truly how I was feeling. But there was something in me that was causing me to simultaneously feel that I could not practice avoidance, I could not just shirk this. For whatever reason I was implied.

I stood and went down the hall, let myself into Paul's haven. Things appeared much as I had left them. I switched on the computer and typed "PASSWORD" in the dialogue box.

OK, I thought. Now for a moment of truth.

I pressed ENTER. The system told me there was an error with my username or password. I tried again. Nothing. And again.

Fuck, I thought. Possibly some agent has acted to prevent me from gaining access to Paul's files! And then I thought, *Shit!* Because without warning there came the sound of knuckles casually applied to Paul Coral's door. And you can guess who that was.

"Hey!" I nearly yelled, spinning in Paul's chair.

Frederick Lu's face was hard to assess. It was possible that he was betraying a genre of sympathy for me, that he believed that he had interrupted me in the midst of some manner of grieving ritual with which he was unfamiliar, but it was also not outside the realm of all livable and/or probable events that the affect now slowly dawning on his countenance was the product of the realization that he had just caught me snooping.

"Good morning," Fred said.

My hands were not so much shaking as vibrating. "Hi," I said. I was really not sure what I should do.

Fred blinked. He allowed his shoulder to contact the doorjamb and he leaned. "I guess you heard."

"I did."

"There's so much we didn't know about him. About Paul."

I nodded. I made my hands into fists and then attempted to tuck them into my lap so their continued autonomous quivering would be less visible. "It's true."

Fred shrugged, and I was unnerved to perceive what looked like a tear beginning along the lower rim of each of his eyes. I think an expression of horror must have shown up on my face, because Fred gasped, "I'm very sorry."

I was quickly on my feet and wrapping my arms around Fred, who was now audibly weeping. The only thing stranger than this turn of events was that I myself felt absolutely nothing. "It's OK," I muttered. I wasn't sure if I was referring to Fred's sudden display, to the uncertain status of our relationship, or to our mutual loss of Paul. Indeed, I was fairly sure that not a single one of these things was "OK," nor did I have any confidence that any one of these minor disasters was going to be resolved to anyone's satisfaction, anytime soon. Above all, it was disturbing to be in such close proximity to Fred Lu. It wasn't something I'd anticipated when I began my day. He was so lean, as of course I remembered, and also so tall in comparison to me, and his body, as I embraced it, was additionally very warm inside his immaculate and exceptionally nice-smelling and very high-quality clothes. I decided it was time to separate. To be honest, I had begun to move on from critical and/or paranoid thought to other more material, shall we say, reflections. "Are you all right?"

Fred sniffed. He was feeling in his pocket. I felt amazed to watch him produce an actual pressed handkerchief. He handled this item so casually, too, as if everyone walked around with one. "Yes, thank you." Fred ministered to his face and patted his lustrous hair. He seemed to want his face to settle back into its usual pert professional mask, but it was not cooperating with him.

"Do you maybe," I hazarded, "want to forgo lunch?" I didn't pose this question entirely innocently. It was intended as a test.

Fred balked but then speedily recomposed. He released a nasal *"Oh."* Then he said, "Sure, I understand."

I tried not to let out an enormous laugh of triumph. I forced my face into a shape I felt approximated innocence. "I just meant, maybe we could go for coffee now, instead? I mean, since we're already talking?"

I watched Fred mentally check his calendar. He experimented with a few substitutions before coming back to me. "That makes sense. Let me just do one thing at my desk and I'll meet you by the stairs."

There were so many things I could think. That was always the thing. And yet the feeling, that feeling, in spite of Paul's sudden death and so many other regrets and so much infuriation, would not stop. It was the feeling of it being my birthday as it had never once been my birthday on my actual birthday, the feeling of it being some imaginary type of Christmas yet to be invented, the New Year, of it being spring for the first time, the face of a tiny kitten who is speaking fluent Spanish and is also a genie who can grant your wish, of being truly implied as the person I really was when another person spoke my name. My heart was a piece of paper. It was a paper fan. It was a dove. In spite of everything, it moved for Fred.

I also knew that Fred was capable of needing things from me. But this didn't mean that he felt, in turn, moved to change his life in order that it become responsive to my needs and wants. That was just the way things were — or, that was where we had left it. There were, according to Fred, "things you do not understand" inherent to his existence.

In spite of our insoluble asymmetry, Fred

and I were now together descending the steep stairs to the cafeteria catacomb. We were in short order surrounded by glittering white tile, a much-contested intervention on the part of a Dutch designer acclaimed for her antiseptic restraint. We weren't speaking, and it took until we were settled across from one another, burned coffee in hand, to begin the exchange.

"Thanks for reaching out." This was me. As usual, there had been a total reset in the course of our transit.

Fred said I was welcome. His face appeared oddly muscular.

I decided I would be generous. "It's good to talk."

"It is."

"How are you holding up?"

"You are referring to the events of this morning?"

"You're asking if I'm talking about Paul?" I asked.

There was a pause. "Well, I wasn't the one sitting in his office chair at nine A.M." Fred gave me a long look, sipped from his cup. "I take it you were just wrapping things up there with regards to the checklist?"

"Of course."

"Never mind, then, Stella."

It was now my turn to more carefully

160

scrutinize Fred. He sounded a little angry, miffed. He took a moment to consider his fingernails. "I have to tell you," he began, "you and I have to figure out a way to work together. I can't have you doing, for example" — he was looking down into his Styrofoam cup — "what you are doing *right now,* staring at me that way. And when I walk into a room, it's like I've committed a crime. I can't have that. I first of all don't deserve it and second it's not, as I'm sure you understand, *conducive.* It doesn't work for what we are trying to accomplish here." Fred pursed his lips, eyes intent on what was occurring along the surface of his drink. At the center of his forehead, a slender branching vein popped gracefully out. "I don't mean to pull rank, and I know that *things,*" he concluded, "have not been very clear."

"Right."

"That's true for me, too. I hope you understand that."

This, by the way, is the sort of sentiment that makes my stomach turn over. I would rather hear almost anything than that an individual is entertaining feelings for me but that he is doing so at arm's length, the better to reassure himself that he can exit the situation whenever he wants. In Fred's case, this was a very, very long arm. It covered the distance of multiple months with ease. Who knew how far into the future it extended. It was likely steadily working its way into the past as well, rearranging events at its leisure. And it made hearing from him about whatever it was he might admit to feel a kind of agony, for any feeling once admitted could just as easily, elastically, be taken back again. Nothing would be said here unless it had already been engineered to be retractable.

Fred began to twist the knife. "I've worried about you, Stella. Some of the things you said. I worried that you might even hurt yourself."

"I don't like that," I told him.

Fred kept talking. "But you really said those things, Stella. To me. I realize that I shouldn't and won't simply let a statement like that go by. I can't. Not now. Not after what happened" — he paused — "with Paul."

I was probably speaking too quickly. "FYI, I was living with someone who was lying a lot and that does funny things to a person, you know? Like, things have names, but if you don't treat those names with respect, the world becomes distorted. That's how it was. Sorry. I'm sorry you got involved with that."

"I know. I've been trying not to be confused by your attachment to that" — he was searching for a word — "that *individual.*" If this was a reference to Monday night, it did make a kind of sense that Fred could currently be concerned, re: harm, re: me.

I opted for euphemism. "Just keep me in your peripheral vision, Fred. That's all I really need!"

Fred seemed to take this remark seriously. He muttered, "OK." He was listening, part of him now like a boy who is receiving an explanation as to why sadistically stepping on small invertebrate creatures is an ethical bad move. He was treating me with strange awe, as if the manifestations of my affect were some species of delicious arctic fish that had to be shipped live from afar then meticulously gutted lest some slip of the blade render the flesh poisonous. I could tell he was drawing from this conversation not so much information about the state of whatever was transpiring between the two of us as "life lessons" to which he would later refer, as he moved on through the series of carefully coordinated events that would form the rest of his "life." And yet there was this *thing,* and all the while this thing was continuing to transpire. And there was some small unscientific part of Fred that did not just perceive this but agreed with me about what it meant.

"I'm just saying, I don't like your desire for total knowledge about me, if you know what I mean, Fred? That can only lead to pain. Didn't Nietzsche have an aphorism for that?"

Fred was silent.

"Look," I said, barreling violently on, "I fell in love with you and it didn't work out. Too bad for me. I know you just want to share some office etiquette protips. I get that! I get it. It's great! It's very nice of you. Very thoughtful. I am trying. I just have to be able to care about you, even if you don't care about me, and that isn't easy. It actually hurts my pride, not to mention my sense of self-respect. I know based on my actions it might not be totally obvious, but I do have some."

Fred allowed the air to cease churning. "I just think," he pronounced slowly, not without softness, "that for me life is easiest when I can care about a number of people."

"You are saying I make this impossible?"

"I am saying that is not how caring about you seems to work."

13

Here's what, by the way, I knew: I, Stella
Krakus, was either onto something major at
the Central Museum of Art, or I was surrounded by a veritable clusterfuck of fever
dreams and their respective paranoiac
authors, into whose ranks I would soon
perhaps, if I was not careful, be able to
induct myself.

If we can turn for a moment from the
beautiful impossibility that was Fred, this
fascinating hyperrational narcissist, if we
can kind of freeze him where he sits, like
the leftovers of that strange arctic fish to
which he compared my feelings, I can attempt to articulate something about what I
had lately learned. I can say that for starters
Paul's research, as read by me on the previous night, had not been easy to parse, at
least not for a newcomer. There were literally hundreds of PDF'ed auction catalogs
and scanned antiques periodicals extolling

the magnitude of sales of earlier American art and furniture, detailing the particulars of various American artifacts. These were haphazardly grouped in a folder titled simply "FACTS." I had begun to make my way through these.

I had been hoping that there might be some obvious thread connecting these various documents of sales, like a single collector. But this appeared not to be the case. Nor was the market in question particularly uniform. There were important American hand-knotted carpets, earlier musical instruments, Hepplewhite, Colonial glassware, weather vanes, and so on, along with portraits, scenic watercolors, theorem paintings, and the like. Eventually I had given up on this cache and turned instead to the only slightly more perturbingly titled folder, "LIES." This one had to make you wince a little, since it seemed to reveal Paul's state of mind. I was willing, more than willing, to go along with him in the supposition that individuals were not being entirely truthful much or most of the time. But I found the distinction drawn between *fact* and *lie* a little rich. Or, to return to a term I introduced earlier, *paranoid.*

Anyway, inside the "LIES" folder were somewhere between thirty and forty historicist academic articles addressing the arts and material culture of the United States. Included was a piece by Bonnie on periodicity in botany engraving and Fred's well-known revision of certain canonical assumptions about Gilbert Stuart's education. (My zebra piece was evidently deemed too "truthful" to make it into this anthology.) What Paul had amassed here was essentially the accepted wisdom, the scholarship. This was what people thought that American art before 1900 *was*.

So, OK, possibly everything that everyone had managed to think about the history of earlier North American/Euro aesthetics was trash. I mean, it was unlikely, but fine, why not say it was possible, if that was what Paul meant by his folder title. We could consider the notion that all of these scholars were not just wrong but consciously and therefore nefariously (?) making things up.

But it did occur to me that Paul might have meant something slightly different. Etymologically, *fact* and *fiction* are nearly synonymous, derived from Latin verbs meaning, on the one hand, "to make/do," and on the other, "to make/form." Since facts are, therefore, as I see it, practically semantically identical to fictions, one may invent one's pleasant facts just as easily as one's comfy, palatable untruths. And I have found that one can lie to oneself very effectively within the confines of one's own mind. I wasn't yet sure if Paul felt the same way. I wasn't sure if he had ever been betrayed, or, if he had, on what sort of time scale. For duration, I felt, makes all the difference.

I was thinking about the last meaningful conversation Paul and I had shared. The blessed solitude of my otherwise uncultivated cafeteria table had been, on the day in question, interrupted by the shadow of a tall, stooped figure.

"Hello, Paul," I said.

"Hello yourself."

"How are you?"

"What an awful question," Paul told me.

If I am recalling accurately, Paul's tray contained an egg salad sandwich sliced on the diagonal, one small bottle of apple juice, a stack of twenty or so white paper napkins, a black plastic spoon, and one dish of pine-green gelatin.

"I didn't know they had that," I said, indicating his dessert.

"All cafeterias are required, by law."

I told him, "Neat."

Paul rotated the plate containing the sandwich so that one of its corner points was pointing directly at the center of his chest. He told me, "I enjoyed your remarks on *Fluidomanie.*" There was a sort of prurient glint in his eye, but I elected to ignore it.

Paul was referring to http://mais-mon-ami-tu-t-es-trompe-d-omnibus.tumblr.com, a blog I used to keep but which is now, as of about a month or so ago, defunct. There had been some important developments regarding Daumier's satirical series on drawing room séances. The mania for "fluid" referenced in Daumier's title had mainly to do with the role of ether and other sorts of imaginary shareable goo in nineteenth-century communications with the dead. As I had contended in my post, ectoplasm, which had recently come on the scene in the acts of certain female mediums, was a curious, metaphorical substance. What were the full connotations of a performance in which a woman spontaneously "emitted" this uncanny jelly? It definitely had something to do with the changing role of women in industrialized society, but just what this role *was* became kind of a sticky issue upon closer examination.

"Thanks."

"Not at all. Nice you're going more material."

I asked to know what this might mean.

"Oh. That you're less driven by questions of technique and schools? You actually dare to read the artwork as an autonomous entity? It's fun to see you try something new. I think otherwise you have a tendency to take a rather bloodless view?" Paul lowered a hand onto one half of his sandwich and raised it to his lips. The triangle of rye was inserted and compacted. Paul continued, "I assume that's how they train you people these days. But you, Stella Krakus, possess an intriguing feral side."

Paul was an unusual sensualist. Crumbs began to collect on the front of his already dander-powdered dark blue sweater. It was not lost on me that I could have chosen to entertain a more generous view of Paul's person. As the department's longtime registrar, he was ostensibly well respected, not to mention knowledgeable, and he was additionally nice enough to take an interest in my writing, such as it was, but I couldn't help finding his physical appearance sort of awful. Now the second half of his sandwich met its end.

I contemplated my cup of thin orange soup. All the food served here was vaguely revolting, and really what I wanted to do was go somewhere and think some more about some works on paper I had lately been researching. "I guess," I told Paul.

"But soon you'll *know,*" Paul was saying, revealing one or two views of the interior landscape of his mouth.

I was forced to look away. Now I asked, staring into my mug of lemon tea, "Was that what you wanted to talk about?"

There came a series of forceful coughs. Paul rummaged in his napkins.

I shifted my gaze back to Paul's face.

He was wiping his mouth, daubing the edges of his watering eyes. "How is that?" For a second he seemed terrified.

"I just meant," I began, "I mean, my blog is so silly."

"Silly?" said Paul. He seemed, if I may engage for a moment in understatement, disappointed. Deflated was more accurate. "Stella," said Paul, "what you write is a lot of things, but silly is not one of them."

And it was funny now, thinking back on this exchange, which at the time had been interrupted by the arrival of one of Paul's interns, whose name I think was Felix. It was as if I had struck some kind of nerve there with Paul, though at the time I did not have any reason to give it a second thought. It was a useful memory, or somewhat more useful, when it came to me now.

171

When I thought about it in relation to G. G. Hennicott's novel, for example. If Paul knew about *Lorelei of Millbury,* if he had been at all sympathetic to that rather unique romance, then perhaps this could have been related to his apparent liking for my *fluidomaniacal* reflections. Maybe he even saw me as a fellow Hennicott fan!

Still, I had no idea what the connection between the book and the map was, frustratingly. Who had made the map? Why did Paul have it? And, most burning question of all, *where oh where* was the original? All the people running around my life were distracting me from what should have been the fruits of my labor, i.e., not drama but cold, hard, calculated knowledge. I would have been more than willing to meet all of them for a séance or some other summoning of the spirits, ectoplasmic goop notwithstanding, if only we could please let the matter of whatever was so troublingly wrong with me be! It was not the most sensitive thought a human being has ever had, seeing as my colleague was only recently at rest, but perhaps Paul Coral might intercede on my behalf, were I able to arrange a supernatural convocation.

There was still a folder to go in what I had retrieved from Paul's computer. This one was titled only "etc." It was a lot smaller than the other two and contained just a couple of text-only documents. I hadn't had the energy to go into it the night before. I could hold out some hope for that now.

But for the moment I was still stuck on Fred's line: "I am saying that is not how caring about you seems to work." It was such an incredibly beautiful formulation, nearly demonic, when you took a moment to think about it. Something worthy of a mind fucker on the exalted level of a Caro, even, and Fred was still so early on in his game! Fred was a lover whose hold over me, though all but disavowed from his side, would not quit. He'd cut deeply, and somehow the incision continued, as if mechanical, automated. Indeed, I was able to expand my lover's aphoristic phrase into something that made slightly more (if syllogistic) sense:

1. Stella loves Frederick.
2. Frederick loves Stella.
3. For Frederick, upon reflection, the verb *to love* is defined as "loving multiple women, when he likes, with varying degrees of transparency regarding this behavior, with said mercurial transparency being a

significant factor in his ability to love."

4. For Stella, the verb *to love* is defined as "loving one person."
5. Frederick understands Stella.
6. Therefore, Frederick and Stella are not in love.

I also, I need to be completely honest, even if it makes me grind my teeth and stamp my feet, had always known about Fred's longtime girlfriend, even before I had reason to Google her on a weekly basis. She was a bicoastal financial advisor. She apparently gave Fred plenty of downtime to pursue his definition of *love*. I have only ever seen her face in photographs, but both *Forbes* and Frederick Lu insist she's real.

14

It was not easy to sit there, to listen to Fred. He wasn't just speculating about a world in which he could both love and not love, he was actively creating this world. I don't mean to portray myself as a total naïf, but this was precisely the sort of dialectic I had gotten married in order to avoid.

The problem was how simple it was to remember the feeling of being with him, even ten months after the event, how near to hand the memory was, his fingers moving lazily as I kissed him, me above him. I said, "You are so sweet." It was so gentle. And a human being can feel so worn out.

It does still make me feel a little better to describe some of what happened. Sort of fake the second night. We were both wanting to fuck all day long. Thinking of it constantly. I immediately took off my clothes. And it was sort of arid, intellectual or something. He did not come inside me.

We were lying down and he seemed concerned that I might become pregnant. I explained that, due to the presence of 100 percent of his recent ejaculation on my stomach, plus the current state of my cycle, which did not involve the availability of an egg, this would be a miracle. Then I said that what he should be more concerned about was the fact that I did not come.

"What shall I do?"

"I can't say," I said.

"Do you want me to go down on you?"

"Yes," I told him.

I don't remember if it took very long, but it was only when he put his fingers inside me that I eventually came. It was shallow, I had to press for it, and it was very clitoral. I was vaguely proud of myself for coming, all the same.

Fred then wanted to know, "Keep going?" Why is it men say this? Do you want me to bite your dick or keep squeezing it or what is it? Surely no one wants that. I told him no.

I was worried that I would have a cramp in my right calf muscle from flexing it so hard as I tried to get there, but subsequently I did not feel anything. I do not remember if I thanked him. I do remember that somewhere I asked him not to be possessive of me, not to "lead me around on a leash." He was somewhat irritable at the time, probably exhausted. A peck good night and then back to my own brick hut.

I became nonchalant myself, thinking this. Being able to narrate such things makes them seem manageable, clichés somehow. I could have said that "my heart had been aching for months," that I had felt so low and not about a lie but about the fact that I could have allowed this to happen for something that didn't seem like love. All the same, it wasn't *not* love. I knew that I, like Fred, had made an argument to myself about my own way of living, about marriage and all else. I had accepted it, valued it — through argumentation. I had practiced my life. I could just as easily not practice it: Or, it was not going to be *easy.*

I considered, in the vacant staff cafeteria, pawing at Fred's chest. I considered telling him that he couldn't keep doing this, that we could not keep having the same conversation in which he told me that he cared about me, kept me on the hook, all the while letting me know he didn't care and didn't have to. I wanted to tell him to stop letting me lead myself on. To stop emailing me every month and letting me hug him and inviting me out to platonic discussions like the current one, in which we would vivisect our still-breathing love. I wanted to say this, even as I wanted none of this, not a single part or iota, to ever, ever end. Because this was, naturally enough, the definition of Stella-Krakus love, and now that Stella Krakus no longer had a husband to distract her, she would be able to live her particular species of love out with even greater specificity and less contradiction, with respect to its peculiar definition.

Fred was waiting for me to say something.

"I guess that's true."

"What is?"

"That I'd want you all for myself." It was terrifying to say such things. "I'm like that. I'm not confused on that point, at least." I attempted a smile. "Thank you."

"I'm sorry, why are you thanking me? Does this mean we're going to see some improvement in office demeanor?"

"Why not?" I told him. I wanted very badly to hurt him now, but I felt that it was unlikely that I would succeed with anything near the devastating effect that would make the attempt worthwhile. "Thanks, you made me realize what it is I need." I produced another false smile.

"Would you mind telling me what exactly that is? As a kind of courtesy?" Fred's reaction was difficult to characterize.

"Ha. Sure. A Band-Aid. I think I cut myself."

And with this cryptic non sequitur placed squarely between us, I bid Frederick adieu. I was like, "Got to answer some email!" There was no way in hell I was going to start being nice to him anytime soon, but as long as he remained ill at ease after a fashion that served my interests, we would be getting along well enough. NB: I never said my loving someone meant that I would always be transparent.

Anyway, I had achieved a minor mental breakthrough, and it was time to see if my hunch was correct. I exited the staff cafeteria by way of the back stairs, headed over to the American Wing. I hung a left, scampered up a priceless lapis and ivory stair, extracted from the famous Quartier Oriental of the first Sapersmythe residence, to the second floor. On the American balcony daylight was describing diverse cased decorative things pertinent to the lifestyles of the robber barons of our nation. I passed a large display of ceramic spoons. I admired a tiered arrangement of silver gravy boats. As I passed, I examined the nearest of these servers, one that had a deft gooseneck handle, by which I mean, the actual miniature neck of a goose. The beak of this finely articulated head of fowl was clamped down over a lily pad. When the boat was filled to capacity, the goose would appear, amazingly enough, to be dipping the leaf daintily into the gravy. I went down the hall, entering one of the 1909-style display spaces maintained in memory of the Fultham-Rhys exhibition. Here furnishings are displayed on raised plinths pushed back somewhat unnaturally against the wall, though one still has a sense of domestic space — even if compacted, even without the obvious, diorama-esque artifice of the period room. It's a dreary walkway, if you ask me, but something that balances the funhouse effect of the wing's numerous period arrangements, which are complete with artificial skies and daylight just beyond the rooms' windows.

All this started shortly after the 1909 decorative arts show I mention, with the museum's first acquisition of a partial American room in the form of a paneled fireplace and attached wall obtained from a mid-eighteenth-century house on Long Island. It was the 1910 gift of one Evelyn Johnson de Woody, wife of the secretary of the museum's board of directors and niece of the museum's first president, who was in some sense assisting in the "decoration" of her husband's clubhouse. The next year an additional section of paneling was harvested from a large farmhouse in Hampton, New Hampshire, by Secretary de Woody himself, who took long antiquing vacations in the Northeast and was evidently not one to be shown up by his better half.

Then Wallace Wynne Johns, a blond man with a very round face who, as his portrait in the Trustees' Dining Room attests, bore a passing resemblance to Pac-Man, was made curator shortly after the creation of the Department of American Objects in 1907. Johns then hired a talented younger man, Jonah Durr Weiss, as his assistant. Weiss, incidentally the museum's first Jewish curator, in turn obtained in 1912 two rooms that had been removed from a federal house in Harvard, Massachusetts, after which Weiss wrote in a letter to his mother that "this Museum possesses the makings of a definitive series of American paneled, or partially paneled, rooms, and I sincerely hope that no one shall stand in our way as we aim to one day have the whole house!" He later complained of having spent a bile-freezing winter scavenging through the thirteen original colonies for Colonial carved wall panels, which "are not released from their settings with ease!"

181

Weiss's major successes were a complete ballroom, "then used as a chicken run," removed in 1917 from Colby's Tavern in Providence, and an upstairs parlor, "then a storage for casks," obtained in 1918 from the Bundt House in Philadelphia. In subsequent years, Weiss and his successors found better luck below the Mason-Dixon, where impoverished white landholders were more easily convinced than the doughty Yanks to sell off magnificent papered salons, elaborate frescoes, mantels, and whatever other decorative elements could be scraped from the walls of their plantation manors and liquidated in order to forestall foreclosure.

These, then, were the artifacts that gave form to most of the American Wing. The domestic spaces were clean, frozen in time, sumptuous, and not particularly spectral. They presented a sort of silent sitcom set of the past, minus, of course, stories of labor and race — which is to say, they were a person-size dollhouse reflecting the aspirations of a very select group of émigrés from Western Europe.

However, this was not where I was going. I made a sharp left and entered, up a small set of steps, a dimly lit room. Though this space is open to the public, it is one of the least visited parts of the museum. We call it our department's "visible storage." It affords the visitor passage among numerous floor-to-ceiling glass cases containing mediocre likenesses of socialites and decorative items of questionable interest and rarity. Really, it is the place we keep works of art that were accepted into our department's collection with the stipulation that if they were not regularly and/or constantly put on display, they would need to be returned to the families of origin. Of course, we don't allow these sorts of stipulations to be written into gift contracts anymore, and we have indeed allowed a certain number of *objets d'art* to fall out of the collection through violation of these very rules. But there are works that, mainly for reasons of history, we would prefer not to lose, and as we cannot fit them into the period rooms (already implausibly stuffed with ornamental accents) or into the meager additional gallery space that pertains to us, we stow them here, arranged in stacks or hanging from particleboard.

I knew where I was headed. I had to work from memory, so it took me a few minutes walking through the aisles, scanning the cases up and down. I was seeking an item whose value was almost entirely anecdotal or historical in nature, an object that had been donated between the wars by a Manhattan-bred heiress, Alice Gaypoole Wynne, whom I have always remembered for her distinctly horsey look, her shocked, melancholic white face and aggressively pomaded cap of dark hair, as memorialized in a 1920 portrait by Kees van Dongen, a Dutch-French Fauvist turned realist. This portrait hangs in a side gallery of the Musée d'Art Moderne de la Ville de Paris, and I saw it there years ago before making the connection one day at my desk. (This was when I was still trying to "familiarize" myself with the sum total of the collection, a project I've since abandoned for personal sanity.) CeMArt seems to possess no corresponding likeness of Alice Gaypoole Wynne, or just plain "Alice," as I call her. However, we maintain Alice's gift in visible storage in perpetuity. Her offering was a familial commonplace book (essentially a glorified scrapbook) kept from the late 1830s all the way into the 1870s by Wynne's great-grandmother, Brunhilda Wunsch Gaypoole, who was a well-known women's and immigrants' rights advocate back in the day. I have never seen an image of Brunhilda, née Wunsch, but one may assume she was less concerned about her hair than her excessively marcelled great-granddaughter,

Alice. Brunhilda is renowned not just for 1859's *Women and Poverty,* her extended essay on women's right to work, but for her early efforts in the organization of aid societies to help educate and organize the dramatically increasing immigrant populations in New York beginning in the final years of the 1830s. We understand that her husband, Gilbert Gaypoole, was either an extremely liberal or an extremely negligent man.

This, by the way, was how I now interpreted the phrase of my dream: *bande d'aide* = "group of aid" = "aid society."

This synonymy, or punning translation, had popped into my head while Frederick Lu and I were shooting the shit. It was a sort of rebus, the dream tying an intuitive knot. The Gaypoole commonplace book is, I should add, one of the few explicitly feminist — or female-authored — items in American Objects. I mean, there are some artisanal quilts and loomed rugs, but most everything else the museum has collected over the years was designed and constructed by male master craftsmen, if not industrially produced. I like Brunhilda's scrapbook because it is something that the museum would never collect today, having, behind it, far more story than market value. It's

185

also basically composed of trash. In this sense, it is a relic in more ways than one.

I should mention, too, that I don't always feel this way about my dreams, as if they contain significant messages or flags, but there was something about the dream in question, that here Whit was sailing away from me on his ancient roller skates, never, in spite of the fact that I was earnestly chasing after him, to return. Perhaps he was about to skate all the way into the Hudson River and sink in those very heavy historical booties! A girl could hope.

It seemed to me that in the past ten hours my brain had been working overtime and behind the scenes. I tried to recall if Paul had ever explicitly mentioned the Gaypoole commonplace book to me, or whether it was that I had at some point seen him in the visible storage staring at it. A specific memory was not coming to me. Yet the thought of this object was magnetic, it sang to me with my weird pun, *bande d'aide, bande d'aide,* and now I saw it, there it was: the commonplace book, on a bottom shelf, near the floor. It was leather bound, with warped and wrinkled pages onto which clippings of magazine mezzotints had been pasted, along with texts from articles and poems, sometimes written in by hand. The book was propped up on a plastic support with small feet and bracing arms. It was unlikely that this position was very good for it; the mode of presentation indicated, if not neglect, then curatorial agnosticism regarding the book's fate. I tried to recall the last time I had come here to stare at it. It could very well have been months ago, even a year. Yet I knew which clipping the Gaypoole commonplace book was open to. Because it usually showed an engraved image of the lighthouse lamp that sat atop Barnum's American Museum, a massive beacon announcing P. T. Barnum's intent to astound Americans by means of readymade and/or relatively commonplace objects, recontextualized via his bizarre rhetoric. There was something about the way in which the illumination of this industrial-strength lamp was described by the engraver, jumping spikily out into the obscurity surrounding it, a little like frayed pieces of lightning, that made the image particularly memorable. Though the text of the article was missing, I did happen to know that Barnum's hall of exhibition, located on Ann Street in Lower Manhattan, had been purchased by the showman and revamped in 1841. In it he displayed a loom run by a dog, the trunk of a tree under which Jesus sat, along with the

Feejee mermaid and various maudlin taxidermy displays and effigies in wax. All this was eventually destroyed by an 1865 fire.

But today the commonplace book showed an alternate image, what looked to be a wood engraving of a certain daguerreotype made famous (to Americanist art historians, at least) by a trial in which the photographer was accused of fraud. The clipping showed a bearded man in a long coat, vest, and pants seated at a writing desk, his hands covering a square of paper to which he is applying a pen, even as a third spectral hand, larger than his and attached to a giant, insubstantial arm, reaches down to guide his writing. In the background, a second spirit stands by, with a vague smiling face, wrapped in a sheet. Brunhilda, or someone else, had inscribed the page next to this extract, "After Mr. William H. Mumler's Picture of a Medium Guided by Spirit Hand and Spirit Child."

I stood staring at this transformation. A page had turned. There was no denying it, the commonplace book had been adjusted.

I reversed course and walked briskly back to my desk. My forehead was hot and I kept clenching and unclenching my own tiny, feminine hands. A notion was irrepressibly presenting itself: It wasn't the commonplace book itself that interested me so much as the family out of which it had emerged.

In my office, I sat down to an exceedingly curt email from Caro. The subject read "First floral display, East Side." This was very like her. The sole bodily content was a cell phone photo depicting an anemic violet cone, an unseasonably early showing by the lilac bushes surrounding the park's Alexandrian obelisk. The email was intended to acknowledge, simply, that Caro and I had once again managed to speak to one another and that, in mostly unrelated news, the world continued to support forms of beauty acceptable to social conservatives. It also indicated that Caro continued on in her belief that she and I had a relationship that could reasonably be characterized as "normal" and "fulfilling." I archived reflexively and turned to a long, halting message from Bonnie that informed the department of recent developments regarding Paul. Bonnie let everyone know that the museum would soon be sending flowers and that a card had been purchased and placed in a corner of the study room in order that we inscribe it with personal messages.

I sat there for a moment, considering this, Paul. This was how it could go. I could feel the smug presence of my own relief at simply not being dead like he was. I was alive, and thus there was some chance that in the intervening time before my own demise I might extricate myself from my affiliation with an existence not merely insignificant but also slightly embarrassing. I envisioned the gentle things I would put into my own message on the card, to whomever it was, the sister. I did have plenty of nice things to say about Paul. But mostly I was considering the fact that I did not want to die this way — which is to say, I did not want to die in *this present,* with my life what it currently was.

Anyway, this was not my life. It didn't feel like *my* life. It was something that had happened to me. It did not feel like the product of my actions.

I knew that I couldn't really go on holding such beliefs. I was living here, in this, so I had somehow "done" it. Maybe it was more accurate to describe my situation as one in which I had done things without knowing. In some cases, I might have looked the other way; in others, I possessed the kind of agency that derives from allowing things to simply go on, without demanding of oneself some sort of reckoning, i.e., I had the kind of agency that belongs to fools and

190

also to certain victims — or, if I were somewhat less generous with myself, persons in comas.

15

I was in the museum's database. The Gay-poole commonplace book had been inducted into the collection in winter of 1930, just as I'd remembered, the gift of Alice, she of overweening affection for hair lacquer, great-granddaughter of Brunhilda, mildly famous feminist, and immigrant rights activist. There was a note appended to the digital entry that let me know that the "gift" had been made "for the preservation and posterity of her great-grandmother's work." There was no mention of any sort of rider requiring that the book be displayed in perpetuity.

I needed to see the thing up close, to hold it in my hands. I knew where the keys to the case were located. These were kept in a box on the wall in the repair and study suite, which was really just a room adjoining visible storage. Standard procedure was to go to the registrar, meaning Paul, and schedule a time to have him go into the case and bring the object in question into the suite for closer inspection. This could be done just before or after normal museum hours. As there was now no Paul, I was unsure what I should do. I could go to Bonnie, but to be honest I didn't really much feel like explaining to her why I needed to view a part of the collection that was totally unrelated to my own area of expertise. After our recent conversation concerning my difficulties with saving face where men were concerned, and now the fairly shocking disruption that was Paul's death, I didn't feel so much like rocking the boat. Besides, there wasn't really a need to.

I remembered that on Monday morning of this week, when I had borrowed Paul's office and computer, I had also been adroit enough to take with me a souvenir in addition to his map and files. I had his keys! Now, I did not know at this moment whether or not I had the correct keys, whether one of them would in fact allow me into the repair and study suite, thus allowing me access to the locked box, the groan-worthy combination to which, I happened to know, was 1-7-7-6. I did not know, but I could try, and as far as I knew, as long as nothing went missing, it would be unlikely that any security footage of me making my consultation would be cause for upset. The cases themselves were not outfitted with motion-sensitive alarms. If someone in security did decide to file an inquiry about my actions, I could hope that it would be processed after I had figured out why this book was worthy of Paul's attention.

There was also the possibility of foul play. I have to admit that I didn't relish so much the fact that Paul was, well, *dead.* I mean, as I went into my bag and felt around, I was feeling for the keys of a dead man. I really don't like touching dead people's keys.

The better to distract myself from such ideations, I went online and searched until I found a biography of Alice Gaypoole Wynne. It had been out of print for nearly a decade and had the not exactly encouraging title *Will to Beauty: The Untold Story of Alice Gaypoole Wynne.* I paid forty-nine cents for it and then demanded that it be sent to my house by early the next morning, which cost an arm and a leg.

Then I did some inane email tasks for the next two hours. Around me, the department maintained sepulchral hush. Perhaps other staff of longer standing were so moved that they were electing not to come in. Bonnie had said as much in her email. One had permission.

It was just after five P.M., then, when I again exited my office. I padded over to visible storage and, after looking first left and then right, began trying Paul's keys in the doorknob of the repair and study room door. The second one slipped neatly in, displaced bolts. I therefore entered and helped myself to keys to the visible storage cases as well as a pair of art handler's gloves.

I reflected that I might now, at this very moment, be doing something that could get me fired. Oddly, this notion stirred me not at all. What felt good, *no,* sublime, was to be actually doing something, to be acting instead of not acting, to be walking upright instead of lying on my pale belly. I could, I reflected, always depend on this quality in myself, even if I burned through all the romantic loves that were granted to me in this world without settling happily on a single partner. Even if I never attained the exalted status of valid human in Caro's (inexplicably beautiful) eyes, I could be this being, this agent, who was convinced of what she must do and who, in turn, did it.

So I unlocked the case and took out the book. I stood, relocked, made my way back to the atelier.

The commonplace book was as heavy as it looked. In a sort of parody of what could by any standard be considered proper study room protocol, I laid out a sheet of near-to-hand paper towels before plopping the book down on the central table. I next went and hunted around the cabinets for some foam blocks to rest my artifact on. When these weren't forthcoming, I removed a pair of L-shaped metal bookends from a shelf of titles on the history of American furniture joining, placing these on the table corners up and covering them with a generous layer of more paper towels. I put the common-place book on top of this shoddy altar.

I wanted to begin at the very beginning of the commonplace book, but the book seemed to have been held pinned open in such a way, for such an extended period of time, that it was no easy matter to crack into the initial pages. It was possible, then, that the museum's stewardship of this item was doing it somewhat more harm than good. What surprised me was that at a certain early place in the codex, the pages had indeed been cracked, which is to say, separated from one another. And it was to this place that I was now turning.

At this crack, this separation, the creator of the commonplace, presumably Brunhilda herself, had pasted in a sheet of paper several times larger than the page to which it was attached. Being several times larger, it had had to be folded up. Gingerly, I now picked it open. The page flopped, releasing minuscule bits of antique fiber.

"Hello again."

I jumped in my seat. The voice came from the doorway. Based on similarity to previous encounters, you may guess the speaker.

"I was just coming to look for you," he said.

I decided that I would feign distraction, perhaps annoyance if things became serious enough. "Oh, really?" I said calmly. I did not look up from the page, which showed the map of Elysia. I stared as long as I could at the engraving, probably a total of four seconds, and then carefully but speedily folded the page shut again.

"Really. I was going to remind you that we have that cocktail for WANSEE this evening and, as Bonnie is a little shaken up, I wanted to make sure that you were available." This was said robotically, but all the same, somehow as if Fred might genuinely care.

I had completely forgotten about the event, but I pretended that it constituted the most highly anticipated calendar item of my day. "Absolutely. I'm really looking forward to it, actually!"

"Great. Thanks for making time."

I scooted my chair back a bit and craned my head around to look at Fred.

It was, if I may say so, sort of like the face behind his face was leaning forward, looking out of his actual flesh face, trying to get an authoritative view of what was transpiring in the room before him. I don't mean that he was necessarily so concerned with what I was doing with the commonplace book, but rather that he seemed to be engaged in surgical analysis of my aura.

I said, "I'll see you later on?"

"You will. And I'm glad we could talk earlier." There was an eerie, hard cast to Fred's countenance as he said this.

"No problem. Always glad to talk. What a day."

"Yes." I could tell Fred wanted to demand to know what I was doing in the repair and study suite and why the keys to the visible storage were sitting out on the table next to my paper-towel arrangement and priceless book. He squinted. "You know, we keep cloths and weights and supports and that sort of thing in the closet outside." He paused. "For future reference."

"Oh my God, yes!" I agreed. I had no idea

why I was speaking to him in this way.

Fred was nonplussed. "I mean, I have found them useful. We are also, just so you know, required by the museum's charter to make use of them. So, for that reason, you may wish to avail yourself."

"Thank you."

"This seems like an interesting excursion." Fred was withdrawing physically, but now his thought reached tantalizingly out to brush against mine.

I didn't say anything. I wanted to get up from my chair but a rage unrelated to our current conversation held me in my place. I hated him for believing that he knew every-thing there was to know about everything in the world.

"You do so much," Fred continued. He seemed weirdly aroused, though his manner also let me know that even in this state he felt no compulsion to act upon corporeal whim.

"Not really." I awaited the next compli-ment.

"You do so many things," Fred repeated, this time with new meaning, though still his tone remained cool. "I'm so curious to know what you'll come up with next."

"Probably nothing much!" I showed a lot of teeth, grinning for his benefit.

After Fred recused himself I had a few minutes left to examine the commonplace book. I began by taking a series of cell phone photos of the map, of the artful huts of the township and the neoclassical fantasy that was the surrounding woodlands. To say that a xerox is lossy is, of course, a gross understatement, and I wanted to be sure I had the best possible views. I'd ponder the minute community, I planned, later on. I next elected to page through the commonplace book, the better to know the woman who had collected all this imagery. There were flowers and regional landscapes, images of the ocean and ships, Europeans in various folk costumes along with explanatory text. There was a section of clippings picturing the schooling of small children; open mouths, pointing fingers.

And then I came to something very, very strange. On some level it wasn't so strange; it was merely an engraving of a beautiful woman on the period model. She had the features of a doll and an appropriately zaftig body. She stood, or, rather, hovered, on a pier in a gauzy dress with an empire waist. The legend below her read "Étoile, the

Singer from Paradise." I trembled a little. A small ship laden with flags was visible in the distance, and both the sun and a faint moon stood in the sky. I carefully employed my phone to obtain pictures. What was strange about this image was that in my parents' apartment, in the house in which I had grown up, there was an engraving nearly identical to this one, framed and hanging in the hallway. I knew this because I had spent many hours standing in that hallway, studying it. Ours was, perhaps, an even finer imprint. Conceivably, this was just a coincidence. Still, I felt unsettled. I gulped, fumbled with the phone. My mouth was dry. Also, it was late.

I had to take the commonplace book back out and lock it into its case again and neaten the suite. Then I had to run back up to my office and do my best using my makeup kit to make it look like I was intentionally dressing day to evening, or whatever they call that on people's style blogs. It was a fine line, too, between looking like I was wearing fairly formal (the better to distract from my outfit) makeup and looking like a birthday cake. I put Paul's keys back in my bag and headed out to the museum's steps, where I paused for a moment to smoke.

My head was full of spirits. I kept thinking of that spectral arm in the commonplace book, probably an illustration from *Harper's*. I thought, too, of the somewhat more contemporary (and substantial) hand that had turned the page of the book, changing the image it displayed. Above all, I wanted to get home as soon as possible and read whatever Paul had written in those documents in "etc." I wanted, too, to study the pictures now stored on my phone. Elysia was not necessarily real, but a version of it was sitting locked inside the visible storage, for whatever that was worth. The first stanza of the poem included with the map kept coming back into my head:

Where is this paradise you seek,
A place where no one mourns,
And nothing irreplaceable is lost,
And nothing lost is irretrievable?

Whatever else one could say, there was something relevant about this as far as I was concerned, since in recent months I'd often had the opportunity to contemplate feelings of intense alienation, even emotional homelessness, in the very city in which I had been born. I felt that I could potentially agree with this line of questioning. Where was the paradise I had not just sought but, idiotically perhaps, believed myself to have successfully discovered? What had happened to that time and place in which love — yes, along with the drinking and yelling and lying and strangely aggressive behavior in bed and everywhere else I seemed to encounter the person I thought was my husband — had seemed unconditional? And why, oh why, was my own mother so incredibly weird?

Something that now and again popped into my head was that my main error had been in seeking my home in the world *in* another human. I didn't fully know what this intuition meant, but it was an idea that returned to me from time to time these days, always taking different forms. And ideas, like dreams, were apparitions that I now studied with greater care. I was troubled, still, by the sense that I hadn't *not* known about what Whit was doing. I hadn't always known, but I also hadn't *not* known. I'd just never bothered to find out.

These counterfactual reveries were interrupted by the appearance of Marco, who was currently exiting our fair institution in pressed slacks and what appeared to be a pressed tote bag.

"Hiya," I said, flourishing my cigarette. I felt a little old, which was sort of nice on a day like today.

"Hey." Marco rushed over. It was evident we were going to talk about Paul.

I smoked some more.

"How are you doing? It's so awful. I can't believe it." Marco was genuinely distressed. It made me realize, by contrast, how scarily numb I had been for the past nine hours. "I didn't know what to do with myself all day. I almost came up to see you." Marco was frowning in the twilight. It was possible that he might cry.

"Do you want a cigarette?"

"Sure." Marco accepted and lit it himself with a lighter extracted from his blazer pocket. "God. Thank you."

I tried to smile.

"Are you OK? I feel like you two were really friends and things. I mean, we all knew him. He was Paul."

"To be honest with you, I still don't feel anything." I thought about this for a second. "I might be a little mad. That seems weird to me."

"That's probably right." Marco was looking at me differently, which is to say, he looked different to me in this moment than he had ever looked before. We just stood there for a while, smoking in silence.

16

Ten minutes later Marco and I were sharing a cab down to TriBeCa. I had convinced him that he should join me for the WANSEE celebration. I knew both of us wanted to be either stone-cold sober or drunker than we'd ever been drunk, and there was no real way of telling how this was going to work itself out. But: strength in numbers. I also happened to know that Fred Lu approved of Marco, and the more I could throw them together in social situations the more likely Marco was to recognize Fred's casual generosity toward those with whom he had passing acquaintance.

I hate this kind of event. There is no way to sugarcoat it. From the moment Marco and I stepped into the copper-plated elevator that glided us up to the top of an unfathomably expensive and formerly industrial edifice, I was not just beginning to suffer but actively suffering. All I could think was how much I longed to already be experiencing the return trip, to be slightly buzzed and sinking safely back down to street level, where I could walk and then tuck myself anonymously into the subway. However, I do have a competitive side. I want, or would really, really *like,* to be less bad at this. And it bothers me that people I don't completely respect, or have come to learn I can't afford to respect, i.e., Fred, are so insanely better at this than I am.

The copper container rang benignly as it slid to a gentle stop. I felt, briefly, that it might be mocking my terror, but there was little I could do to retaliate against a non-sentient mechanism. The doors, parting noiselessly, revealed an open floor plan as well as the major wealth that affords a walkthrough overlooking the Holland Tunnel stuffed with persons who are present only because you are sharing your money with them. There were maybe a hundred people here. This was for starters. The floor was poured concrete, very pale, nearly white. Multiple arrangements of tastefully minimalist sofas encircling maximalist neon area rugs gave the impression that the condo was a sort of hotel lobby, intended to be inhabited not by its owners but by guests, and that these guests were likely to have somewhat tenuous relationships with one another. The utterly intimidating decor was completed by Rauschenberg silkscreens and more recent works I could not identify in my ignorance of the art of the end of the last century.

Marco strode out of the elevator, freakishly enraptured. He paused, glancing back at me. "You OK?"

"Yes," I burbled, experiencing terror. I felt my shoulders start to hunch up.

Marco grimaced. "Come on. I'll find you some booze." He took my arm and all but dragged me into Babylon.

There were twentysomethings in the unisex catering uniform of our era, white shirt plus black pants, swishing around with trays of drinks. Marco engaged one handsome individual (to whom he would probably have had more to say under alternate circumstances) and pulled down something made out of vodka and champagne for me. I could see Marco a little more clearly now, and I was starting to seriously admire his fortitude. He was capable of play, I saw, and would probably go far in this world. I, however, wanted to slink to a distant corner to drool on myself and await the angel of death.

"Here you go." Marco meaningfully

wrapped one of my trembling hands around the drink.

"Thanks."

Marco also took a cocktail for himself. "Thank you," he told the server. I watched the two of them wordlessly come to an understanding that they would seek each other out at a more advantageous instant later on. I could only admire the grace on display.

"Thank you," I echoed Marco. I felt like I was twelve and a half. My face was flushed, greasy.

"So" — Marco turned back to me, sipping — "do you know these people?"

I gulped down half the contents of my glass. "Oh God," was what I said.

"Interesting," said Marco.

"No, no, I don't know." I was looking around. The crowd was slightly younger than usual, and it occurred to me that Fred was possibly making some adjustments or additions to his social stable this evening. There were, judging from the sizable eyewear and a few instances of cape dresses, some Chelsea gallerists in attendance, and even a few of their artists, one of whom was wearing yak-fur pants. The gallerists nodded a lot. They were pretty women in their forties who were aging magnificently and making tons of bank doing something they didn't hate. As far as the current setting was concerned, they were noncommittal. This was fine for them, cocktails were plentiful, and if they got a new client out of the deal, great. Otherwise, this night was low stakes. I worshipped them. I mean, privately I worshipped them. I would never *be* them, but you could see that this was the way things could be if you were living right. They left the neuroses to the creatives they represented and went on subsisting very, very well, thank you.

Some higher-up administrative types from the museum had also made the scene. They were the people in the crowd who seemed most thrilled to be here and wholly in their element. They were inhaling alcohol and walking around loudly greeting anyone willing to be accosted. Some of the females of the functionary class had on their "liberal" jewelry options this evening, wooden blocks on string or modernist brass triangles. They were feeling casual, optimistic. They had gone with a bright lip. And then there were a ton of other people I could not place — I mean, you of course had your circle of CeMArt curators, all squished together for moral support, trying to pretend they were just standing around casually. And there were the ladies with unfortunate nose jobs and unnaturally high metabolisms dressed in revealing pastel jumpsuits or vaguely southwestern getups. These were people with more money than sense, who were, for the successful curator, an occupational hazard and even necessity. They never knew what they were doing anywhere they went and therefore required constant attention.

I espied Fred, who was in the midst of attempting to train one such woman to exchange social niceties with another hetero couple, both of whom had suffered alarming amounts of Botox to be injected into their foreheads, jowls, necks, and possibly eyeballs. There were newcomers as well: many very plain male executives in well-cut, looser suits and a few circumspect women milling around. They were corporate. They had come from WANSEE, and they clearly liked this space. They felt it was appropriate to the mission of a major art museum; plus, it had actual artists in it. The relevant boxes had been checked off. Staring at these clean, toned capitalists made me extremely nervous, for I knew that, by talking to them, I had the power, in my radical awkwardness, to disrupt the flow of not just the confidence in the room but also the capital. And though I did not much care for

WANSEE or what seemed to be its ambitions to secure all of the earth's moisture, I did to some extent care for my job, and I did not feel like giving this job away during the course of a cocktail party.

Said Marco, "I think I recognize a few people."

"Listen, you should really feel free to mingle."

Marco just laughed.

"Please," I begged. "And please don't laugh at me. I'll do better if I'm left to drown on my own."

"I'm not laughing at you."

"You should! It is laughable. Please, I'm fine."

"Oh, Stella Krakus. Whatever you say."

I thanked him.

"No, thank *you*. See you later?"

"Maybe," I said. I watched, twitching, as Marco made his way into the gelling crowd. I let myself be swallowed up by various indiscriminate jostling shoulders as the party seemed, in the course of fifteen minutes, to double in size.

I sweated, bobbed, completed my drink, secured another. I managed to run into an auction house employee I knew vaguely from grad school, feigned bottomless nostalgia, and monopolized this hapless woman

211

who, praise Baal, did not have either the presence of mind or powers of recollection to ask about Whit. Then someone tapped a glass repeatedly and Fred's long-anticipated toast began. Everyone pivoted up into photographable position.

"Hello," said Fred. He opened with a fairly long homily, even for him, thanking Davis and Darren Axelmundsen-Coates, whose home this apparently was, for letting everyone traipse through their doors. The couple was somewhere in the assembly, but it was difficult, from my vantage at least, to see them. Whatever these two had done for Fred Lu, one thing was certain, it was not limited to this event.

Languidly, Fred eased on to the matter of WANSEE, what a crucial partner the conglomerate was, how it/they really understood the contemporary arts and the needs of contemporary audiences for the arts, and how he was so endlessly grateful for valuable and refreshing conversations with so-and-so, who was executive director of this and that, and who had accomplished those and these extremely accomplished accomplishments.

This, to be honest, made me feel like a microbe that was living under the shoe of a cockroach that was living under the sink of two of the most doltish frat boys you'd ever want to meet on a Billyburg corner at midnight midvape who'd just moved in together to explore their dreams of becoming middle managers. How could I possibly be a curator if Fred was a curator? I wasn't a curator! I was just a human-shaped supply of erudition and random bits of data that kept the paintings from falling off the walls. Fred was meanwhile engineering the walls, inventing whatever it was that would come after walls, and whatever scruples had to be sacrificed to this illustrious undertaking, these were not keeping Frederick Lu up at night. As Fred talked and talked, I felt myself dissolving into the condo's temperate air. I was a form of human decoration to this scene. It was laughable, as previous iterations of tonight's occasion should have better instructed me, that I could think that Fred was nurturing any kind of undying feeling for me. It was a fucking joke. That he bothered to try to talk to me about what had transpired between us at all was not just an act of mercy on his part, it was the best a someone like me could ever hope to obtain from a someone like him, so why wasn't I endlessly grateful and comforted and even kind of ecstatic? Why wasn't I converting our dead-end romance into a species of professional success and getting on with it? I was crazy to think that he could genuinely care about me. *Collaborate with,* fine, but love, never. I was a moderately interesting iteration of my class, just another serviceable brain in a city already replete with geniuses.

During the course of my reveries, Fred had metamorphosed. I became aware of this and hushed my thoughts in hopes of catching up with his discourse. I had to listen very carefully, because what he was saying now was a little bit hard to believe. And I think other people in the room were having trouble believing it, too, judging from the hushed murmurs and small movement in the crowd. What Fred was saying was that WANSEE and CeMArt's partnership would extend beyond the generous funding provided for the current exhibition of American paintings. It would become somewhat more permanent. WANSEE was unveiling a new venture, and if anyone in the room wanted a treat, she would navigate on over to CEO Vincenzo Bamberg's recent TED talk, a discussion of the coming of a new mode of networked collective life, the so-called smart city. Such "technologically responsive" communities, with their "miles and miles of fiber connectivity" might (here Fred cited a recent *Economist* feature) bring about global compliance, if not actual peace, before the end of the century. And Fred was more delighted than ever to proclaim that a satellite version of a newly conceived CeMArt franchise would be included in each of the "smart cities" WANSEE planned to construct in the coming twenty years, and WANSEE was planning quite a number of cities, where mankind would surely take refuge not just from everyday inconvenience and security issues posed by fundamentalists but from approaching environmental collapse. Adding a museum to these model cities was a way of engineering a more satisfying user-generated experience, of "retaining complexity," as Fred put it. Fred tacked on a winking pleasantry to the effect that he himself was not a fanatic or an ideologue, but he did know a next-level business opportunity when he saw one. And he was sure that by sharing information freely we could eventually work out a version of the data-driven economy that would be to everyone's liking, from artists to stock analysts and back again. The applause that followed this speech was dense and prolonged.

The throng thinned a little and retired to the edges of the room. There was a fresh round of hors d'oeuvres. I took a few steps forward and very nearly caught Fred's eye. I say "very nearly" because our eyes did touch, in that nonphysical way, but this was only because Fred's gaze was on its way to meet that of another individual a few feet to my right, a tall and slender woman, who from the back appeared fairly young, pleasingly dressed in dark clingy things. This was not Fred's girlfriend, for Fred's girlfriend was not much taller than me and had black hair; this was someone else, a Mediterranean blonde with delicate features. But from the way Fred moved to meet this someone else, to touch her hands and place his face in proximity to hers, I felt certain that they were more than friends and had been so for some time.

I swallowed. I really wasn't sure that I could do this anymore. Anyway, I basically already didn't exist here so it wasn't that hard for me to leave. I was even kind of drunk.

I at last experienced my fantasy of descent in the copper elevator, was restored to street level, walked a few blocks, and descended once again. The C roared up, a broke-down, 1990s affair.

When I got home, I was feeling pretty dejected. Frederick had won, and he had very possibly won not just the museum but the entire coming century. It seemed to me that there was very little point to most of my work, such as it was. I was a functionary. The institution functioned. You might have thought that this kind of realization would inspire rage, anti-fascist fervor, something. It didn't. I felt, in the throes of game loss, like a diminutive pyramid of feces deposited by some museum patron's fur-baby Chihuahua.

Torpor ensued. It was all I could do to force myself to get out my laptop and return to Paul's files. I went into the folder titled "etc." Here there were three documents with the file extension ".txt." These were titled "PLAN.txt," "work.txt," and, appropriately enough, "morework.txt."

I began with "PLAN."

This was a series of notes, a sketch. Paul was, I guess it's fair to say I was horrified to find, not so much at work on a conspiracy theory of the Department of American Objects but, gasp, on a great American novel. I almost started screaming at the computer. I mean, in fact I may have spoken aloud, "YOU'RE DEAD AND ALL YOU HAVE TO GIVE ME IS THIS?" But I regretted it instantly. I silently begged

forgiveness. Memento mori. Anyhow, I like
novels.

■ ■ ■ ■

THURSDAY

■ ■ ■ ■

17

"Compose a novel," began Paul's "PLAN,"

in which a poet speaks. He does interesting things you wouldn't expect a poet to do, like holding down a job. This is done to make him seem plausible. And to help us see through him.

Behold the poet at his labors: he is composing a long poem about the history of art. It is a history about all of art, not just fine art but anything humans have made with a certain smiling, translucent attention. It isn't a real history, since he is a good poet. At any rate, it is not a narrative. It is a task. Soon anything we might have known about him will be replaced by these gestures.

This will take place gradually. Day by day, the poet will adopt the past as his own.

The poet is living in a kind of house

located inside a museum. The house is a ruin, though very clean and perfectly restored. We don't know how the poet got inside and there's no explanation of how no one ever catches him or how he eats or where he sleeps or how he travels between these rooms, which are on occasion separated by entire centuries.

The poet doesn't have a real person's history, a personal story — at least, not anymore.

All he's ever wanted is to be the greatest American poet who ever lived.

Not an easy task. But he is a real soul, a true soul, and that's the thing that has to be conveyed. The poet is authentic. That is the whole reason for the novel, why he is talking to you here.

He is an open door.

This was the end of the document. I considered sardonically retitling it, "A_scintillating_tale.txt."

Whatever one might say about Paul, never let it be said that he was not interested in himself! Yet there was an eerie vacancy at the center of this elaborate vow to self-portraiture, and it complicated the literary navel-gazing. "He is an open door." Perhaps I had even already seen this in Paul; the door swinging easily on its hinges as a diverse crew of available identities swarmed on the other side.

The next morning I got up and puttered around the house, waiting for my heiress biography to be conveyed by UPS. Even if all was lost, I wasn't about to let this doubtless juicy hagiography just be kicked into limbo. I planned to be there to sign for it. And so I was.

"Have a pleasant day," the man told me.

But it was going to be a long and extremely unpleasant day. If I was interpreting last night's tea leaves correctly, it might even include Nicola di Carboncino's announcement of retirement, which, one presumed, he could now proffer without worry or shame, knowing that Frederick Lu's plans to catapult CeMArt into next-level relevance had been broadcast to the public. I, on the other hand, could have the pleasure of contemplating the reduction of something I had believed was a proverbial mountain into a proverbial molehill. My agonizing love for Fred would shrink in importance in direct proportion to his rapidly gestating greatness. This would be fun.

If I cared to, I could additionally compare myself to Frederick Lu more objectively. I could think about his achievements, and then I could think about mine. Or I could just stop thinking about my achievements and only think about his.

I got on the train. I decided to allow myself to be distracted by *Will to Beauty.* I stared into its florid cover. The book had, after all, been written with just such an end in mind (i.e., distraction), particularly when it came to people of my gender.

Alice Gaypoole Wynne was born in 1895. At this time, she was just Alice Marguerite Gaypoole. Her paternal grandfather had been a banker, and his son, her father, was also a banker. Alice attended the correct cotillions, came out when the time was right, summered overseas, learning how to buy dresses and look at art, as well as the inverse, in Paris, to which libertine capital she would return from time to time.

She met her husband, William "Willy" Wynne, at a sports club in the Hamptons when his horse bit her on the upper arm, causing her to vociferously cite the famous designer whose creations she was wearing, "I declare, that mare has a taste for Fortuny!" Willy was smitten and asked for the hand attached to that witty arm a mere month later. Thus Alice was brought up and married well and living in all the correct ways by the time of the Battle of Gallipoli, but she still had to get through the rest of her life. This was going to be the hard part.

Somewhere along the way, Alice realized she enjoyed not just buying paintings but also making them and so began to practice art. A resourceful secretary Alice had employed shortly after her marriage, a woman by the name of Mabel Styke (pronounced "stick"), convinced her to start up an exhibition space if she wanted to meet au courant artists, and this, then, was how the Elysia Club came into being. The biography attempts to reduce these events to a minor detour in Alice's existence and is not particularly forthcoming as to reasons for the unusual name.

Of greater interest is a sculptor and art critic Alice encountered by way of the club, an attractive blade by the name of Otto "Boy" Pastt, who swept her off her feet with poetry and spaghetti dinners, bringing her just a bit closer to the common man, or so the biography opines. Boy became her first lover. Boy was not, however, faithful. This led to clashes between the paramours. Boy claimed that Alice was married and therefore owed her husband certain services. Why should he then be denied the company of alternate ladies? Alice, enraged, banned Boy from the club and tried — successfully — to have him fired from the staff of a publication unimaginatively called *The Journal of the Arts.* But Alice's revenge had side effects. Boy's expulsion became cause for general mutiny from the Elysia Club, and in late 1930, Alice and Mabel Styke were forced to close it down. The biography tries to make this seem like an entertaining farce and lingers over letters testifying to Alice and Willy's tearful reckoning regarding the state of their union and subsequent reconciliation.

I was at my stop. I closed this torrid account of heiress life and dragged myself out of the car. People seemed particularly violent to me this morning, and I almost lost a toe to a certain determined stomper in a beige raincoat and large bow-shaped barrette. I brawled my way up to street level and walked against the wind. Everything felt like it was farting purposefully and precisely into my eyes.

In the museum, in my office, I checked email. I remembered, or rather saw on my calendar, that I had planned to meet Cate for lunch today. Because of waiting for *Will to Beauty* to arrive, I was pretty dramatically late to work. It was almost eleven A.M. The office felt more populated than it had on the previous day, but things were still slow. There was another potentially oppressive email from Bonnie, this time with a link to Paul's obit.

I needed to do other things, but I also couldn't seem to not take the bait. Besides, I was becoming increasingly desperate for personal information about the man and poet. I clicked.

PAUL CORAL, PRIZE-WINNING POET AND FIXTURE AT CEMART, DIES AT 57

BY TESSA ZHUK

Paul Coral, a poet and expert in the history of American art, whose formal style and skill with lush description won him a devoted following, a Taft Prize, and numerous grants, died on Tuesday in Manhattan. He was 57.

His sister, Lacey Coral, said he died of an apparent overdose of antidepressants prescribed to him as sleeping aids. It is not known whether his death was an accident or a suicide.

Mr. Coral arrived on the New York poetry scene in the early 1980s, at which time he also began working as the registrar in the Central Museum of Art's Department of

American Objects. His first collection, "The Telephone," was selected for publication in the prestigious Oberlin Press Series in 1984. Isabelle Crave, writing in the New Republic, hailed Mr. Coral as "a brilliant craftsman and philosopher-poet of the soul's decor." Coral published only two additional collections in his lifetime, but he won a critical following, especially among artists and other intellectuals, who were attracted to the brilliant interplay of form and thought in his work. The poet Sadie Beckett, one of his most ardent supporters, called him "a direct line back into the material spirit."

Paul Anthony Coral was born on July 22, 1958, in Rochester, NY. His father, Lars Smitey Coral, was an engineer with Kodak and his mother, Ellen Smith, a homemaker. A successful student, he was accepted into Dartmouth College, where he earned a bachelor's degree in the History of Art and Architecture in 1980 and wrote his first poems. After graduation, he drove to New York City and presented himself to Cal Winters, then chair of CeMArt's American Objects department and one of the museum's most beloved leaders. Mr. Coral's self-presentation was so impressive that he was instantly accepted into training to become the department's registrar.

Over the years, Mr. Coral grew to be known not only for his work within the museum but for a style of poetic narrative that, with mysterious meditative clarity, led readers into unforeseen landscapes as well as to startling conclusions. In "Wednesday," the narrator enjoys a stroll on the grounds of a house that seems to contain all of American history, or, at least, selective and haunting parts of it.

A female spirit
held an anchor over his heart
as if the arbor were
an albumen *carte de visite.*

Elsewhere, Mr. Coral pursued more specific histories, such as that of the city of his father's birth, including its slow adoption of New York State's 1799 statute for the abolition of slavery, not fully accomplished in Schenectady until 1827. His lyric essay on the subject, "The Pines," whose title evoked the Mohawk origins of Schenectady's name, was excerpted in Granta and appeared as a full-length collection in 2001. In 2002, Mr. Coral was awarded the Taft Prize for this book.

His other poetry collection was "Superimposed Worlds" (1994).

Mr. Coral never taught formal poetry courses but gave well-attended readings and lectures from time to time at several universities, including the University of Iowa and Columbia University. In addition to his sister, he is survived by his former wife, the writer Ella Voss, most recently author of the novel "Philip Crystal." Ms. Voss, who remained a close friend of Mr. Coral even after the end of their marriage, said, "We have lost a great poet. But harder for me than this is losing a true friend."

I found a link to a review of Voss's most recent book. *Philip Crystal* was about a boy (the "Philip" of the title) growing up in a fictional suburban community in western New York, a pseudo-Rochester, where many of the men work for a single industrial entity, Halex, a thinly veiled version of the Xerox Corporation. It is the late 1970s, and the company has expanded exponentially during the preceding decades, making millions for its investors and lining the pockets of management and various research departments, while also transforming substantial amounts of local land into industrial zones. The corporation has also recently designed a state-of-the-art research facility within the neighborhood where Philip and his family live. Philip's father, a Halex employee, struggles to keep pace with his colleagues, suffering from the attentions of inappropriate women and an affection for alcohol. The Crystal household is a fraught place, where the parents politely ignore each other and Mr. Crystal is seldom home in the evenings. Philip and his older brother, Jason, are left to their own devices. Jason, the elder, is able to provide access to certain material pleasures associated with cold war teenage life, but things turn sinister when Jason falls in with a circle of boys who go in for more perverse recreations. (Here the novel was compared to Yukio Mishima's *The Sailor Who Fell from Grace with the Sea*.) Though the review was unwilling to give away the book's culminating cum shot, its terminal glance into the face of evil, the denouement seems to include Philip's witnessing of an event that will scar him — and probably the reader, too — for the rest of his life.

I clicked the window closed and shivered. It was time for lunch.

I was going to meet Cate at a diner called The Green Light. It was overpriced and on Madison but our options, especially re: atmosphere, were limited in this area so we did our best.

I have known Cate for something like fifteen years. We met the second week of freshman year in college and since this date have maintained an allegiance that is nearly perfect in its combination of mutual understanding and respectful distance and/or easygoing neglect. I never feel that I need to act in elaborate ways to keep up the friendship, which is pretty much all anyone can ask.

Cate is a tall brunette of Argentine and French-Canadian extraction, and she is fancy. I'm not exactly sure what it is she does to make her money, but she calls herself an art consultant and appears to be in business for herself. Our continued acquaintance probably has something to do with the fact that our lives have run in complementary though not identical tracks. Sometimes I do get the sense that Cate finds me useful from some professional point of view, but I have yet to discover what this point of view might be and therefore have difficulty taking offense.

Whenever Cate encounters me, she always begins by noting how cute I look. "Oh my God, you look so sweet!" she bellowed today. The nearly comic difference in our respective heights may have something to do with this feeling on her part.

"Hi there," I said.

We embraced awkwardly for a moment.

Cate was wearing a pair of sweatpant-shaped pants that were made out of gray suede and what appeared to be a black cashmere sweater under a jacket that had been cut to look like a bomber but was made of embroidered silk. Sartorially, she had been on a sort of trompe l'oeil kick for a while. Her sneakers were pristine and free of logo. She appeared to have stepped out of a music video and/or progressive skin-care commercial. She was radiant.

We sat down. In what seemed a miraculous single continuous gesture, Cate flipped through the menu, raised her hand for the server, and ordered each of us a set of matzo ball soup and salad and side of fries. With this out of the way, she arranged herself facing me and wanted to know, "So, how's my girl?"

"Yeah, I'm OK." I recounted the story of Whit's appearance at the "Land of the Limner" reception on Monday.

"What?!" Cate was laughing. "I'm so sorry. It's not funny. I really know that!" She did not stop laughing. She also began crying. "I think in the past I really could not see this side of him, but now it's pretty hard to conceive of him as a bigger fool! Oh my God, you poor thing, you must have been in a fury."

I shrugged.

"Who else was there? Did everyone *see*? I feel like you should be able to sue him! He must be totally out of his mind."

I reminded Cate that I was, sadly, already in the midst of suing him for something else.

Cate sighed. "I'm so sorry. That's very true. You are of course already suing him!"

It takes a lot to cause Cate to abandon one of her riffs of spontaneous joy. While things lasted, others had been, at the very least, amused by my relationship with Whit. Some individuals had even taken a kind of comfort in the idea that something as improbable as our love for one another could endure. It was problematic, and not just for me, to come up against the disastrous conclusion of our affection.

"Oh, look!"

This was Cate. She was pointing at the window. I mean, she was pointing *out* the window, but it took me a moment to see where her finger wanted my eyes to go.

"That's your *colleague*," said Cate, in a conspiratorial tone.

It was Fred. He was going down the street, deep in conversation with a young blond woman in her early twenties who was wearing, bizarrely but not entirely unattractively, a short mink cape. The young woman was somehow familiar, even if I had never seen her face. I realized, with growing alarm, that it was she whom Fred had approached after his latest WANSEE-related homily the previous night. She had been his primary audience then, and now here they were. Together. Again.

"Wow." Cate's eyes were very big, her mouth very small.

My face was frozen so I suppose I gave her a blank look.

"Big fish. Big, big fish."

"What do you mean?" I said. I already knew I was about to have zero interest in the arriving food.

"The younger win," Cate told me.

"What?"

"Win, of course."

"Win what?" I hoarsely repeated.

"Her name!"

I shook my head.

"W-Y-N-N-E. Electra. You must know her. Electra Wynne? She dates, um, oh God, what is his name?"

I stared.

"Shit. I think it's Bam-something? Bamberg? Swiss or something. Father's a very big man."

I was having difficulty breathing. "I don't know that man," I managed to whisper.

"Oh, yes, you do! He loves the arts. But anyway. What a feather!"

I reiterated my inability to comprehend.

"For his dunce cap, silly. Whatever, fuck him, I'm hungry."

18

I didn't go directly back to the office. I went a couple of blocks out of my way to a bookseller who did a combination of trade in rarities and literary works of the present. She had Paul's two books, with their historical cover art, which I bought along with Ella Voss's recent tale of mid-century horror. The bookshelf was thickening.

I strolled, smoking.

The *Wynnes.* Had they won?

Alice Gaypoole Wynne had furnished the museum with her great-grandmother's scrapbook shortly after the affair with a man named Boy had reached its disastrous end. Perhaps she was hoping that her sacrifice of a familial treasure to a major NYC institution would somehow redeem her after that ill-conceived alliance. As for the scrapbook, the commonplace book, it was kept by a very serious woman, a woman who had worked to change society, yet it gathered together rather unserious items, like the picture of Étoile, the pretty lady who came from "Paradise." Brunhilda had collected images from magazines and other ephemeral sources. Her book contained illustrations associated with entertainments of her time and played with the spectator's ability to differentiate artifice from reality. Barnum's lighthouse lamp was real, but it called attention to a space that housed humbugs, everyday objects falsely described as historical treasures and wonders of the world. Mumler's spirit photograph, showing the ghostly hand, was a similar ploy for the spectator's fascination and trust. It was both real and not. You could believe these things and feel awe at what there was in the visible world, or you could mistrust these things and smile at the entertainer's ingenuity. This contradiction or option was likely a major cultural aspect of the social world in which Brunhilda did her work. One wonders if she viewed these tricks and sleights as mere entertainments or if she saw them instead as a tool for teaching skepticism among more recently arrived sectors of the American population. And then there was the map she had included, depicting Elysia, a place hearsay claimed did not exist. I wondered, for one enticing instant, if she were not herself the author of *Lorelei of Millbury,* itself so full of illusions that appeared real, as well as illusory realities. And yet I could not quite understand what the map had to do with the novel.

This commonplace book had at some point come into the possession of Alice Gaypoole, the first of the family to marry into the Wynne line, who, I felt I could say with some certainty, must have looked through it and appropriated the name "Elysia" for the arts club she was starting downtown. There was something likable about this, particularly at a time of ubiquitous patronymics. Alice, a more modern heiress, had created the arts club as a space of fraternization, perhaps sororization as well, in which she could freely experience not just culture but romantic love, particularly with Otto "Boy" Pastt. Then paradise had gone awry, and she and her team had closed up shop.

I would need to examine the intake books for roughly 1929 to let's say 1932, which I planned to do as soon as I got back to the museum, to see what the deal was, but I wondered about other parts of the Elysia Club's collection. It must have been substantial, purchased from its own artist-members. Off the top of my head, I didn't think the department had received any of them. Something of an interesting twist in itself.

I was fairly well sunk in these thoughts, depending on my legs and some basic sense of direction plus habit to just carry me back to the museum without the direct participation of consciousness. This was why I did not notice at first when Whit walked right up to me.

"Missed you the other night!"

I almost screamed. I did not scream, because it was broad daylight in one of the most expensive zip codes in the city, and this would have caused some consternation among the locals. However, I wanted very much to scream, among other, more vivid expressions of dismay.

"Sorry, I seem to have startled you." Whit was nearly blushing. He gave the astonishing impression of sobriety. "I really didn't mean to do that."

"Hi, Whitaker," I said. "Are you here to tell me that you've signed?"

"I," said Whit, but he couldn't figure out the rest of his sentence. He left the pronoun there. He was wearing some sort of pale trench over a gray spring suit.

"OK, well, I'm going to leave now. Don't come to the museum again. Don't try to accost me on the street. Don't try to contact me or see me. Don't do any of these things. Forget that you ever knew me. You are a lying, cheating bastard, plus I think you are mentally ill, and I want you out of my life." Here I noticed that we were standing at the base of the steps of the museum. "Now kindly fuck off while I go indoors and continue to support myself by means of my current profession." I began moving up the steps. My heart was hammering. I was surprised that my body wasn't being thrown from side to side by this organ's exertions.

"Wait!" This was Whit.

I kept going.

"You won't even listen to me say that I'm sorry!" Whit had yelled this after me, a new accusation to add to the collection.

A couple taking a selfie with their aluminum stick looked over at me. "Give him a chance," one well-meaning half of them advised me.

I'm not one for recriminations masquerading as apologies, but under the circumstances I did feel that Whit's request was owed a reply. I paused where I was, turned, and marched back down to the bottom step where Whit was heroically awaiting me.

"I knew you'd come back," he breathed.

I looked Whit squarely in his face. I

considered the too close arrangement of his eyes, crowded up on either side of his small, straight nose, probably some sort of birth defect. I contemplated the look of relief and triumph that seemed to be washing over him. I said, "You will sign the papers and this will have a result. We will be divorced, and we will be divorced forever, and that is too bad, because I loved you and wanted to spend the rest of my life with you. I don't want to see or speak to you again until you sign. And then, after we are divorced, I also don't want to see you or speak to you again, ever. I never, ever, ever want to see you or speak to you again." I sighed. "Now, before I go, I'm going to leave you with a little something to remember me by." I began to squat down.

I wasn't, by the way, conscious of what I was doing, precisely. It was as if some outside force were gently guiding my body, arranging my muscles. It was effortless. Whit, meanwhile, appeared to be so over-whelmed by the fact that I had walked back down the steps and deigned to speak to him again that he, too, was in a kind of dream state, though, I might add, his was of a slightly different nature than mine.

I could hear him murmuring above me, "Do it, Stella. *Do* it," which exhortation allowed me to comprehend that he imagined that I was about to give him a blow job in public.

I was at a good height now and pulled my right arm down, making a fist, so that I would be aiming upward, for optimal damage, and I punched Whit as hard as I possibly could in the testicles.

Whit was instantly down and writhing on the sidewalk.

I made a speedy but calm exit. A few people seemed to have taken notice but were inclined to give Whit a wide berth. It was true, I reflected with satisfaction, that he had also given me verbal permission to do what I had just done.

The selfie-stick couple was staring at me with a disturbing combination of repulsion and glee. "That was perfect," one of them told me, nodding.

"Thank you," I said.

"What happened, if I may ask?" the other wanted to know.

"Oh," I said, "he actually asked me to do that."

"Really?"

"Yes. He's crazy." And with that, I went indoors.

19

I really felt, though, as if some outside force had entered my body and given me the strength and timing to do what I had just accomplished. It was as if another hand had closed over my hand, wrapped it into a fist, instructed it as to the best route upward into Whit's testes. The intent was all mine, but I couldn't get much of a grip on the sensorial miasma of simultaneous knowing and not-knowing through which I'd just instinctively glided in order to supply Whit some well-deserved pain. Maybe this would call my former partner's ambient attentions to what had — very factually and genuinely — transpired between us, i.e., that for the final two years of our marriage he and a woman who was not me had been surreptitiously enjoying condom-free sex on the regular. Though I wasn't holding out particular hope for Whit to realize the absurd magnitude of his infidelity, that he had for all intents and purposes been engaging in nonconsensual bigamy, it was possible that he might take a few moments to reflect on the upshot of our relationship's actually ending. I felt that perhaps he had not quite grasped this finer point, i.e., that this was for the duration, and one almost had to feel sorry for him, traipsing mournfully around as if there were something left to reclaim. Generally, it was sad, and not even because *he* was so pathetic and sad.

If I hadn't been as angry as I was, I might have shed a tear. I was grateful for the inspired will-to-nut-shot because this act was allowing me to do something I had not done for a very long time, which was to be disappointed and to be, very simply, hurt. So much aggression had been visited upon me — I mean, so much obfuscation and anger and then my own pursuant flailing, during the course of which I seem to have managed mainly to hit myself in the face rather than disengage from the marriage — that I hadn't had time to exist as a person who had been harmed by another person. I had been very busy keeping up the pretense of being a person whom someone had attempted but then failed to harm. This was not who I really was and the pretense had become exhausting.

I pondered this for a moment. It was a different kind of narrative, the one I was producing, than the one you usually think of in relation to revenge. Because with revenge the express goal is to enjoy, or at the very least be certain of, the other's suffering. I suddenly felt that all I wanted was merely to be certain of my own suffering. It made no difference to me how Whit felt, and in a sense the low blow was kind of an arbitrary signifier. It could have been any number of gestures, as long as the end result was Whit's momentary nullification. On the one hand, Whit had been left struggling, sack throbbing and stomach full of knives, which was unfortunate and not very nice, but on the other he also wasn't upright, towering over me, in the early stages of sexually assaulting me, or, what could have been even worse, capable of speech.

I was walking slowly into the back of the museum.

The security staff must have come to an agreement with the powers that be, because I saw Gary, a Trinidadian expat in his early thirties, at his normal post. I tried waving, but a crowd of gangly Scandinavian tweens in matching backpacks surged through the hall, and he had to turn his attention to preventing one of them from ripping the arm off of a wooden cherub.

It was funny, because I abruptly had the impression that the whole phenomenon of personal revenge, the legendary human appetite for it, could mostly be explained in terms of what I had just experienced. Here I am not talking about blood feuds or genocide, just events scaled to fit within a single human life, events that do not expand to affect an entire population or culture or historical age (though perhaps everything that happens is always affecting everyone, I really don't know!). What I mean is, I had not known that this would be what I wanted. I did not wish to be revenged against Whit. I didn't wish to know that Whit felt pain. I really did not wish anything in relation to him at all! I just wanted to see him incapacitated and separate from me. Or: I wanted to see my own agency, as divorced from his. And I wanted to know the exact extent to which I had suffered. And I wanted to be able to feel the pain, rather than merely comprehending, intellectually, that events that were designed to make me suffer had taken place.

It was a tease. I was still entirely too capable of looking at my own situation from a disquieting variety of dispassionate angles. I still saw it as "someone's" interesting story. It was easy to have the sense that I had been robbed, not even of love or property, but of the ability to care about my own life. It wasn't just, how was I going to get back there, get back into those scenes in which Whit was dishonest and I did not comprehend the terms of my own existence, but rather: How was I going to get back into living anything?

I wasn't entirely sure that I had ever done much living. If you had asked me about this twelve months ago I would have told you that I was in the thick of things, that I had so much real life going on, I didn't know what to do with it. I would have talked about how very much I was leaning into my career, and how very much I was married to a man I cherished, how very much I loved the city where we lived, how very much the arts were approaching a late-republican golden age. I would have been lying, but I would have believed that what I was saying was true, and I would have believed this because although I could feel the difference between truth and a lie, I had become accustomed to ignoring this perception. For this genre of perception had grown inconvenient, most of all, as it turns out, in my own home. (Take it from me that lying to someone you love really fucks with that person!

If you do this, you are no longer loving them and should abandon them pronto. Do not convince yourself that they are the one at fault. You are at fault. But the damage you do can be minimized by a speedy exit. Dear cheaters of the world, I have but one word for you: *leave.*)

Anyway, I was going down to the archives. I mean, I was going down to the archives, and I felt really fucking bad, but it was good, because this was feeling something.

These archives were, in case this was not clear, of the museum's own internal activities. Though the museum houses several other libraries and archives, it stores the records of its operations outside — or, rather, below — these more bookish spaces, with their reading rooms and vaulted ceilings and semiopen stacks. The rows of filing cabinets we on staff refer to as the museum's "archive" are actually materials that have been rendered obsolete by digital memory, but which are crucial enough that they are grudgingly maintained in real space and on the premises, rather than being burned or shipped out to North Dakota. These are the records of the museum's catalog when it was an actual catalog of paper cards, as well as the original longhand and later typed versions of the museum's acquisitions records.

This paperwork is maintained in a storage area that is also home to a variety of pallet-lifting devices, platforms and plinths, various promotional discards including a series of giant foam-board cutouts celebrating the fauna of medieval Japan, a broken plaster cast of a discus thrower everyone has agreed is actually alive and who is named Lefty because of his missing crucial arm, as well as other miscellany. The area is guarded by a man named Rainer, a Czech with a strange whistling voice who seems to be about three hundred years old.

"Good day," said Rainer.

"Hi. I just want to check something in the files," I said, raising my ID. I have introduced myself to Rainer on several occasions in the past, but he doesn't seem to remember me. As I have come to trust that he won't, on the other hand, reject me, I didn't bother with further pleasantries.

"Yes, yes," Rainer said. On his desk, he had a wall clock facedown and appeared to be dissecting it. He noticed my gaze. "It stopped!" He brought his hand down on the desk with a brilliant bang.

"Too bad."

Rainer seemed at a loss as to how to interpret my reaction. "Well, not really," he said, as if we had known one another all our lives. "One shouldn't take these changes too seriously."

I smiled, nodded, walked by.

As I didn't want to engage Rainer further, I decided that I would do my best with the paper files on my own. There was a series of cabinets that seemed to be for acquisitions, and on opening one of the uppermost drawers I discovered that its contents were organized by year. After a bit of looking, I located the year 1930 and flipped around for another ten minutes, pulling files and replacing them, until I found the record for the commonplace book: "Gift of Alice Gaypoole Wynne, to be exhibited in perpetuity." (This was something I needed to make a point of asking about, whether we did not list information of this kind in the online catalog because it encouraged copycat requests, or if there was another reason for our reticence.) There was a brief description of the physical appearance of the book and its contents, and it named the member of the American Objects' staff overseeing the acquisition, "J. D. Weiss," the young curator who had written to his mother regarding expeditions to pillage the decorative arts of British America. Attached to the back of the official intake record was a typescript. It was a letter.

Dear J.,

You will know already dear, thoughtful Alice wants you to have this. And you must do as she asks and always keep it somewhere the public eye can touch it. Things here at the "cutting edge" are grim. Don't laugh and say I am fibbing. We've overplayed our hand and now receive boyish signs that even our surrender won't be accepted. I doubt very much the club will survive and have resigned myself to it. The pen is so much mightier than the sword, and even the heart, etc., etc. Well, so it is. Alice claims there is more to tell and will write directly as she is stateside. What a mess. I do very sincerely wish the very, very best to you and to as much of your great institution as my modest shout from down here in the next county may reach. We are relying on you, even as I remain

Your friend,

M.

There it was. This must be Mabel Styke, writing on her employer's behalf. She was likable, odd. And judging from the letter, if I was reading its somewhat coded terms correctly, the Elysia Club had not quite met its end. And "boyish signs" must, for example, refer to Otto "Boy" Pastt's retaliations against Alice. The letter was undated, but the intake form itself gave me "Feb. 2, 1930," as the day of the acquisition. I'd need to look later for a subsequent acquisition, perhaps including paintings collected by the club.

I began pulling files and paging furiously through. I ventured into the rest of February, March, April, May, June, July, and, then, in that month least hospitable to work, I found something. There was a series of forms all dated the same day, "Aug. 2, 1930." There must have been at least fifty of them. They appeared to have been either very hastily or very cautiously filled out. Perhaps it was some combination of the two. In the space for description of the item, the administrator in question had seen fit to include only the phrase "Recent Americana." Where the name of the donor should be inscribed the form read "Generous Benefactor." J. D. Weiss was again the curator in charge. I flipped through the pages and was relieved to find at the bottom of the last a note advising me to "See addendum for detailed account of the gift (letter)." I lifted the page, ready to discover the document that would explain to me what this history was that I was at once ignorant of and did not know how to look for. The next page was simply another intake form, for a Peruvian necklace, circa 200 to 600 A.D. I flipped some more, attempting not to become desperate. I discovered additional intake forms. There was nothing else included in the folder.

I stood there. The air around my eyes felt thick, possibly it was visible. I wasn't sure what I could look at; I was experiencing that level of frustration. These fucking folders!

I was thinking something else, and I wasn't sure if I could possibly be right. It didn't make any sense, but possibly it made the only kind of sense I'd lately come to know, as in, it could involve publicly punching a man in the jewels and then walking nonchalantly away. I mean, I hoped it wouldn't involve publicly punching anyone else and/or proximity to additional genitals. I shook my bag and listened to the jingle of Paul Coral's keys.

I replaced the files as quickly and as accurately, with respect to date, as I could. In 1930 a gift to the museum had been improperly recorded, and the letter detailing this acquisition was lacking. And though I knew it was a species of magical thinking, I couldn't help suspecting that Paul might have been the one who had carried it away.

On my way back upstairs, I rummaged, via my phone, through old emails from my museum account. I knew there was one in which a department emerita, one Celeste Hardy, offered to send any takers a galley of her forthcoming book on children's portraiture in Virginia before the nineteenth century. Paul had accidentally replied all.

I remembered this because of his kindness and the elegance of his note. It wasn't often you saw a straight man offer such earnest interest in a mediocre intellectual project undertaken by a woman. I mean, he had written to Celeste *purely to be supportive,* and not because this support constituted some sort of act of charity or penance or step in a course of professional advancement, either. At the time, I was still very new in the office, and this message had kind of blown my hair back. It probably seems weird, and it is very hard to describe in retrospect, but he was just so guilelessly humane. It was as if, in reading this personal note, out of nowhere, in the midst of light administrative drudgery, I had come upon a piece of unexhausted time.

But more relevant to my current activities was the fact that in this email, directed to all and sundry of American Objects, Paul had seen fit to include a mailing address that was not his office coordinates. And so I knew, as the saying goes, where he lived.

20

I had one further errand for the day. I wanted to see what I could find out about Otto "Boy," who I assumed was one of the Elysia Club's earliest proponents and most passionate active members and, later, a rather foul antagonist. Did he even remind me a little of Whit? Of Fred? I tried to imagine what a person with such a nickname would be like. I wasn't sure if the supposed individual I came up with was the type of person I'd want to be alone around. Or, maybe he was the type of person one wanted to be around, which is to say, alone with, like, *constantly* and *exclusively.*

He did not, as it turned out, have a Wikipedia entry. Such, I guess, can be the fate of those who do not ally themselves appropriately with the appropriate institutions. A platform aggregating and synthesizing the content of various archives along with metadata drawn from globecat.org told me the following, under "Biographical notes":

Otto Pastt (1879 [1880?]–1960) was an art critic, lecturer, sculptor, and administrator from Buffalo, N.Y.

Pastt served as art critic of the *New York Saturday Post,* 1911–1917; *The Journal of the Arts,* 1918–1929; editor of *The Call,* 1931–1933; and lecturer at the Art Students League. In 1933, he was made technical director of the first, but short-lived, New Deal art program, the Public Works of Art Project (PWAP), established to provide work for artists in the ornamentation of nonfederal buildings, and served under Ed Moran until its activities were suspended in 1934. He subsequently transferred, along with Moran, to the U.S. Treasury Department of Painting and Sculpture (later termed the Section of Fine Arts), which from the early 1930s on administered the funding for competitive government commissions and grants for single artists, to decorate buildings and other federally maintained spaces. At the Section, he acted as sub deputy advisor, and as the editor of the Section's *Arts Bulletin.* Pastt subsequently entered the U.S. Treasury Department's Division of War

Finance. Here he was in charge of organizing exhibitions and overseeing the design of posters by so-called "combat artists," to stimulate the sale of war bonds. He was the author of a number of pamphlets and articles on American art and architecture, notably "The Concept of Picture Making" and "Views of Federal Buildings, an Illustrated Record."

From the description of the Otto Pastt papers, 1900–1950. (Unknown). GlobeCat record id: 234193907

There was a link to an archival collection at the right, "Pastt, Otto, 1880–1960. Otto Pastt papers, 1840–1967, bulk 1900–1960. Unknown (ISIL: DSI-AAA)." I followed the link, which led me to a GlobeCat page with an error message: "The page you tried was not found. You may have used an outdated link or may have typed the address (URL) incorrectly." Still, there were a lot of ledes within the biographical text. I tried copying half of it and pasting it into Google in quotes, just to see if there might be a page in existence at a different address. There was no such page, although I did come upon a link to a site called "Archives Directory for the History of Collecting in America." Here again, after clicking through, I landed in aporia: "Error: 22 — Unknown error."

I sighed. I reread Boy Pastt's biography. I was interested in *The Call*. Either it had enjoyed a very brief run, or Boy a brief tenure. Perhaps both. Subsequently Mr. Pastt had retreated, or maybe advanced (?), into the minutiae of federal administration. I directed my browser to globecat.org and entered search terms for the magazine. Its nondescript two-word title did not inspire confidence as far as database research was concerned, and, sure enough, I was not greeted with results that would help me. This was the thing with minor publications, minor figures. You needed text with real specificity to discover them online, but then the likely scenario was that your specific piece of text, whether title or passage, hadn't been digitized or wasn't cited in other materials, and much of what you otherwise had to go on would be buried by other, more canonical instances of similar terms. I mean, if you had given me three months to dig up information on Mr. Pastt, then, sure. I would have gone in person to Washington and read his records. But even then, when it came to the materials most useful to me, his earlier career before he became a full-fledged bureaucrat, I would have had only hints, correspondences, not the genuine article.

I wasn't being particularly methodical. But as of this afternoon on the museum steps, I had one man down, so to speak, and there was new space and new time in the mental landscape pertaining to yours truly. I decided to make a more aggressive effort. I steeled myself against disappointment. To my original search terms I now added "Pastt, Otto" and the word "Elysia." I tabbed over to activate the search box, shut my eyes, and hit RETURN. I waited.

When I opened my eyes again there were two results. One was an irrelevant (though fascinating, I am sure) DVD from 1998 regarding self-led wine tours and the storied notion of *terroir,* but the other was an entry for *The Call,* and clicking through I was elated to learn that the museum's library possessed all six issues on microfiche. In fact, this was the only location within New York City that had relevant holdings. The University of Buffalo owned hard copies.

I noted the call number and threw myself down to the library like I had hollow bones.

It was getting to be late in the day, and the resident fellow was not excited about being forthcoming. "Mondays are really the day for microfiche," Dani, who was a girl, said. "M for M, but with a different meaning."

I tried to get her to understand that we were talking about, at most, a single box, like twelve envelopes, nothing.

She said, "Please don't lie to me, Stella. Do you know how to use the machine?"

"Yes," I lied. I have seldom needed to access microfiche or film in my research. Again, because of the way in which digitization has tended to work across time periods, more of what I have needed was available to me online or via university digitization initiatives. The twentieth century is either so well known to us that its archives seem remote digitally, or the nineteenth is a time we've already so much forgotten that what's to hand seems exhaustive. But this may have more to do with how grants have been disbursed than anything else, i.e., history is still just money talking.

"Great, because I don't have time to show you right now." Dani was just standing there, expectant. "Yes?"

"Don't you have to go get the, um, fiches?"

"Oh, no. I do not do that." She pointed to an adjoining room/closet. "Help yourself. And, seriously, if you have any problems, you know what to do."

"Call you?" I hopefully offered.

"No, the opposite of that. Or, I mean, just don't have any problems. You can't have any problems, because I can't help you right now because of the reshelving project."

"Thank you," I said.

"Oh, and we are closing in thirty minutes."

"Thank you," I repeated. "Your hair looks nice."

"Stop," Dani said. "I know you don't know how to use the machine."

"I definitely know how to use the machine."

"You definitely do not."

"I'm off," I said, "to go use the machine I used to use all the time in alternate libraries you never saw me at using the machine because you didn't know me then or anything about my use of the machine!"

Dani, whose hair I had complimented and which was like a pewter cap, like hoary silk, like something she had gotten done professionally at terrifying cost, and had put on a card and forgotten about, had already started doing something else.

I pulled my face back together and strode into the task.

It wasn't that hard to find the fiches neatly slotted in their box. As Dani had foretold, my troubles began at the crucial moment at which I had to cause the fiches, these pieces of film, to interact with a desktop device that was something like what one would imagine a photographic enlarger could become, if a feature of the *Starship Enterprise*. It was fifty pounds of beige plastic, lenses, gears, and lightbulbs, and when I at last discovered its "on" switch, it roared to life with an enthusiasm that suggested the presence of copious additional hardware, if not an outboard motor. Next to the machine sat an elderly PC whose sole task it was to provide visual proof of the existence of files generated by the machine, and to allow the user to convey said files to his or her email account. The PC regarded me blankly. I ignored it. I began fussing with the mechanical parts that seemed most likely to be interested in admitting my fiche. After a few attempts, and the permanent corruption of one corner of a fiche (one and a half pages of *The Call* would, alas, never be legible at this library again), I got something up on the screen. Knob adjustment was now the way forward. The page came at last into eye-stabbing focus.

Do not doubt that you hold in your hands THE CALL: Volume one, Number one;

blazing a path into a super-modern world, a world willfully turned against weak tradition and assured in its own ability to imagine, draft, and build in and for the future, without recourse to a confessedly incompetent past. Once we might have said, "These are the days when the ivory of time-worn experience is being split into shards for inlay in some frivolous comb or thrown carelessly to the junkman. For a new golden age is under way — in ethics, in government, in lifestyle, and in the arts — an age gleaming beyond the boilingest inundation to tarnish its enamel. Even if, in matter and form, the age proves, in due time, to be but of golden oak: for the moment it glitters, — and it is yellow." Now we have lived enough to know that we hold in our hands not gold but sapling branches. They are humble but vital, and can bend. The era progresses apace, sometimes uncertain in her steps, since still younger than she wants to be, though she is now wiser by far. These are times for the arts, when the arts must lead the charge, calling out, "Onward, friends! Here lies the way to the future!"

This peculiar arabesque apparently constituted the "Editor's Note" for the first issue.

It was signed "The Boy." Talk about your mixed metaphors. The thing made my teeth hurt.

I began skimming, scrolling, reading bits of articles, removing and introducing fiche after fiche, trying to imagine who the hell the intended audience for this fascist nonsense might have been. But more than this, I wanted to find my prize. The catalog had told me that it must be in here. I was also racing against the clock. Would that Rainer might spontaneously ascend from his dungeon to break all of the timepieces in sight . . .

Then, there it was. It was just a little piece of text, centered within a space normally, I guessed, reserved for advertisements.

THE ELYSIA CLUB
We take insufferable pride in the
everywomen we have decided we
indubitably are.

This was the first notice. It appeared in the second issue of the magazine. Then, in the third issue:

The public is advised that THE ELYSIA
CLUB is *à la revanche.* It will not be
stymied, knows all, and is one of the

most haughty and unique, if not best, feminine institutions known to this or any other city built by *man,* and how odious this term is. (Men, how disgusting!) We are beyond maleness. It is unnecessary.

I winced at this satire of feminist discourse. Previously I'd thought this style of critique, such as it was, didn't show up until the later 1960s, but now I supposed I could state with some conviction that I'd been wrong about that. This was obviously not friendly writing. I wasn't exactly sure what the adverts were meant to accomplish, but I did not think that one was meant to feel fuzzy in the general direction of TEC after digesting them. Possibly the use of the adjective "insufferable" included a sneering pun in the direction of women's recently obtained ability to vote? I imagined Otto "Boy" smirking to himself as he typed up these unpleasant apostrophes, hunt and peck. One thing was certain, the ladies had gotten under his skin.

I rubbed my eyes and took an image. I emailed the image to myself.

The voice of a nonplussed Dani came on over the library PA. "Hello, patrons. The Central Museum's library will be closing in five short minutes; yes, that's just five minutes. I regret that circumstances have prevented me from advising you as to the library's closing at an earlier juncture, and then at subsequent regular intervals. I hope you will understand and behave as if you had known this twenty-five, twenty, fifteen, as well as ten, minutes ago. Thank you, one and all."

I made my own preparations.

On my way back upstairs I realized that maybe the thing I wanted to do now was pay a visit to Caro. This had nothing to do with my most recent discoveries. Rather, my desire was entirely tied to the mezzotint depicting the singer "Étoile" that had appeared to me yesterday, by way of the Gaypoole commonplace book. Something, i.e., our ongoing cold war, made me really want to know what Caro thought of this. You see, I like to observe her when she's forced to interpret evidence on a dime. I also can't lie. I don't hate putting pressure on the woman. I packed up my office things, went back downstairs.

I mention this portion of my trip only because, as I came out onto the top of the museum steps and surveyed what was left of the pinkly dying day, I happened to see, below me on the street, a pair of familiar figures. A young blond woman wearing a short mink cape that basically made no sense over her additional getup, which was tight and black, was being helped into a similarly tight, black vehicle by a slim man of grace, who was Fred Lu, and he closed the door and waved as she was driven away and then turned and commenced strolling downtown with his oxblood murse.

If I tell you that there was a feeling in my heart as of its being impaled by a short, sharp stick, and then slowly and deliberately beaten against the ground until it was absorbed into the unfeeling earth, please do not think I am exaggerating. There was no line of reasoning, social, moral, aesthetic, or historical, that could convince me that I had not suffered a second great loss in the confusion of the implosion of my marriage, in losing Fred Lu, if ever I had had Fred, which indeed maybe I did. In spite of Whit's deception, I could not wholly blame Whit for what had happened here. Here I was on my own. Besides, Fred wasn't even the one wielding the pointed stick.

I was.

21

I knew early on with Fred, or, rather, I knew very suddenly, what was in store. It is possible, too, that what I at the time construed as being "in store" was something that had already happened and which had already hurt me, and yet I waited. I waited to be hurt, because this was a form of hope. If I waited, I was not yet living in the event. This was what I did during my week of meditation, or pseudomeditation, after our brick-hut congress. I tried to keep the event off me.

I think about that time with a shortness of breath. You have to understand how little I wanted, then, to be sure that my actions had meaning. I wanted to feel that there was some other material force in the world guiding my life. I shut my eyes and attempted to empty my mind and invite it, whatever "it" might be, to be present to me. This procedure was not a success. Whit's face was, meanwhile, as I recall, increasingly scary to behold during this strange week, during which the implications of my own actions, if not Whit's, slowly dawned on me. I think Whit's outrage was not even produced by some intuition that I had been unfaithful to him. I think he was mainly furious that I still had not recognized his own inattentiveness, if not the long-term cheating itself. Any normal woman, Whit felt, would have been more careful about, would have been more attentive to, even *obsessed with,* his attentions. No normal woman could stand being ignored as he was ignoring me. She would die from it. And not only did I not die, I viciously attacked him by refusing to give him the pleasure of my jealousy. I gave him no pleasure. I was distant, distracted, cold.

During that week, I sat on the floor with my eyes shut and knew nothing. I stipulated, with a version of myself that kept track of events in the present yet was not exactly *part of* present time, that I did not know yet and was waiting. The event would someday come.

But how can I say it? Even then the time was beautiful. Perhaps I should have leveled with myself and left my husband. But perhaps then the time was more beautiful than it had ever been before. I remember how I got in my car that Sunday after Fred and I had slept together and I drove back from Delaware and it was a thick, dying, gorgeous afternoon, with dark gold and then orange light. Inside, I was exploding. Someone was shouting inside my head: "You are alive!" I did not know where I was. Inside my mind I was on my knees. I whispered, "Please tell me what to do." No one said anything. I tried to repeat what Fred had told me. "Trust yourself," I said aloud. I pulled over and sat in the car and wrote this phrase down. But whom, I asked, would I trust? What was "yourself"? Reading a contemporary Buddhist tract later that week I came to the conclusion that doubt of this kind is due to a lack of consonance between mind and body. I found that I had emphasized my own connection to the earth excessively. I could even feel this, or so I thought, in the lack of certainty in my shoulders and in my head.

Now entering Basset's Prints, I corrected my posture, lifted my chin. This would be, at the very least, a more revelatory week than that one had been. Caro was at her desk, a little figure.

"To what do I owe this pleasure?"

272

I tried to smile.

"Are you off from work? You came over to see your mother? You should be careful, Stella, because your mother might get the impression that you don't hate her."

"Ha!" I said, trying to imitate Caro's tone.

"What?"

"I just mean, hello, it's great to see you."

"I don't think I've seen you this much in one week since you were about five years old."

"You make it sound like I was kidnapped."

"No, Stella, I am trying to say that you have always been extremely independent. As soon as you could walk you were off to see what Stella could do for herself in this world."

"Not to mention, self-interested."

"Well, dear, one must survive. Now, what was it you wanted?" Caro was wearing a pair of purple, blue, and red "mock" tortoise reading glasses, and now she poked these down a bit lower on her nose. She seemed to be in the middle of cooking her books.

I took a moment. "I actually wanted," I began, grasping my phone inside my bag, "to show you something."

"Really?"

I removed the phone from my bag, brought up the image of "Étoile, the Singer

273

from Paradise."

Caro received the device. She switched on a lighted magnifier she kept on her desk and allowed its lens to intervene between her face and the screen. "Well," she said, handing the phone back.

I waited for some response.

"That's very interesting."

I didn't know what to say. "Does it" — I paused — "remind you of something?"

Caro blinked. "I saw the obituary," she said.

Because I was unsure what her admission betokened, I remained silent.

"I wondered how long it would be before you brought this up. I wasn't sure if we would need to discuss it directly. But now you're here, making that demand."

"What exactly are we talking about?"

Caro pushed her glasses farther down. "We are talking about the same thing we were talking about at lunch the other day. We are talking about your friend and mine, *Paul*."

I tried to keep my tone dispassionate. "We're talking about Paul Coral?"

"Yes, we are most certainly talking about him, dear. We are talking about him because he played an important role in my career, and I don't see, at this juncture, why you should not be aware of that. In fact, in order to avoid any potential sloppiness, it seems essential that you know some things, since you continue to require answers. Lord knows what you will come up with if I don't set you straight. And/or, what sorts of damage you will inadvertently wreak upon your own inheritance in your supposedly admirable quest for truth. Sit down," my mother told me.

I sat.

"Paul and I met in 1980. It was when he first got his job and he wanted to know everything about everything. He started coming into the shop."

"I thought you didn't know him."

"Goodness, Stella, you take everything I say so extraordinarily literally."

"Because," I shot back, "words have references?"

Caro removed her glasses. "First of all, words have 'referents.' Second, I'm not really sure why you assume that everything you encounter must be limited to those qualities discernible at very first sight. Often what we see on first glance is merely a trick expressly designed to deceive us."

"Great," I told her.

"You think I'm being arch or paranoid, but really I am attempting to offer you some

275

useful advice. So you've shown me an image of a commercial mezzotint, circa 1820, perhaps earlier. You recognize, of course, that I am in possession of an uncannily similar print, a finer and more complex intaglio item reminiscent of the etching revival of the 1840s in France. It is an American work and hangs in my home. The etching revival, as you know, did not reach the United States until the 1880s. *But never mind that,* you think. You think also of Francis Seymour Haden, who studied Rembrandt and brought Rembrandt's ideals back into the benighted world, but Haden lived in Britain and was not at the height of his powers until the 1860s. You think, *What a fine image you have hanging in your hallway, Mother.* How wonderful to have such a fine revival print, which yet manifests American subject matter, which has a whiff of the fun of commercial culture and yet so much of the romantic panache of the revival. No print such as this can exist, am I right? And yet *I* am in possession of one such print, that rarest of all rare things, something which cannot exist."

"OK," I said.

"And what can this mean, you ask. You search your mind for every possible explanation, in the process conferring more and more value on my excellent print. Even if you know nothing about prints you would feel a certain *frisson,* wouldn't you?"

"I guess. But that's obviously a red herring."

"Very good, Stella. Occam's razor. If something's too good to be true, it isn't. A useful point, alas, when it came to your marriage." Caro did not miss a beat. She rattled on, "And how, then, did I come to possess this ravishing print, which hides its inauthenticity so intriguingly in plain sight?"

I had already for a while been unwilling to sign on for this particular language game. "I don't know," I informed my inquisitor.

"But of course you know! I have a counterfeit. It's not even a good one. No, no, it's a *great* one, because it imitates something even better than the actual history of printmaking. In its own way, it's a kind of masterpiece."

"This sounds like a eugenics project."

"Stella, my darling, you cannot just waltz in here and expect me to elucidate all of human history for you at the drop of a hat."

I sighed. "So Paul made that, is that the idea? And he worked for you. And I imagine he made others."

"He did. And the reason this is important is that for nearly a decade he kept me in business. It may not surprise you to learn that *les nouveaux riches* do not always want *vrai de vrai.* Sometimes they would like something a bit better than the genuine article, they expect that, they expect that that's what money can buy, and Paul and I learned over the years how to supply what they wanted. He had fertile ground. What, after all, is your department at the museum but a physical record, a kind of syllogistic proof, even, of the development of the tastes of a class of Americans with more money than sense? Before I had a refined command of the international market, it was an extremely convenient thing to do. And we did it."

"Paul used items in the collection?"

"Yes. And what you may not know about him is that when he was young, when he was up in New Hampshire as a student, he had studied with a master printmaker, an expert in engraving, etching, and aquatint, and he understood the techniques. I would never have gone along with it if it were not for that, that he had traditional knowledge."

I raised my hand, which still contained the cell phone and therefore looked slightly ridiculous. "I'm sorry, but are you suggesting that what the two of you did was *OK*?"

Caro blinked.

"I'm just saying, Mom, this seems potentially illegal."

"Oh, I don't really know about that. I'd estimate that about ten percent of circulating works on paper aren't genuine. They're quite tricky to authenticate, particularly if they were originally produced as multiples. Any dealer worth their snuff will tell you that right away. Then again, I've seldom been asked to authenticate anything I was selling! I chalk it up to my customer base, quite solvent but really a bit desperate, in some cases."

"I see."

"Do you? Do you, really? I imagine you are hoping to do some damage here, at the very least privately rake me over the coals. Perhaps you even want to expose your own mother as a fraud! For starters, my dear, a private school education is not free!"

I thought about this for a moment. "Some people get scholarships," I offered.

"Yes," Caro all but shouted, "but those people do not live on 89th Street!"

There was, as ever, a certain tautological tendency plaguing Caro's thought, but I'd never known how to release her from the care of the ouroboros she'd long ago made into a cherished spirit animal, and I wasn't about to attempt that particular philosophical jailbreak on this day. What I said was, "It's a nice print."

Something moved. "I think so, too," Caro pronounced. Then, "Paul was really very talented. I think he was very nearly, in his own way, a great artist."

"Have you read his books?"

"Oh, I don't go in much for poetry. What I did see seemed extremely pleasant, but, you know."

"You can't judge it?"

"Precisely. I can't really *assess* it. Not the way I can something graphic."

I nodded. "Did Paul ever, as far as you know, create any maps? Did you ever sell anything of that nature?"

Caro appeared to consider this query with genuine uncertainty, to the extent that this was possible for her. "No," she said at last. "That isn't something we ever did, not that it would have been a bad idea. Stella, perhaps you have a mind for this business, after all." Caro smiled, thinly, in my direction.

"Thanks," I told her. "That's interesting to hear. But no maps?"

"No maps. No maps for poor Paul."

I got on the subway at 77th. It had been, I reflected, a full enough day. The air in front of me was sort of swarming with something or other, but my body felt relaxed. Farther down the car, someone, a girl in green pants, I saw, was crying, and I watched a woman with two very young children reach across the aisle and hand her a package of Kleenex. The girl accepted this small piece of assistance. I looked away. I didn't do anything on any of the trains I was on for the next thirty minutes. I just sat there, letting it sink in, whatever it was.

At home I decided to force myself to check my personal email for fallout from the most recent Whit debacle. It was possible there would be, fun now over, some screed of threats or even a lawsuit, considering Whit's particular skill set. There was, however, radio silence from the Ghiscolmb sector. It was Marco who alerted me. "Is there any chance this is you?" was the alarmingly foreseeable subject of his email. Included in the body text was a link to a popular gossip site. One of the site's editors had posted a video, taken, by some act of cosmic mercy, at sufficient distance from the scene that my face was not legible. Two distant figures, one recognizably male, the other a near-midget female, stand together in intimate conversation. Then one of the pair — this is the female — abruptly further reduces her height with respect to the other and pops her fist violently up into his crotch. The other, pain hilariously evident even under crackles of wind and running commentary by the videographer, drops to the ground and commences writhing, as the female stalks impassively off, climbing the museum steps like the angel of vengeance she has become.

I replied to Marco, "Absolutely not!" I then forwarded Marco's message to Cate, adding, "If anyone asks, it's not me ;-)" I went to seek some water. When I returned, Cate had already replied. "You are such a good shot," she said. "This makes me so proud."

I smiled. It occurred to me that assault charges from Whit would necessitate his admission that he was not honoring the terms of our separation agreement, and, not only this, that he was harassing me at work. There were literally hundreds of witnesses who'd seen him with me on Monday night, and at least one or two of them could easily be convinced to embroider the tale of how scared I'd been when I confided to him/her that I did not know how to shake my creepy estranged husband, though of course decorum had had to be maintained for the duration of the party. And then there was the fact that he probably didn't want his name associated with an Internet meme celebrating his emasculation for the rest of his life. I took a few screen caps at choice moments and considered creating my own choppy GIF to help get the ball rolling.

But then I didn't. I closed my laptop.

I went into the kitchen and made myself a decent omelet and ate it standing beside the counter. I did the dishes. I walked once around each of the rooms in the apartment, taking stock of the eclectic furniture situation. I rolled a ragged cigarette from a pouch of stale tobacco I keep at the back of a kitchen drawer and smoked half of it out the window before pitching the rest away. I got out Ella Voss's and Paul Coral's respective publications. I was pretending as hard as I possibly could that I had forgotten all about the presence of Paul's keys at the bottom of the tote. I retired to my bedroom.

I flipped around Paul's collections. I really wasn't sure what should interest me here. I had acquired *The Telephone* and also the more recent *Superimposed Worlds.* These just looked like poems to me. I mean, I was very glad to have these two collections, because I cared about Paul and his work. However, I was unsure what his published verbal exertions could mean to my current conundrums. I skimmed dutifully, but nothing was coming up. I turned to Ella's latest.

The cover showed an image of a child's hand grasping a lilac bloom. It had been described by various luminaries as "gripping," "important," "strange," and "upsetting." A photograph of Ella Voss graced the lower left-hand corner of the back cover of the book. She appeared exceedingly unassuming, like someone's drawing of an older woman. She was expressionless, her neck wrapped in a prissy paisley scarf.

A few pages in, we are treated to a family dinner scene.

"The best part," Jason was saying, pointing for emphasis with a fork that was held, his father felt, perilously close to his right eye, "of the story —"

"Jason," said his father, "do me a favor, son, and lower that."

"What?"

"The fork," his mother clarified. She blew on a morsel and gazed expectantly at her husband.

"Yes, sir." Jason frowned. He took a slug of milk from a tall glass. "Anyway, it switches to the point of view of this guy who gets sent to this other planet where there's total peace and harmony but it's only so peaceful because there's this, this, uh, big machine that's controlling everyone's brain. Except it's kind of like a plant, you know? Like, it's living?" Jason emptied his glass. He canvassed his father's face.

Charles Crystal nodded. His wife, a blonde, had once been reasonably pretty. Her face was heart shaped and worn. Now she got up from the table and refilled her son's glass.

Jason's pale eyes widened. "So, get this, then the guy shoots the machine until it dies, because he thinks everyone is a slave, and he wants them to be free, even if that means that they have to have war and poverty and all of that. And then the machine dies, because it turns out it's actually not that hard for it to die, and all these people, all these millions of people on the planet, are liberated. But then, get this, he has to take over for the machine. He *has* to. He doesn't want to but they make him do it." Jason was staring at his father.

Charles Crystal smiled indulgently. He observed the smooth, tanned brow of his elder son, which was bright with enthusiasm and dismay. "Well," he said at last, "I guess that man became president?"

Charles Crystal chuckled, pleased with himself.

"No —" Jason was starting to say.

"Dad?"

"Yes, Philip?" Charles Crystal turned to his younger son, who was seated beside his wife. "What can we do for you this evening?"

Philip was nine. "Dad, I want to know if Sherry is going to get better soon."

Sherry was the Crystals' dog. She was a chocolate lab and was currently in the late stages of a difficult pregnancy.

Charles Crystal approved of his younger son's interest in the female condition, and his eyes danced briefly over to his wife. "Well, do you think something's wrong there, son?"

"I dunno, Dad. She just seems so heavy, like she doesn't want to do anything anymore."

"What?" Jason was meanwhile demanding. "Jesus Christ, Philip, the dog is knocked up. Can't you understand that?"

"Oh!" said their mother.

"Jason!" Charles Crystal warned.

"I know that," Philip muttered. He looked down at the remaining mashed potatoes on his plate and slowly stirred them. The child was different. Though he did not cry or otherwise trouble his parents at night, they were aware that he seldom slept. Charles, en route to sample a leftover drumstick or cold ham, often passed the child's open door and found his younger son lying on his back, eyes open, motionless in the light of the moon. Now, outside, the mellow song of the ice cream truck had begun. Philip did not seem to hear it.

Charles Crystal was reaching into his pants pocket for his wallet. The boy should feel his care.

"Philip," Charles Crystal said, "are you finished with your supper?"

Slowly, painfully, the boy nodded. He continued staring at his plate.

"Well, then, young man, you should go find yourself some dessert!" Charles Crystal removed a crisp dollar bill from his wallet and passed it smoothly across the table, dropping it beside his younger son's plate.

The boy sat there.

No one spoke.

"Go on," said Philip's father.

Trembling, the boy reached out one still-dimpled hand and lowered it over the bill, unconsciously crumpling the money into a ball as he took hold of it, and wordlessly left the table.

When Philip had gone, Charles Crystal turned to address Jason. "Do you really feel that's the sort of talk your brother should hear?"

Lisette Crystal stood on cue and retired with her plate and Philip's plate into the kitchen. She had barely touched her food.

Jason was frowning. "I don't know, Dad. I think maybe he needs to remember that that dog's gonna have puppies. That's all."

"He's only nine! And he's a sensitive child. He's not like you, Jason. A man has to know whom he's dealing with. Philip may not be ready to understand all that you have already understood. We must be patient with him."

"You can say that again!" Jason continued to eat. "Say," he said, "d'you think I could go back in there," he indicated the kitchen with a toss of his head, "and have the rest of Philip's?"

Charles Crystal considered his elder son. "I don't see why not. Just remember, when Philip comes back indoors, go easy on him."

Charles Crystal is an engineer with Halex, but something is wrong. Ideas sift through his fingers unsubstantially, soft as ash. Sometimes he cannot understand what his colleagues say. He has taken to sneaking into the desk of a younger Halex engineer at night, stealing that man's work, passing it off as his own. Diet pills and scotch, along with sporadic secretarial assignations, relieve his anguish.

Philip Crystal is allowed to stay home from school. His mother, Lisette, imagines herself drawing a witchy circle around her son. She purchases unnecessarily large quantities of canned food in case of nuclear holocaust, now that colonial projects are failing. The dog, Sherry, becomes more and more obese.

"Halexvale," a seven-mile industrial park abutting residential suburbs of the novel's pseudo-Rochester, comes to include some two hundred chemical plants. Countless leaks and spills result in toxic silver contamination of sediment in the pseudo-Genesee River bed (the novel names it the "Gentle River") as well as soil in and around the city.

In 1981, a pipe ruptures near P.S. 2, a school at the southern border of Halexvale, releasing thirty thousand gallons of methylene chloride. Worried parents yank most of the 594 children enrolled at P.S. 2 out of school. Classes are briefly canceled, but then the school rapidly reopens in triumph, after state health officials discover high concentrations of chemical vapors underground but, as they are keen to emphasize, insignificant traces in the school building.

Sherry the dog gives birth in a closet on the day of the spill, and Philip is at home and can witness the biologically instructive event. By afternoon he gets it in his mind that he will be the first to tell Jason what has happened and at last prove he understands canine reproduction.

Eavesdropping on his mother's late-day telephone conversation, Philip is able to discern where Jason will spend the afternoon. When the coast is clear, Philip removes his bicycle from the garage and pedals into the grid, arriving at the raised ranch home in question and dropping his bike on the lawn. The door is open, but there is no one present anywhere on the upper two floors of the house. Philip is about to leave when he remembers something his brother has told him about basements of houses, that this is an important and underappreciated portion of the home. Philip goes downstairs and in one windowless room in the basement his brother and friends are raping a very young boy probably the same age as Philip. The End.

■ ■ ■ ■

It was very late, and I put the novel down. I felt clammy, sick at heart, having given my attention over to a work that had forced me to visualize things I very much did not want to visualize, making me complicit in their recurrence, even if only in my mind's eye. I was seduced by Voss's prickly detailing of surreal events. *Philip Crystal* also put me in mind of Lorelei's otherworldly retreat, but how different were these two accounts of ex-urban utopia: Hennicott's elegiac; Voss's explicit, vaguely noir.

And I thought of Paul, about the time that he had spent inside of American Objects' false building, behind the façade of the customs house, in a dozen different false living rooms.

■ ■ ■ ■

FRIDAY

■ ■ ■ ■

22

It was Friday. At my desk in the morning I had received an email from Caro with no subject, the body of which simply said, "Nice to see you. XXO."

My active evening notwithstanding, I still had some questions about the mystery known as my job, as well as its contextualizing historical surrounds. I was also trying not to think about Paul's keys.

The temporal location toward which my mind was now tending was a bit on the earlier side. I considered the 1930 donation of Brunhilda Wunsch Gaypoole's commonplace book and the lack of proper documentation of other items that had come along with it that August. I had no hope for the digital catalog, however I still did a due diligence search. Alice Gaypoole Wynne had, according to the database results I received, made but one donation in her life, i.e., her great-grandmother's scrapbook. Though this was very generous and good, when you thought about it, an heiress of her standing would in any and all cases have given more, if she had things to give. I pondered this fact for a moment. *If she had things to give, which she indubitably had, see Elysia Club collection.* What could have impeded Alice? Who or what could have stood in her way? For the moment I didn't have time to consider the question further, but it was one worth asking. I would need to return to this later.

There was something I had for too long avoided doing, and it was time to remedy this. I needed to go downstairs and view what I imagined to be Fred's show of earnest, on-the-nose American excellence.

I dragged myself back into the wing.

The title "Land of the Limner" had been elegantly emblazoned on a purpose-built false wall before the relevant galleries in intricate, ribbon-like script, as if cut with the tip of a sword.

I was in a hurry, so I didn't linger over the introductory text. I passed behind the pony wall into the first windowless gallery.

It was dim in the room, not to mention that the walls had been painted flat black, so that the setup felt puritanical in the extreme. Overheads cast halos on a series of eighteenth-century works, full-body portraits of the Dutch for the most part, accomplished on wood paneling by individuals more or less able to paint. It's a moment in aesthetic production that you pretty much have to look at to believe, because you have centuries of ridiculously, hubristically accomplished painting in the Netherlands, and then you get to ye olde New World, and crap looks like this. This is to say, it was a far cry from Van Eyck. Females in ostentatious silk heels and triangular ankle-length dresses were described flatly, in mostly unmixed colors. They held flowers. Their dresses were embroidered with additional flowers. They stood, blushing, facing forward, the better to render their anatomy easy to depict.

I found myself particularly drawn to one portrait, a woman in a vertically striped skirt who held a long rose, the blossom of which was nearly as large as her face. She was holding the rose up to her nose, as if she might sniff it, but her gaze was turned out of the portrait, toward us. I went in for a closer look at the label. This told me that the portrait was attributed to someone known by convention as the "Wunsch Limner," since the last name of the person depicted was likely Wunsch and nothing was known of the artist beyond his (or her, though likely *his*) accomplishment here. The date attributed to the painting was "ca. 1790." I would have preferred to just go about my business now, viewing the rest of the show, but I recognized this all-too-familiar last name from my research. It was a very uncanny coincidence if it was a coincidence, but probably it was not a coincidence. In fact, there was no way in hell it was a coincidence. I took a picture of the lady with the rose. I knew it was not necessary to do this, seeing as I myself had but a matter of days ago wrangled image files for every work in the show, but it seemed to me somehow crucial that I capture her for myself again, now and here.

I went into the next room. It contained early-nineteenth-century works. These were mostly British patrons, though again a baby Wunsch, similarly the work of an anonymous limner, made itself known. How, I berated myself, when I had been working on the checklist, had I failed to notice this pattern, the ubiquity of this surname? I paused for a moment to admire the advances in modeling and conveyance of three-dimensional space that accompanied the advent of the year 1800. Congratulations, Americans! Although, on the other hand, there really was something to be said for the previous room, with its awkward pictures of the daughters of rich upstate ranchers of Dutch and German descent. It showed you something that the art historian seldom has a chance, and probably does not want, to discuss, i.e., the fact that the history of art, or the history of the production of aesthetic objects, is not merely a narrative of progress and increasing skill in the relation of realist detail, or just the invention of new ways to convey politics to an in-group. There is also branching and back-tracking. And there is isolation, and there is miracle. And there is something people call "charm," which is what happens when nothing works in a given painting. But what you get when nothing works is everything.

Subsequent rooms contained genre paintings of adorable pets (the Internet would, I felt sure, reward Fred) and additional portraits by the eccentrics of the limning world, mid-nineteenth-century painters who combined photography with painting or painted the same image over and over again, such that it seemed less like a painting and more like an infinitely reproducible work, like a painted sign with its conventions for lettering and graphic cheer, or even a lithograph. There were religious works and enormous family portraits.

Then I came to the modern rooms. Some of the canvases here showed fleshy heiresses nine feet tall, about to extend a dimpled ivory pinkie into the twentieth century, if their ruthlessly cinched waists would permit them to move that far from the supportive furniture of their drawing rooms. There were scenes of street life, tiny canvases depicting nightlife haps and the interiors of various interwar galleries, lubricated with illicit hooch and packed with female painters in backless dresses and male painters in rumpled suits, and then a lively daytime painting contest. There were also a few little-seen Stettheimers on loan from various private collections, a Kuniyoshi. What surprised me most of all was that the small canvases, these group scenes I mention, were the museum's own. I had never seen any of these paintings before.

I had to give Fred credit, it was pretty much an incredible show. Seeing the progression of this style of working on the East Coast just felt so specific, and I wasn't even thinking about what Fred had done as a pseudo-innocent attempt to self-promote anymore. He was promoting himself by doing something actually useful and culturally relevant. Or, now the dismal thoughts kicked in, he was *actually* shamelessly promoting himself by doing such good work, had shamelessly strategized every move here. I really could not tell. He was *too* good. Would I feel better about what he had done if he had just guessed and randomly came up with the right thing to propel himself into the art-historical stratosphere?

This was the thing about Fred. When he was close to you or you felt close to him, he was the hero you had always sought, who understood the truth of the world, and you believed or wanted to believe that he knew what the right thing was, perpetually and unquestionably, and that was why he was doing whatever he was doing. But when you took a step back, everything changed, and he was a ruthless jerk. I could not decide where I wanted to stand. I truly did not hate Fred and did not think of him as an evil mastermind, but neither did I feel that he was the Second Coming of Christ. He was a pretty man who was good at his job, and he fucked like a total sweetheart. This was, I kept trying to convince myself, the beginning and the end of my commitment to him.

I went back upstairs to the department.

The question was, I kept reflecting, how long would Fred continue to tolerate closeness to someone who chose to remain agnostic with respect to him and his talent? By remaining in the same department in which he worked and continuing to consider him human, was I putting my own career in jeopardy? And: Would this remain an abhorrently distracting feature of my life, for the rest of my life, were I to stay here? Would he continue to claim, in exchange for my determined noncredence in his god status, my heart?

Fred was cool, but he also had standards. Perhaps more than anything he had standards. He would demand a fee. This was one thing I could be sure of. Obviously neither side of his family had gotten as rich as they had by giving, even immaterial, goods away.

I, on the other hand, was the descendant of parents who were both the very first in their families to make good. They were trying their hands at venality-as-lifestyle, as it were, and I still had a choice. I didn't have to go along with it. I didn't have to believe in the meaning of these exchanges. I could elect to follow the laws of some other system.

But so far this hadn't really worked out for me. I had struggled and written a dissertation about public irony as it existed two centuries ago. And I had married a funny man who seemed to like me a great deal, but who had no real ability to understand or accept what it was that drove me to do things like write 100K+ scholarly words about transatlantic rudeness. Like me, Whit wasn't a worshipper of the system, which was what had made him good at interpreting and occasionally manipulating the law, but he was also and indubitably a fan of the path of least resistance. His fragile conception of himself, unwieldy, feeble, and essentially as permeable as wet tissue, could not bear up under any kind of stress. I may be misanthropic, but I know what I am and I am not a fan of the least resistant path. If I want a way out, I will cut it myself.

In my office I began doing a bit of looking into the Wunsches of New York, who I felt might be relations of Brunhilda et al. They were a German family who had owned an enormous piece of land, nearby and including what is now the town of Hudson. In the late eighteenth century, they had successfully sold the portion of territory now containing Hudson off to a dotty former Brit who was not into the Crown and who had been having some difficulties keeping up his whaling and shipping business on the island of Nantucket during the fraught years of the Revolutionary War. Much of the Wunsches' archive was maintained at a historical museum south of Albany, which some bountiful bequest by a twentieth-century descendant of the family kept free of mildew and parasitic worms. This archive had a website, and on this website was a phone number, which I, being an enterprising person, called.

The first thing I needed to confirm with my interlocutor was that the Wunsches whose archive she upheld were plausibly the same Wunsches whose eligible daughter, attesting to the especially pronounced reproducibility of women during this time, had been painted with a rose by a limner back when New York State was a wilderness.

"Yes," said the lady on the line. She expressed surprise that I, working at CeMArt (she had caller ID), was not already aware of this connection. "You have the right ones!"

I thanked her.

"There weren't that many wealthy Palatines back then," she assured me. "You can be confident!"

The next question I had for her was whether the famous nineteenth-century feminist reformer Brunhilda Wunsch Gaypoole was a relative.

"Of the Wunsches?"

I averred I meant the very ones.

"Of course! She's one of them!" The speaker paused. "She had a very interesting husband, as I recall. He was a publisher on the side."

"Oh," I said.

"Sort of a Leonard Woolf."

"Really?"

"Well, of course she was rather less prolific. But Gilbert helped her publish. *Apud Gilbertium Lacunam Felicem,* 'At the House of Gilbert Joyous Pool,' to translate rather literally, if you've seen one of the title pages? There was a novel, along with the social writings. It came earlier. Not so well known."

"Right," I said. This was *Lorelei of Millbury.* I reflected, with a thrilling shiver, that I had been correct. I told her that I had another question.

"And what might that be?"

I said that I wanted to know if she had ever heard of a place called Elysia.

There was momentary silence on the line.

"Hello?" I said.

"Still here!"

I repeated my request for information related to a place, real or imagined, by the name of E-L-Y-S-I-A.

The voice came back over the line. " 'A place where no one mourns, and nothing irreplaceable is lost, and nothing lost is irretrievable'?"

I didn't know how this person knew that she could get away with this with me. But she did. And could. I replied, "Yes. A place 'with tears dry and wrongs righted, where nothing that occurs in dreams knows human fear or cruelty.' Do you know anything about it?"

" 'Dear seeker, careful one —' " The woman started laughing and she couldn't go on. "OK, OK, you've got me. Who's this?"

Suddenly my blood ran cold. *Had I just accidentally rushed the club?* "Oh," I began, "I'm, um, new. I don't know. I just had a question."

"Of course you're *new,*" said the voice, souring abruptly. "Everyone who calls is *new.*"

I refused to be intimidated. "New to *this,* you mean?"

"Yes, of course, *new* to this! What d'you think I mean?"

Oh lady, I thought. "Well, I was just wondering, you see, if you don't mind my asking, I've been doing some research regarding a commonplace book kept by Brunhilda Wunsch Gaypoole —"

"Yes, you're very lucky to have it in your collection."

"Thank you."

"You're welcome."

"Well, I was just wondering, in the book I had come upon a map."

"Yes?"

"It describes a place named Elysia, and it seems as if you are familiar with the poem that accompanies the map. I really just wanted to know if you had any further information about —"

"The map?"

"Yes, about the map."

"Are you affiliated with an institution?"

"What?" I said.

"Are you affiliated with an institution?"

It was an interesting question. "Yes, of course."

"I ask because we have different rates for private individuals versus larger bodies. You'll have to give me an email address and then I'll get back to you with an invoice as well as the documents you are requesting."

"I am requesting documents?"

"Yes! You are!"

"OK," I said, "any hint as to what these might be?"

"Oh, there will be a complete description. Fear not!"

"And when might I expect these, the, er, documents?"

"Oh, certainly by midafternoon, I should say."

"Great," I told her. "And, actually, I'm just going to go with 'individual,' if that's OK?"

"It's fine by me."

I spelled out my Gmail address.

23

After I had hung up the phone, something made me turn in my seat.

Fred was standing in the doorway of my office. "Sounds like you're doing some intriguing research," he said.

I smiled. "Always."

"It's nice to see."

This was the cue that we were going to play the game of pleasantries. I wasn't totally opposed to this, although I could think of better things to do with the next hour. The main thing that annoyed me about this game was that Fred always got to decide when it would begin and when it would end. Here my input was less unwelcome than irrelevant; Fred, being the more puissant of the two of us, had to take it upon himself to perform the role of game master. It wasn't, again, that I was so bad at the game. I just wasn't quite as invested as my lover.

The emotional affair continued: "How are you doing?" I offered.

Fred indicated with his body that he was exhausted. He was not incapable of physical humor. "May I come in?" he wanted to know.

I made a gesture to the effect that, yes, of course. And Fred shut the door most of the way and seated himself on a rickety period piece that had once been part of the collection but which a curator before my time had identified as a subtle reproduction and which had subsequently been deaccessioned into my office. The chair resembled a converted umbrella stand to which a cushion had been haphazardly stapled. It groaned in protest even at Fred's meager derriere.

"It's been kind of an incredible week." I really didn't care that much about Fred's show but now was the time for me to express my awe, and if I didn't make a good display, there would be trouble.

Fred smoothed his hair back. His face was getting plainer. He wanted to be himself. "It has. I'm kind of overwhelmed." He sat with his legs apart, hands on his knees, leaning over. He was wearing black slacks, a light blue button-down with sleeves rolled up. I eyed the veins on his forearms.

"That's understandable. You do so much."

"Not really. Not enough."

"It's hard to imagine how you could do more."

"Ha!" said Fred. "I guess so. But there is so much to do."

"It's true." The pleasantries were really starting to wear thin. If things continued this way, soon I would have to resort to complimenting him on his clothing, with exhaustive treatment of each individual item.

Fred sighed. "It *is* true," he repeated, with new emphasis. "I try to keep a balance." This last comment, by the way, was for Fred tantamount to a major confession. He did not easily admit to any kind of difficulty in relation to work.

I decided that I could make this quality time together somewhat more useful for myself by trying to extract some information from Fred regarding the future. I said, "I was amazed about the collaboration with WANSEE. I mean, franchises of the museum, wow. I imagine that will really help with revenue."

"I know!" Fred smiled. "The board was *very* reluctant at first."

"Why was that?" I knew exactly why, but Fred would enjoy answering the question and I wanted, for reasons of both affection and self-interest, to give him that pleasure.

"Well, you know, what are we going to put in these places? How will they possibly reflect the core mission, and so forth."

I nodded. "I'd imagine they would be concerned about dilution" — I paused — "of the institution, I guess. If that's an apt metaphor."

"No, I think that's exactly right."

"So what convinced them in the end?"

"I brought in statistics on the number of people who graduate with doctorates in the history of art each year and the number of jobs available to them. And I gave a little talk about the state of inheritance tax, and the artworks people currently give and would *like* to give, that is, would like to be *able* to give, based on my own research. And I showed some figures regarding the recent changes to the museum's collection — and to collections of the few comparable museums around the world? It's clear that if CeMArt would like to maintain market share it must continue to scale. We are also probably the only major collection of pre-nineteenth-century Western art anywhere in the world that does not have significant government funding. And the City of New York is not about to give us ten acres of parkland to build on for free anytime soon.

If you think about the Louvre, how it com-
mandeered its own medieval foundations at
one point? This is a literal expression of
what is possible in Europe that is not possible here. And the contemporary collections have become so unbelievably aggressive. And then there's Saadiyat and things
of that nature. We don't even need to go
into that."

"No," I agreed. I didn't know what he was
referring to.

"So this makes sense, I think." Fred
looked up from the carpet. His large, fine
eyes searched me out. He wanted to know
if I was willing to go along with him.

"It does," I lied. And then I lied some
more. "Also, it seems incredibly exciting."

"That's how I've tried to think about it!"
The sudden enthusiasm betrayed his own
doubt and even reluctance to undertake the
very measures he had, ostensibly, already
undertaken. "I mean, can you imagine being someone incredibly young and having
the opportunity, for all intents and purposes,
to direct her own museum? It's not like
you'd have to travel to Mars."

I started to wonder what Fred was trying
to tell me. Was he offering me a promotion,
and/or exile? Would I, Stella Krakus, be
granted the distinct pleasure of picking up

shop and transferring my existence to Nevada or São Paolo or Abu Dhabi, or wherever it was going to be? Here I could be in remote dialogue with dear Fred, be his loyal extension and creative emissary. I could attempt to realize my own vision, and if I were lucky and successful enough, perhaps I would someday distinguish myself to the extent that I could return to New York City and have some sort of viable job by the time I was fifty. What an idea!

But I tried not to let it show too much when Fred's machinations terrified me, and so I said, "Of course not. I mean, it's not like *anywhere* is really that far away anymore!"

"Ha!" said Fred. But all the same he seemed slightly sad.

"Hey," I said, attempting to catch our respective emotions up to speed, "it's not like I said I'm taking the job."

This made Fred crack a lopsided smile. "I didn't say I was offering."

"I know. You're not running this entire place —"

"Yet."

"Right."

Fred was loose, liberated by my intuitive understanding of his plan. He could trust me as much as he needed to because I didn't have any power. But he enjoyed and respected my intelligence. He was someone who had never stopped liking a good time.

"It's sort of unbelievable, the current climate. Everything's going to be different, so very soon. Change is the order of the day. But we can also define it, that's the thing. That's the thing, I think, that makes this distinct from other periods in human history."

Fred was becoming messianic and obviously felt at home in this state. I wasn't sure if I myself felt so sanguine about climate change, whatever Fred meant by that phrase, though clearly he wasn't exactly or exclusively referring to the earth's ecology. This sort of ruthless cheer was one of his go-to modes. I used to like this about Fred, this quality he had, because it suggested that he knew what he wanted and was not afraid to obtain it however it could be gotten, hook, crook, etc. He wasn't ashamed of creating a world in his own image and then adding a house to that image. Inside that image, in that house, he could privately dwell. He clearly respected his own self-sufficiency, maybe even considered it a kind of political good. When I was still with Whit, this aspect of Fred seemed like a safe and comforting bet and therefore made Fred an excellent sidepiece. Fred's vision of life corresponded to his own desires in a way that was novel to me. It was eminently rational. He had painstakingly measured the height and depth of his needs and created an appropriate container for them. I saw the little house, too, sitting there inside that imaginary world. It fit Fred so well. I had, fool that I was, walked blithely up to the front door and I had knocked. From inside the house there had come a noise as if someone had fallen off his chair. And someone rushed to the window and looked out and I saw that person's face. It was Fred. Fred, I called out, open the door. He peered out his window, surprised to see someone standing in his yard, otherwise completely neat and obviously long empty. Fred, I am here. I am here, please let me in. The Fred in the window made signs indicating that he was not permitted to open the door to anyone. Could you, I suggested, at the very least open the window. Fred considered this. He opened the window just a crack, less than an inch. He put his mouth down to the aperture. I've never done this before, was what he said, before closing the window again. From behind the glass, I saw him mouth, *Things are perfect the way they are.* Then the lights in the house Fred had constructed for himself in the world he had created for himself went dim. No matter how many times I knocked on the door and no matter what I screamed up at him from his cabbage garden, he never came to the door again. To be honest, I wasn't even sure he lived there anymore. But I was still standing there in that garden. Maybe I was enraged, maybe stricken with grief, it was difficult to say. I seemed, even to myself, an implausible player in this drama. The ground was sandy, and I'd recently retreated to the base of a tree to wait out eternity. Fred had sent a number of friendly but efficient messengers to let me know that I could stay as long as I wanted, but that I shouldn't expect anyone to answer my calls. The messengers were polite but basically firm. Also, when rhetoric and repetition failed them, they simply disappeared into thin air.

I examined Fred's face. I had become completely motionless in my own real desk chair, but also under that imaginary tree. You could have mistaken me for a statue, inside of Fred's imagination, and at this point I think some of the messengers did. I think some of them thought that I had stopped being human long ago and now they just walked by me without bothering to convey the message. And because my legs were now basically marble, it was not really possible for me to get up from under the tree, and so I resorted to a Jedi measure. I had begun, over the millennia, to construct an exact replica of the world of Fred's imagining within my own mind, with a single small difference, that here there were not one but two of me, and the second one of me had arrived to carry the first one of me out. If my mission was successful, I would be able to see the world beyond Fred again, I would remember what this was, and I would be able to leave him, if I wanted to. I didn't need, you see, so much to escape as I needed that choice. I needed to learn how to have that choice, to make it something that I could do, because without it, I could not be with anyone.

"Stella?"

The bubble popped.

"Sorry," I said. "I was doing some reading last night and I didn't sleep as much as I probably should have."

"That's OK." Fred did not ask me how I was. He said, "I've been thinking about Paul."

"Yes?"

"Haven't you?"

I nodded. I said, "I didn't realize that he

318

used to be married."

"It seems like that was a little while ago."

"Have you read many of her books?"

"Ella Voss's? Mostly about them."

"It's interesting."

"What about it?"

"Well," I said, "just how it is when two writers are together. If that ever works out."

"I'd imagine it's like it is for anyone. You can either be with someone or you can't. And for a long time even if you're not with them you'll think that you're together."

Fred was being extremely forthcoming.

"Was that how it was with the two of them, do you think?" I wanted to know.

Fred blinked. "I have no real way of knowing, of course. But it is hard to say if they ever stopped being together, is what I believe."

"Yes," I said, "it seems like it can be that way." I changed tack. "Do you know if there will be a memorial?"

"Oh, I should think so," Fred said. "I imagine we will hear about that later today. Will you attend?"

"Of course," I said.

"You and Paul were close, I thought."

"It's funny," I said. "I was about to say that I'm not really close to anyone, but then all of a sudden that just seemed totally untrue! Yes, we were close. I just don't know anymore what that means."

"That you were close?"

"No, I mean, I guess, to be close to anyone."

"You'll figure it out."

I found Fred's remark extremely annoying. "I'm glad you have such confidence in me!"

"I always have."

"Thanks, then."

"Yes," said Fred, drawing himself up in the fragile chair that loudly protested his maneuver. "Well, I'm glad we could talk."

"Of course," I told him. Then, in an attempt at levity, "I'm almost always here!"

Fred performed another strangely sad smile. "So am I."

24

I just sat still at my desk for a little while after Fred left. I felt I held my own well enough in these encounters, but this was really the best I could hope to do, as I couldn't set my own terms, the way that things between us had been constructed or come to pass, depending on how you thought about it. I just kept trying to catch an edge of some kind. I wanted to be able to see underneath this thing, to recognize the way in which it was fundamentally unsound, but for whatever reason I seemed completely unable to do this. Or, everywhere I checked, things appeared to be in basic working order. Fred and I just seemed not to be having the kind of relationship I'd imagined I would have with someone I felt this way about. And apparently I was the only one who was totally, or even in part, dissatisfied.

Maybe I was even fascinated that something like this could be possible, that you could be willing to alter your life for someone, and it just would not matter at all. I am not talking, by the way, about anything having to do with Whit. This really has nothing to do with Frederick, either. What I am talking about is the rest of my life, going forward from this point on, the self I wanted to reproduce, perhaps in gorgeous aquatint, standing before the sea in a light, high-waisted dress a year from now, myself a sort of Étoile, because this was all I felt I had to offer anyone. And this self seemed not to matter to Fred, and this was what crushed me.

I tried to rouse myself. I mean, how many times was I going to rediscover the impossibility of this relationship before I learned my lesson? More than anything I wanted to *learn* from it, not to feel merely laid low. It just made me so incredibly angry, was the thing. I mean, at myself.

In a fit of pique, I logged into my email. It was my go-to in all moments: joy, sadness, arousal, ire, whatever. It had nothing I needed, but it had in the past made me promises that had changed my life, and now I wanted to read new vows addressed to me, swearing that I would be liberated from my current condition. I mean, in the present the inbox never had anything I needed. It was only in retrospect that I realized how this or that message had changed my life. And maybe what I wanted, even more than to receive a message that told me that now, again, everything was different, was to be able to know what I was reading when I saw it. I wanted to learn to know when my life was about to change. I mean, probably everyone wants this. I just didn't know how strong a wish like this can get.

For now the inbox was arid. It offered fulfillment of Fred's prediction (a gathering scheduled for the coming Sunday afternoon), as well as a message with an attachment from someone named "Kotz, Ona," directed my way from "G County Hist Soc." In fact, this was something. In fact, there were several attachments. One of these was an invoice for twenty-one dollars for scanning services. The other two items were PDFs. One was a history of Greene County and the other seemed like a cheaply made booklet, published in 1803, with the intriguing title *Elysia, Town of Unexampled Prosperity. Including a Map There Of.* The email itself contained the message "Trust you will find here what you need. All best, O.K." These last two letters were, by the way, presumably the initials of the sender.

I downloaded the two documents.

The history had already been abbreviated for me. On the three pages "O.K." had seen fit to scan and email me, she had also digitally highlighted several key passages. These sections explained the existence of a member of the Wunsch family named Wilhelm Wunsch, who had lived at the end of the eighteenth century and at the beginning of the nineteenth. He was not born in the New World, but rather ventured over to join prosperous relatives when he was in his early twenties, and his major claim to fame was his education in the art of engraving, something he had completed just before his passage.

Wunsch eventually became a merchant and gentleman farmer, like all the males in his family who resided in the neighborhood, therefore taking a step up in the world. In spite of a female child from a previous association, whose mother was apparently lost to polite society, he was given a piece of land and permitted to marry, in order to secure certain local allegiances. But he seemed all his life never to have forgotten his early education and was renowned throughout the area for his strange puttering, business schemes, and small inventions, such as a mechanical bed that allowed the user, by means of a crank attached to the wall, to wind him- or herself into an upright position, thereby enabling the sleeper to simply walk away from bed rather than needing to go to the trouble of getting up out of it. Wunsch was also credited with the invention of several drawing machines, including a mechanical arm that allowed the sketcher to sit in one room while his drawing transpired, if he so pleased, in another.

But the most famous, or infamous, as the case may be, of Wunsch's inventions, was a town. This particular municipality was never built, but Wunsch had engraved a map of it. As botanist John Bartram suggests somewhere in his 1751 *Observations,* it's a good idea to plan ahead, since "knowledge must precede a settlement." This was in Wunsch's profligate early days, and at this time it was apparently his custom to loaf around Lower Manhattan, occasionally traveling to the wharves to observe the progress of immigration, which fascinated him. It was said that in this place and at this moment he acquired a "sultry" female companion, a gypsy, chanteuse, or dancing woman by the name of Étoile, a person of unknown origins and motives, with whom he for some period resided before returning north to the lands cultivated by his relations.

Wunsch was mildly storied, if not quite infamous, for his hawking of the nonexistent town in print, the beauty of which was also hauntingly — or so the Greene County historian maintained — described in song by his winsome consort, who attracted crowds of the newly arrived by means of her siren voice. I raised an eyebrow at this, contemplating the precariousness of Étoile's situation. I wondered, for example, if she ever sang in praise of something other than Wunsch's imaginary conurbation. Étoile and her German lover must have made a pretty pair and probably scraped by for some brief period on the funds raised by means of leaflets and songs, but their attachment was based in fiction, if not fantasy, and therefore could not last.

The highlight in the PDF ended.

I turned my attention to the second PDF. O.K. had here seen fit to include the entire publication, which was to say, all four pages of it. *Elysia, Town of Unexampled Prosperity. Including a Map There Of.* was the most interesting commercial pamphlet on the culture of the dawning of the nineteenth century in the United States that I had never read! Presciently, or exploitatively, or perhaps by way of some combination of the two, it promoted the culture of an intentional community located some one hundred miles up the Hudson River, beyond the depraved reaches of the city, a place blessed with the "pleasing uniformity of decent competence," that would, no doubt, have satisfied the wandering soul of a Crève-coeur, if not the insoluble melancholy of a Rousseau, with its simple prosperity and promotion of autonomy and personal responsibility. Few details were given, save the promise that the bearer of the pamphlet might make his or her way northward to the town, there to find occupation that would guarantee the "transmission of a glorious inheritance to posterity" by means of exhaustive exploitation of any new American's "inestimable rights to the wild." I reflected, frowning, that manifest destiny in miniature was still manifest destiny and therefore pretty nasty stuff.

On a subsequent page, the purchaser of the pamphlet was informed of the names of several imaginary coach services as well as one "Mister Spheer," who operated a fictive ferry. Those who wished to travel by foot were advised as to roads and warned of the vagaries of climate, of beasts and bandits. Following this text, there was a muddy map. It showed the grid of a township near a river. Above it clouds parted, revealing the face of a grinning neoclassical sun.

This con was not, as far as I could tell, *my* Elysia.

So Brunhilda's father had been a utopian evangelist of a kind. And a salesman, and a huckster, if not a prodigal son. He reminded me a little of Frederick Lu.

Without knowing it, I had been waiting for something big, but here was this. Elysia was a ploy, a humbug. I didn't know what any of this had to do with the beautiful map of the commonplace book, though it did further increase the fascination exercised upon yours truly by that document. I was curious about the origins of that map, who it was who had intervened into Wunsch's sad little scheme to produce something of beauty.

This left me with the women. Or, rather, it left me with the ways in which each had left to posterity what she had left. Brunhilda was of course the author of several serious books on the matter of the political future of women in the U.S., and so in some sense she constituted less of a conundrum. I knew I shouldn't really be thinking like this, but her life felt safe, accounted for, knowable. And perhaps she had also been a novelist. It made some sense. She was energetic and needed a speculative realm to populate with figures who were able to live as she herself wished to live.

What intrigued me more was her great-granddaughter's existence, what had transpired somewhat down the line, as it were. Why had things devolved rather than improved? Why had there been so markedly less liberation for Alice than for Brunhilda? Weren't white women of privilege supposed to have obtained new and exciting forms of agency in the twentieth century? What, moreover, had become of poor Alice — not to mention the Elysia Club collection? If I were understanding the acquisitions records correctly, it seemed as if numerous works of art had come into CeMArt only to disappear.

Back on the databases, I chipped away at this final question by searching for donations made by Alice Gaypoole Wynne in the catalogs of other major American museums. I found that in the mid-1930s, Alice had made several generous gifts to major East Coast institutions. They were mostly of modernist realist paintings, tough female nudes beside deco furnishings, pale blue smokestacks, gourd arrangements. These could very likely have been materials collected during the Elysia Club years. I Googled a few of the artists in question; a number had been in residence in Greenwich Village at the appropriate time, though I was not sure how much this meant.

I wanted to know more about what had happened to Alice later on in life, and so I removed *Will to Beauty* from my desk drawer, picking up where I had left off in the later 1930s. She and Mabel Styke were clinging to each other, or rather Alice was clinging to Mabel, and after the end of the club, Alice did her best to keep busy. She went in for philanthropy, especially around education, and supported the Art Students League. She traveled and maintained her home. She began researching period fabrics and lighting design. She kept a succession of small, anxious canines, memorializing them upon demise in needlepoint.

Then, just when her life couldn't seem to get any duller, she was embroiled in scandal. Some fifteen years earlier a close male cousin, Benedict "Benny" Wynne, had married a sensual young woman, one Jane Masters, former cocktail waitress and beautician, thought to be a gold digger by the rest of the Wynne clan. Benny, whose arteries had been rendered impassable by years of delectation of pork products and perhaps also cocaine, upon matrimony could not resist promptly dying of cardiac arrest, but not, it turned out, before siring a daughter. The progeny of this short-lived and importunate coupling, a "plain" child christened Doris Fortunata Wynne, stood to come into a great deal of cash at age eighteen, and the Wynne family did not want her luscious mother, Jane Masters, in the way of so much lucre, for the story was that Masters would surely exercise an unhealthy influence as far as her daughter was concerned. The plan was, therefore, to get Masters declared unfit and Alice, now in her fifties and no longer marcelling her hair, established as the ward of the child of error, thus keeping Jane's brassy talons off the Wynne estate.

The Wynnes were an incredibly powerful New York tribe, and they probably shouldn't have had much difficulty pulling this plan off, but they did not know enough about their own kin. They did not know, for example, about Alice's storied past with Boy, as well as her ill-advised attempt to be revenged against him. The Wynnes were busy putting the supposed gold digger and woman of loose morals, Masters, in a deleterious light, paying the tabloid press through the teeth, and had simultaneously embarked on a vicious suit to get the woman declared unfit as a mother. Alice was offered up, publicly, I might add, to more serious journalistic outfits as a lonely but happily married woman who had never been able to have children of her own and who had always felt like something of a mother to poor, wayward Doris Fortunata. Likenesses of Alice in full philanthropic mode, rail thin and towering over urban youth in smocks at a pottery class, were disseminated in *Time* and the *Evening Standard*. Alice became renowned as a rabid advocate of early arts education as a means to reduce public nuisance. Doris Fortunata accompanied her on staged visits to museums and trade schools. They stood or sat side by side at various benefit galas, in the stands at horse races and at tennis matches, on the deck of a continent-bound steamer as a curtain of confetti fell — in each instance captured in glittering grays for the society pages.

Perhaps Boy saw his chance, who knew. Perhaps it was Jane Masters herself. The source of the images has never been discovered, but this was how began one of the most notorious, if previously unknown to me, smear campaigns of the midcentury. PATRONESS WAS SOMETHING MORE, ran one headline. Another, weirdly lyric:

ECHOES OF BOHEMIA'S SIREN CALL. Franker: PAINTED NIGHTS OF UPTOWN SOCIAL SURFACE, IN SCANDAL. And: FORTUNE WAS HERS, BUT SHE LOVED ART. Today this exposé is forgotten, but back then Alice was described as an indiscriminate adulteress. Candid photographs of her avant-garde turpitude between the wars — Alice leering drunkenly through ribbons of smoke, or writhing in transparent evening wear, or receiving a kiss from a famous lesbian — were published. Anonymous testimonies appeared, about her double life and the depths she had enthusiastically plumbed during those two louche decades, when she, a married woman, passed her time with artists, critics, poets, and philosophers, among other lowlifes, at the Elysia Club. The coup de grâce came when a shockingly intimate nude of a woman who was unmistakably Alice arranged *L'Origine du monde* style in black and white surfaced. Adding insult to injury, this lover's-portrait-turned-revenge-porn must have been snapped by Boy himself.

It went badly for the Wynnes. Maybe some of the allegations were even true, not that anything that anyone wrote even remotely mattered once the photographs came to light, with their ineluctable visual testament.

Alice was declared unfit to be Doris Fortunata's guardian, the case against Masters the supposed gold digger fell apart, and significant amounts of money, even by the standards of the Wynnes, were lost. Alice's husband did not divorce her, but rather disappeared to Mexico, where he seemed able to indulge certain increasingly time-consuming personal habits, e.g., bennies and transactional sex, in peace.

Alice herself ended abruptly: Even before the close of the scandal, she had begun to exhibit symptoms that we would today associate with early-onset Alzheimer's, and by 1950 she was delicately institutionalized by whichever relatives had been deputized to keep tabs on her. Though the biography seems to want to portray this as a sort of blessing, that Alice at last forgot her cares and began living in an eternal present before the time in which she had been pilloried, this fate seems pretty terrifying, given her husband's neglect and her family's humiliation and hatred of her, due to what the press portrayed as AGW's sex yen, re: artists.

I paused in my reading. I was mentally cycling back through various overlords of CeMArt when it occurred to me that there had been a midcentury Wynne trustee. He was not a Wynne in surname, but his mother had been a Wynne. And then I remembered the name, Wallace Wynne Johns! He had been the first curator put in charge of American Objects. And he, of the Pac-Man face, was the one responsible for Jonah Durr Weiss's eventual hire.

I was racking my brains, trying to think where I could find the best records to help me out. What I wanted was a copy of the museum's catalog that would have post-dated the gift but predated the scandal. Because the catalog was digitized so much later on, the paper catalog could, of course, have been altered in the intervening years. Anyone could really have done anything they wanted to these records, particularly within American Objects, which at that time had a staff of three, including its secretary, out of which two individuals were probably, if not secret lovers, then best friends. I realized that the missing document in the ac-cessions records could have been removed long, long ago, and could be anywhere by now, if it hadn't been set on fire, shredded, or buried in Central Park. (It was the fantasy of a simpleton to think it was perched safe somewhere in the apartment of Paul Coral, someone I apparently be-lieved could deliver me from all evil but who I needed to remember was dead!) I therefore had two hopes: One, that Mabel Styke had made scrupulous duplicates of all her correspondence and that this was included in an archive somewhere; two, that I could come up with some bureaucratic notch somewhere within CeMArt that neither the intermedial nature of our institutional memory nor the contrivances of unscrupulous curators had been able to efface.

As far as possibility one was concerned, I wasn't going to hold out hope. I realized that *Will to Beauty,* Alice's biography, had been written less as an entertainment than as a work of feminist history and I was fairly sure its author must also at some point have come to this realization. Of course, the book had been marketed how it had been marketed, complete with a totally unbelievable but nevertheless happy ending. But it was essentially about a woman whose family wanted her forgotten. Mabel Styke, Alice's secretary, would have needed to do a lot of legwork if she wanted her hapless employer's records to end up in a public archive.

I was therefore left with option number two. This was when I remembered *The Four Seasons,* one form of CeMArtian institutional memory — of gossip, really — that was less easy to alter or erase. Unrelated to the hospitality arts, this was an early curatorial bulletin circulated exclusively within the museum proper before the advent of the Second World War when issues with staffing and other resources had caused numerous extraneous activities to cease. *The Four Seasons* was jokingly named after a set of nonexistent statues that should be included on the front façade of the museum, but which, due to exorbitant cost, were never carved, and which appear as four pyramids of unfinished blocks resting serenely atop columns, even to this day. They are eyesores, but somehow no one notices them. I happened to know that the CeMArt library had a bound set of this niche mag in two volumes, and I rushed downstairs to try to get hold of the relevant one. I even knew where we kept them. I was standing in front of the shelf where they were stored, and I could already see the gap, mocking me. Bells went off in my head.

I performed the fastest walk one can possibly get away with within the museum's library, which is mostly just a regular walk, up to the circulation desk.

"Dani," I hissed. "I have an emergency."

Dani, who was a millennial with hair dyed an impressive gunmetal gray, pivoted. "Really?" She was not eager to become involved.

337

"I can't find something!"

"Is it in the catalog?"

I was holding up the available bound volume of *The Four Seasons,* which covered the wrong years for my purposes. "I don't need the catalog. I'm looking for volume two of this guy."

Dani squinted. "Perhaps another patron is using it."

"Dani," I said, "there's no one in here."

Dani lobbed her gaze around the room. "You are correct," she said.

"Are you telling me that this has to be missing?"

Dani blinked. "Oh no, not necessarily. Senior staff have borrowing privileges, just within the museum, of course."

"So can you tell me if it's checked out?"

"That I can do." Dani tapped away. Her face came back. "Checked out. Not missing." Then her face went back to the screen. "Oh," she said. "Hmm." She seemed perplexed. "I'm not sure what we do in this case" — she was sort of speaking to herself now — "if the person is, um, not ever going to be able to return it? If there's a communication procedure." She sighed. "Like because he's *dead.*"

25

The problem was that once out of the library there was nothing preventing this set of journals from ending up anywhere one wanted to take it. I ran back upstairs, panting, to Paul's office. I already knew he had nothing on his shelves, so I am not sure why I bothered.

"Jesus Christ," I said to no one in particular, now fearing the onset of a bloody nose. I sort of waved my hands in the air and tried not to jump up and down from rage. "Ugh, ugh, ugh," I grunted and stomped back to my office, not caring who saw me coming out of Paul's door. *The Four Seasons,* volume 2, could be anywhere right now, I kept trying to remind myself. I was feeling a sick mix of dread and delight. I went into my email and searched around until I found Paul's email containing his home address. I stared at it and then shakily wrote it down. It was in the East Village. I cleared my browser cache. And left the museum.

Paul lived in a walkup. In some ways this made things simpler. It would be easier to avoid neighbors and to disguise where I really was going. I tried to open the front door nonchalantly, as if I did this every day of my life. I did not succeed. I spent maybe two minutes jostling the key around before the lock on the steel door finally gave in. It wasn't a great building. Probably there was rent control. I mean, I would have killed to be able to live in a place like this. Was that morbid of me? I really didn't think so!

I went up the interior stair wondering if at this point I was technically already doing something illegal. I mean, I was definitely already doing something illegal, but how bad would it be if I were caught at this point? Would it be tabloid level? Alice Gaypoole Wynne–level public humiliation? I'd definitely lose my job, unless, of course, I could convince the authorities that Paul had given me his keys, told me I had access. But the problem would be, then, that I had not revealed my possession of Paul's keys even after the revelation of his demise. Maybe I could claim grief? A form of temporary insanity? I wasn't sure. I was already in the building, so there was no use turning back now, or so I had decided to permit myself to think.

Paul lived in apartment 5B. I let myself in and was greeted by an antiseptic smell. I didn't really know much about what happened around death and its aftermath, so I had to assume that decay became a problem in almost no time at all, which was incredibly gross. I slipped inside and shut the door behind myself, gagging softly. I felt very young. It was palpable to me, when I walked into Paul's place, that I was entering a bygone era, but this was different from studying the more distant past, because you could actually interpret the fact that your own existence had not been foreseen at this (the past) time. It was relevant to you. And I felt the year of my own birth weirdly implied by Paul's classic 1980s apartment, with its twitching, rhinestone-encrusted cat clock in the kitchen and its venetian blinds and clip lamps and ashtrays and spare, sort of deco, masculine disarray. There was a living room with ceiling-high built-in bookshelves, and I dreaded the possibility that *The Four Seasons* had been fitted in someplace here, among myriad titles it could take me days to hunt through. I sort of whimpered to myself and looked around for Paul's desk. There was no desk forthcoming. I realized that it must be in the bedroom, which was also, presumably, where Paul's body had been, and so I was not particularly eager to find said desk but knew I needed to do so.

The bed was just sitting there, made. There was also a worktable with lamps clamped to it and rolling cabinets underneath. I inched over. Above the table hung several architect's renderings of what I understood was the original plan for the American Objects galleries. And below these framed plans I saw something and didn't even want to pray that it might be what I needed, but oh it seemed the world was occasionally kind, and it looked as if this book bound in red buckram could very well be the book I wanted, and I took hold of it, just as I heard, with a feeling of consternation I cannot describe for you in human words, the sound of a key being fitted into the lock on the front door, turned.

There are two classic responses in this scenario. The first of these is, of course, to hide under the bed. Knowing, however, of the probable recent presence of a corpse on this particular item of furniture, I nixed this route. The closet, then. I thought, nonsensically, of R. Kelly's early aughts operatic film *Trapped in the Closet. Blue Velvet*'s slightly

342

more hysterical take also crossed my mind. Did Paul's have the requisite slatted door? It did. Oh God, it was tempting. My heart fluttered, got very hot. I actually had no choice. Someone was already moving in the entranceway. I let myself into the closet, which smelled like cedar and the inside of a shoe and cough syrup, which was altogether a bracingly male perfume. If Paul hadn't been so recently deceased, it would not have been so bad an odor to have been smelling. Mostly, I decided to pretend that Paul was alive.

The individual who had let himself into Paul's house was moving around. There were some sighs. I was able to determine that this was probably a woman, based on the clicking of footwear. The person, I could also tell, had just seated herself in an armchair in the living room very close to the door of the bedroom. I wasn't sure what she was trying to do but I was definitely scared that the reminiscing session, or whatever, was going to take a while. Perhaps it was his sister. Maybe she was living here now, in which case I was pretty much absolutely fucked. I thought a little bit about possible outcomes: Perhaps I waited until she fell asleep, then snuck out. Or maybe she would go out for food or something else and I would have a window. In any case, I would need to wait.

I settled in. I mean, I did not move, but I allowed my body to become accustomed to the fact that it was going to be where it was for a pretty long time.

The person in the living room was not doing anything.

I waited.

Now the person in the living room began to speak.

"Paul," she said. "Shit."

For a while there was nothing.

"Shit," she repeated. "I remember we used to be so loving. Do you remember that, how it was? Do you remember when I was teaching at Iowa, and you came into my room with a daisy after class? It was over the summer. I was teaching and you were there for that reading. I had never experienced so much kindness, and now you are dead. I'll go on living, but I don't know if I can ever explain to anyone what it is like to have you dead, Paul. We aren't even married anymore. It's been so long since we were married, but I can go on talking to you, because of what you meant to me then. I know you understood that, what that meant to me, for us to be together as we were. But you didn't understand anything else about the life I was trying to live. You thought you wanted something for yourself, but you could never come around to the idea that I was not the one who was keeping it from you, I was not the one keeping you from your authentic self. My fictions did not prevent you from becoming the author you believed you were. Your failure to appear in the world in the way you desired to appear had nothing to do with my writing. I don't know what that failure was. I was so glad when I got free of that, Paul, when I got free of that blame. Self-deception made you live a bad life sometimes, Paul, and you tried to drag me down to your level. But I could never hate you for that."

Someone texted me.

I don't have an elaborate tone or anything like that, but anyone who is not a moron who hears my minimal *tock!* as of a tiny mallet striking bamboo knows that someone else — who may *be* a moron — is nearby.

The female person who was sitting in the chair exclaimed, "What!" I could hear her get to her feet. It wasn't that she was scared, exactly, but more I think that she had not been prepared for there to be an additional outrage so close to the other outrage earlier on this week. "Who *is* that?" she demanded.

It was interesting, because she did not run

out of the house, which is what I would have done. This indicated a different relationship not just to physical threat but to the notion of the worth of life. This person had already accepted the fact and/or inescapability of her own death, which was not something that I, personally, had done.

But it was, in some sense, helpful. She could take the lead.

I decided to step out of the closet and introduce myself to Ella Voss.

"Hello," was what I said.

"Oh, thank God you're not a man," was what Voss told me. "You're also tiny and I could throttle you, what a relief."

Ella Voss was in her fifties and gave the impression of always having said exactly what was on her mind to everybody. She was a sturdy woman who had not been fated to be thin but who had lived in a city long enough to train her body to approximate the ideal. She was also successful and maybe even rich, and there was no way her author photo was doing her any kind of justice.

"Have a seat," she told me.

"I'm really sorry about this," I said.

"Paul's dead, so I'm not worried. Anyway, you're not his lover." She considered me. "You're someone he knows from the museum. Right?"

I nodded.

"How amazing! What brings you here?"

There was something about her manner that inspired absolute calm. She couldn't have cared less if I robbed Paul blind or vandalized the apartment or even, as I may have mentioned, attempted to do harm to her.

"I needed a book."

"Ha! And now you have it?"

I nodded. "I think so." I wanted to look down and ascertain whether the book I held in my hands was in fact *The Four Seasons* but really I felt that it was of primary importance that I continue gazing deep into Ella Voss's turquoise eyes.

It was beginning to grow dim in the apartment and Voss reached over and switched on a light. "Now you have your book, well. And yet I imagine there is something more." Again, she wasn't aggressive. This was an extremely pleasant conversation.

"I read your novel!" I burst out.

"Really?"

"Yes."

"Which one?"

"The new one. Actually, last night."

"So, then, you and I are somehow in the same boat."

I didn't know what to say.

"I just mean, I think I startled you, and now you have startled me. And each of us is still trying to understand Paul, though I suspect for very different reasons."

I made some sort of involuntary noise.

"Yes?" Voss wanted to know.

"I, I just mean, is he there?"

"What do you mean?"

"I mean," I could only say, *"there."*

"I'm sorry?"

"In your novel."

Voss considered my statement. "What causes you to pose that question?"

"I mean, it's horrible!"

"I'm sorry," said Ella Voss. "You're very vehement. The thing about Paul you need to know was, he suffered from block. That really bothered him more than anything else. He never did what he imagined he should do, and this was extremely bothersome to him, debilitating and maddening, really, and it caused him to make assumptions about other people, particularly those he was close to. I wasn't always like I am today. I used to be capable of being hurt."

I didn't know what to say to her. I tried, "I wanted to take his advice."

"You have no idea how much a person can change in one lifetime. I am not even talking about Paul, here."

"I didn't always feel like Paul cared about work," I told her, feeling strangely young again.

"He probably didn't."

"I didn't know what Paul was doing."

"Well, Paul was unusual. He didn't care about art history as much as your average art historian and he didn't care about poetry as much as your average poet. It's difficult to say where that left him."

"Alone?" I asked.

"I don't know about that. He was a miracle for a while. As I was saying, Paul didn't really care about history, at least not in a narrative way. There's some honor in that, but then you also run into problems."

"Such as?"

"Honesty," said Ella Voss.

■ ■ ■ ■

SATURDAY

■ ■ ■ ■

26

I left Paul's apartment soon after this exchange. It felt in the end like I'd been paying him a long-overdue social call, like we finally knew one another a little better, much as he'd always wanted.

I went home and got into bed in my clothes and went to sleep. My overworked brain had become uncommunicative, and it had been so long since I had slept in this manner, just dead to the world.

The next day it was Saturday, and I awoke and knew I was ready to attempt to read Paul's files again.

I went back into the folder named "etc."

I now had two options: I could read either "work.txt" or "morework.txt." I thought about skipping perversely forward to "morework.txt," but then I thought better of it. I would just look at whatever Paul was calling "work."

I opened the file. It began, in medias res,

Should I, too, begin to publish under a pseudonym? I think about a possible ancestor. Her name is a long, bunchy name, a bag in knots. Her name is Brunhilda Wunsch. When she composed her novel, she easily Anglicized. She was G. G. Hennicott, taking part of her husband's name. This is smooth. Doubtless I am a weak person. I could not travel where she went. I know what I know and want to live it in another way but never quite get there. I never quite get to being other than the person who I am. I know too much. I live in too many houses.

So Paul had read *Lorelei*! And he had known about Brunhilda's double identity and perhaps wished that he were capable of something similar. But this was a short text, possibly a foray into the novel detailed in "PLAN.txt." I turned to "morework.txt,"

Some people here around me are lovers. I am not opposed, but this environment is not so good for that sort of thing. Better by far to concentrate on the work we've each set ourselves. Look at F. and S. What can they hope for? F. has no heart, and S. no eyes. It makes sense that a blind person would like someone who can't feel, but she can't understand that what he doesn't feel is not the same as what she doesn't. He sees all too well, and additionally the world rewards him for it. To a writer they'd seem like characters.

But am I a writer, given the modes and results of my research? Is this how I am to learn that I am not a true writer, that I do not see even these two in this way, as characters? And they are so often in the house! I should be able to do something with them, refine it all as a new work, but I remain exhausted, impotent. What can his advances mean? What is the meaning of her acceptance? I'm already an old man. I go around these rooms and everything could be a harm to someone somewhere. Put in some footnotes if you care about fact now. Try to say what happened. There is a playing card for Ella, the painting for myself. A print for Stella and a mirror for Lorelei. But do I now come to a wall? I have worked as hard as I felt myself capable and more, yet I cannot seem to walk backward. I am numb nearly always, as in a dream. My hands hurt.

Then, later,

But perhaps I should say I did see F. and

S. today. I've come to view them as an emblem. They are a possible emblem for what has gone wrong. It is almost beautiful. And, in fact, it is beautiful and if I weren't in pain half the time I would tell them so. I can imagine their faces! But I am not merely miserable. I am brilliant at it. I stood at some distance and observed them near the pond a little after lunch. She listens. And I know he is not insensitive to that. But he will never leave his world in order to enter hers. Too much is left up to chance there. If only Stella really were a historian. I imagine I could write about everything by way of her. But enough. Elsewhere, the day has been sunny and cold.

There was something about the way Paul wrote that made it easy to read on and on. I wanted to read all of what he had written. It was like ice cream. I grew sated as I went. I liked, too, that he had seen me, that he had the decency to notice my errors. Paul was probably not the world's greatest novelist, but he was pretty good at confessing, as poets tend to be.

What did he mean by "There is a playing card for Ella, the painting for myself. A print for Stella and a mirror for Lorelei"? If the "print for Stella" was one of his counterfeits — perhaps, to keep things neat, the Étoile possessed by my parents — that would suggest that the other items noted were a counterfeit playing card, a counterfeit painting, and a counterfeit mirror. Did Paul's counterfeiting experience extend beyond what Caro was aware of? Could he also have been working with antiques dealers up and down Madison? Not to mention, was what he had told Caro about his education in printmaking even true?

"Work.txt" and "morework.txt" were at once revealing and confusing files. Each was an ambient autobiography, notes toward a narrative that was always just about to coalesce but never quite did. The documents were written mostly in present tense. Sometimes asides, reflections on identifiable works from the American Objects collection, were thrown in. I couldn't tell if I was biased because of my preexisting connection to this material, but I thought, in spite of its significant shortcomings in relation to plot, that a lot of the writing here was pretty intriguing, though, again, not much like a novel. It was an uncanny catalog. There were lists of materials and forms:

- softwood
- banister-back chair
- easy chair
- gate-leg table
- century vase
- girandole
- verre églomisé
- mahogany
- mahogany veneer
- tulip poplar
- yellow pine
- gessoed and gilded
- white cedar

The lists went on and on. Objects were considered from multiple angles, and I felt as if I could see them here in writing more clearly than I could in life. "Morework.txt" closed with an incomplete sentence involving a directive: "Rooms 734, 737, 740, 743 [here insert lavish, empirical description goes on for pages]." In spite of the final unfinished line, the writing seemed important, already a book of a kind in its own right.

I took the liberty of combining the two work-related .txt files with "PLAN.txt" and retitling them "american_objects.txt." I removed all save this new document from the flash drive and ejected it.

I needed to get ready to go out.

As far as my social life was concerned, we have already seen that it was basically nil. Until fairly recently, I had made up for this lack by nightly entangling myself on the couch with my husband. (I watched something; he slept.) Now I compensated with daytime dates with Cate and anodyne research.

On this particular evening Cate invited me to her beautiful Brooklyn Heights home where, presumably, I would discover beautiful people. I was, and let me put this in the form of an understatement, a mess. I did not know what I was going to say to anyone about my present condition. I wasn't even unmarried, for crying out loud! And I also did not have anything to wear that was likely to produce in these people's minds an effect of anything other than sloppy neglect or an academically aggressive attempt to be hip that went way, way in the wrong direction.

I considered for a moment reprising Monday night's *tenue de soirée* but determined upon reflection that this outfit was now permanently cursed and would probably need to be the subject of some sort of exorcism ritual. I emptied the closet out onto the floor and stood at the center of what felt like a roiling pile of boot-cut pants that had never looked reasonable on a short person, as well as ill-advised maxidresses, corduroy skirts, and tops embellished with strategically placed pieces of lace. I dressed, I realized, like it was 2003, and it had been a long time since I looked anything like good doing it. Part of me wanted to shed a little tear for this pile of idiosyncrasies lying at my feet, the sartorial wages of unchecked desire and extremely poor taste. But standing here I could see, all in one place but also in terms that were somewhat acceptable to my tender self-esteem, how many things I had been doing wrong. I mean, I wasn't transgressing against other people, except I guess visually, which was sort of a nice thing. But this wasn't a way that I needed to be anymore.

I kicked the clothes, dumb signifiers that they were, to the corner of my room. Maybe tomorrow I would see about pulling out a few basic items and donating the rest to Housing Works. What was left in my closet were the navy blue pants suit I had worn to my interview for my current job, my wedding dress, and a gray T-shirt dangling forlornly from a hook on the back of the wall. I selected this last item, put on my interview pants. Most of my shoes were for work and, when I added them to the present outfit, made me look like an off-duty CIA agent who was trying to play a quick pickup game with her kids in the driveway after a long day of devising new strains of fascism at Langley. I also looked like I was trying not to look short. The only other shoes in my closet were a pair of white Keds I had not worn since discovering that hipsters liked them, but tonight such an association was really going to be the least of my problems. I tried them on. I stood in front of the mirror.

At first I could not tell how I looked. Maybe nondescript? I picked up a book and tried holding that over my face to see if that helped with the project of assessment. The body looked, well, normal. Small, but normal. I appeared to be to scale. I removed the book from my face. I considered how the body looked with the addition of its face. I looked, I reflected, fine. I looked, by luck and by accident, like someone who wasn't trying that hard to put herself together, because really I was trying, and with a great deal of exertion.

I went into the bathroom and scrubbed my face. I put on a little makeup. For the most part, I put on mascara. I combed my hair and added some water to it so that the wave would come out, thinking of Alice's interwar style. I spent a little while looking at the gold wedding ring sitting alone on a side shelf in the cabinet. I closed the cabinet door. When I felt that I was assured of being sufficiently late, I left the house.

27

Cate's partner, Reihan, met me at the door. He and I are afraid of each other. For years we have been trying to avoid finding out how exactly much it is that we do not get along. He went to the same college as Cate and I did, but he is five years younger than we are, and Cate met him only upon her return to the university campus as a graduate student. She "snapped him up," as she says.

As luck would have it, Reihan and I were wearing the exact same outfit. I mean, he wasn't wearing Keds, but pretty much everything else was the same. He managed to let me into the house so that we could deliberate about this matter in the vestibule. "Should I go upstairs and change?" he wanted to know.

I really did not want to offend him. "Well," I began.

Reihan turned his face to the side a bit

and his eyes shifted. He softly engaged my gaze.

It was only at this somewhat belated juncture that I realized he was kidding. Reihan smiled.

"Oh, hahaha!" I exclaimed, because I imagined that this was how people were laughing these days.

Reihan was like, "I had to offer."

"Thank you so much," I said. Then I tried a compliment. "I like those pants." But this exchange was evidently going on too long now and had lost its charm, because Reihan was already crossing the threshold into his home and I am not sure if he heard me.

What was happening was something between a party and a dinner party. Reihan and Cate were causing people to stand around with plates. Cate appeared in a long skirt with a big belt and a white blouse. She seemed to be in a movie about life on a modernist ranch. I wasn't sure what I was going to be able to contribute to these goings-on.

"Hi," I said. "I'm here." I handed Cate a bottle of wine I had found on the top shelf in a supermarket. It was a Rioja and on the label there was an image of a dove carrying a bottle of wine in its beak.

"Wow," she said, taking this specimen

from me. "Thank you." She looked me up and down. She nodded. "You've done it," she pronounced.

I wasn't sure if she meant that I had committed some sort of grave error that might not be reversible, or if she simply meant that I had managed to dissimulate my nakedness with clothes one more time and she was proud of me for this act. But we were basically in public, which is always a confusing environment for me, and so I decided that I wasn't going to follow up on this one.

"Sorry I am late," I said.

"I know!" Cate told me, giving me a look. "I expected you to be the first one here!"

"Really?"

"No, of course not!"

"Oh," I said.

"You are the last one here, but that is also great, and I am glad to see you." Cate gave me a small, dry kiss. She smelled like oranges and the beach and some kind of food.

I had been given a clear drink containing alcohol and now I was standing alone in Cate and Reihan's kitchen. I was trying to stave off terror by pretending that each succeeding moment was always only arriving and not actually present to me. It wasn't that I was not there at the dinner party, but it wasn't that I was there, either, which I felt was a pretty good compromise. I was awaiting the inevitable moment when Cate would come to rescue me, and we would share a few precious minutes alone, sometimes sneakily imbibing directly from the bottle, before Cate would be called back to the rest of her guests and everyone would look up and see that I was the one diverting Cate from the better part of her life.

Tonight, Cate was not separating herself from her party. I could feel the juncture at which I would normally be joined by my savior arrive and then pass away again. I contemplated the elegance of Cate and Reihan's brushed-aluminum refrigerator, which was not really elegance so much as expense. I picked at my mushroom tartlet. I knew that I probably appeared strange.

But what my painstaking control over the situation could not account for was the appearance of a short man I had never seen before in the kitchen. And by "short," I mean that he was my height. "Victor," he said, offering his hand. "I'm Catherine's cousin."

This felt a little ridiculous. I really didn't see what the point of this was.

Victor politely ignored the fact that I seemed to have forgotten how to speak, if ever I knew. "I think you're a little bit famous," he said. There was a minor accent here. He was not from the northern side of the family.

"I'm not famous," I muttered.

"No, I think you really are. I think I maybe saw you on Reddit the other day!"

I was assuming that this person was mildly insane. I mean, I would probably need to talk about it with Cate later on, but for now I would attempt to exercise kindness and withhold judgment.

"I am not," I said, "on the Internet." With this point clarified for his benefit, I waited patiently for Victor to continue.

Victor smiled. "You're extremely modest."

"There is no way for you to know that."

"You're really a person of great ability, you know. Other people would like to learn from you."

"I find that hard to believe."

"If you like."

I drank some more of my clear alcoholic beverage. It was hard not to continue in this vein with this person. It didn't really seem to matter what we were talking about. It sort of enraged me to be having a conversation with no subject, but I also really did not want it to stop. "So you're saying that I should just drop everything and become some sort of guru?" I had no idea what this meant, but it seemed like Victor had already demonstrated that he did not require sense on this particular evening, or perhaps ever.

"Sure. I think you should do that."

"OK."

"Yes, I think it's a pretty good idea. You'll have maybe something like a dojo, where people of all ages and even genders will come to receive your teachings, and I think very probably the world will change."

Now I knew exactly what Victor was talking about. I took a moment to progress through the interconnected stages of disbelief, anger, mourning, and acceptance. Cate and I, I decided, would be having words.

Victor was, weirdly, only watching this occur. He was probably a person who liked cats. He waited patiently, knowingly, for the emotional shit storm to subside. His face was generating this bizarrely sympathetic expression.

I drank a lot more of my drink.

"Your fame is great," Victor continued, "but of course it's anonymous fame, so you haven't really had a chance to enjoy it. Let me ask you something, do you know everyone at this party?"

"I know Cate and Reihan," I said.

"But you don't know anyone else here?"

"No."

"Recognize anyone? Anyone you think recognizes you?"

It was true, I reflected, and maybe even a little strange, that among the ten or so people currently gathered at Cate and Reihan's house, I didn't know a soul, not even tangentially. Either I had been relegated to their D-list, or, seeing as it was a Saturday night, perhaps they were attempting, kindly and subtly, to push me out into lesser-known waters.

I shrugged. "No. I don't know anyone. And no one knows me." It almost felt good to say it.

Victor said, "In that case, famous person, allow me."

What happened next was that Victor introduced me to the present company as a woman named Sylvia and everyone in the room was like, "Hello, Sylvia." And Victor told everyone that probably they didn't realize it but they were standing in the presence of greatness. But he did this in such a way that no one felt like they were being told something insane or otherwise maniacal. They just sat there quietly as amused awe bent their brains a bit and relaxed them. Victor knew what he was doing.

Victor spoke in Spanish, like, Cate, can you make it possible for us to gaze into the Internet?

Cate's game face at this moment was inspired, because she had a pretty good idea of what was coming, having already been so impolitic as to share with her relative my secret identity. But she could also see that I was going along with Victor and even looked somewhat at ease, which, for me, at a party was an event like the appearance of a narwhal riding a unicorn. In Spanish, Cate said something like, Yes, Victor, I am not a millennial but my husband very nearly is, and so one can indeed look at a projection of the Internet in our living room. And Cate went away and brought back a laptop that Victor was permitted to manipulate. And Victor manipulated the laptop a bit before introducing me to the crowd as a mathematician from Stanford who was just in town for a short visit and who had had an unusual afternoon one day while she was here and then had also had the uncanny experience of this unusual afternoon going viral, but such was our age. "Isn't that true, Sylvia?" Victor said.

"Yes," I told everyone. "A strange man approached me and, I'm really not kidding, he told me that women are bad" — I paused for effect — *"at math."*

"Really?" murmured a lean woman reclining on the sofa. "He knew that you were a, um" — and here she was not sure what word to use — "math expert?"

"Yes." I was nodding. "He is a philosopher. I mean, a professor of philosophy. Actually" — I began embroidering — "he works at Princeton? Anyway, he recognized me, as I am a quite well-known *math expert,* an international expert of math, and he just came up to me, here on my *vacation,* and he said this. And then —"

Victor interrupted, not unkindly. It was possible that my embroidery was going a little too far outside the lines. "Yes, and then what you are about to see occurred!"

Reihan, as if on cue, made the lights go down. Victor caused the now apparently somewhat renowned video to play. "Oh, I've seen this!" the lean woman began to offer, but was shushed by the rest of the audience. At the moment of contact and then response there were howls of delight. The room burst into applause. Then the lights went up and I spent the rest of the evening being congratulated on my fabulous timing and aim as well as being asked to explain the topic of my current research at Stanford, which was something I appropriated from a recent but not too recent *New York Times* feature on an actual mathematician, intimating that I was doing a lot of important thinking around the fact that water does not spontaneously explode.

This was almost all of the rest of the evening. Some of the rest of the evening had to be taken up, once everyone else had left, with figuring out how Victor had managed to do this, and Cate, Reihan, and Victor were finally forced to confess that they had planned to orchestrate this bizarre scenario starting at around six P.M. when Cate had had an early drink and gotten loose and couldn't resist sharing my recent exploits.

Cate was languidly stroking my hair. We were eating a secret cake made of some kind of artisanal ice cream that Reihan had forgotten to serve to the guests earlier in the excitement of the sharing of the video on how to punish a testicle. Cate said, "Can I make a confession?"

"Can you?" asked Victor.

"*May* I?" Cate repeated. She was looking at me.

"Sure," I said.

"Would you feel really bad if I told you that I was maybe concerned that you might not have a good time at the party? I feel like you kind of hate this kind of thing. I feel bad inviting you, but then I feel like I should. I don't know. It's my own dilemma, I suppose."

I thought about this for a minute.

"She seems all right to me." This was Reihan. He was currently eating a lot of cake. He sort of jostled Cate's leg with his leg to indicate that she should desist with the descent into guilt.

"Well, Sylvia, I mean, *Stella*! God! Stella is about the most resilient person I know, but that doesn't mean she has to like everyone. You know *I* don't." Cate leaned over and somehow gracefully kissed Reihan's knee.

"Hmm," said Reihan. Then, "Mmm. This cake is really excellent."

"You made a good choice," Victor confirmed.

"Do you want some more of it?" Cate was getting up. "I know I do." Then she said, "Stella, come here for a second."

I was a little tipsy so it took me longer than an actual second to find my way to my feet. I traipsed after Cate.

In the kitchen Cate said, "I'm serious, you know. That could totally have backfired and I don't know what made me do it. If I told you it was like there was some kind of invisible force in the world this afternoon, would you believe me? It was guiding me, making me do what I did. I never doubted it until after we went through with it! Isn't that weird? And for the record, it's really more than OK with me if you don't like people! It's one of my favorite things."

"About me or about anyone?"

"Yes."

"Which 'yes'? Are you sure you weren't just drunk?"

"I've been drunk before."

I considered this. I was fairly drunk myself. "You know what I think, C., is that that was you. That's what I've come to believe. When it feels like there is that weird hand, I mean, I know that *feeling.* That's actually you."

"So that's *me*?" Cate was serving both of us some more cake.

"Yes, that's you. That's you encountering yourself."

"Haha," said Cate. "Maybe I am a nicer person than I think!"

But then I had to be put in a cab and sent home because my level of intoxication had become not just excessive but incapacitating, and, no, Victor and I were not married the next day because, as we all know, at this point I was still married.

■ ■ ■ ■

SUNDAY

■ ■ ■ ■

28

On Sunday, a heavily aftereffected version of myself made an appearance at Paul's memorial. I wore sunglasses for as long as I could afford to and not seem obscenely rude, as well as a fair amount of blush. The occasion was copiously attended, mostly by people I did not know. We were served couscous and dips and slices of raw vegetables and fruit, and writers spoke. The event had been organized by writers, and it was only toward the end that the museum staff had a chance to make their farewells. Nicola di Carboncino spoke for a hot second and then Bonnie got up and asked everyone who had known Paul at the museum to raise their hands so that others in the room would know who we were. She said how glad we all were to have been invited to share in this appreciation of our colleague. She said that he had been a beloved, but in some ways not so very known, person at the museum.

Not that we all hadn't known him, and appreciated him, and felt his support. But that he kept aloof in an attractive way.

It wasn't faint praise, exactly, but it struck a lead note. Perhaps others feared that they themselves would be subject to such a description after death, at which point they would have little opportunity to defend themselves, except via the agony of haunting. Possibly Bonnie was still smarting from the incident of the unfinished exhibition checklist. She was, after all, somewhat petty.

Fred lurked near the door and left early. Ella Voss was also in attendance. In the aftermath I approached her and handed off the flash drive containing Paul's writing.

"It seems like maybe he had another book," was what I said.

Voss examined me. "Thank you," was all she seemed to feel like saying. She was in short order accosted by various literary acquaintances, and so I also made my exit, the better to get home.

Once there, I stripped down to my undergarments, fixed myself a jar of cold water, and climbed into bed. I sighed, feeling at once drained and cozy. I was sitting atop a proverbial heap of information, but at least at this point there did not seem to be anything I needed to react to with any kind of urgency. I was toying with my phone in the way that one does when one has little to do and is enjoying the fact that one is not obliged to reply with a panicked swiftness to incoming info. I slipped into various apps, slipped out again. I began swiping through the week's photos.

I came to the images I had made of the map. This was not the map of Wilhelm Wunsch's 1803 pamphlet but rather the map of American Objects, of the Gaypoole commonplace book, the original siren that had summoned me into this system of affiliation. I began pinching and stretching, as one may do with photos on phones of our era. And as I pinched and stretched and found myself standing before the now greatly enlarged arched doors of the attractive huts of Elysia, I felt, for the first time in a long while, satisfied. I didn't want much, other than to be in this location, playing with forms of the mediation of the past. I ventured into Elysia's wild surrounding garden, its park of incongruous beasts. I zoomed in on the vegetation, on the grimacing faces of big cats. Examining the uppermost canopy of one particularly complex copse, I found an unexpected pattern. I had to zoom out, relocate, zoom back in again. I stared at the phone.

WO IST AM TAG IHR ZEICHEN? WO SPRICHT DAS HERZ, read the words. I zoomed further. The words continued: *SICH AUS? UND WANN IM LEBEN, WANN IST ES FREI, — WAS UNSER WORT NICHT NENNT, WANN WIRD, WAS — TRAUERT, GEBANNT IN DIE NACHT, SEIN WUNSCH IHM?* For he was not just a huckster, nor your average artisan. Wilhelm Wunsch was a micrographer, or microcalligrapher, an artist who draws with tiny letters, and this map, though similar at first blush to the map contained in the pamphlet, was truly nothing like it. It was not just an image but a letter, a longer poem. Minuscule words were hidden within the vegetation of Elysia's woods.

I have some German, so I was not entirely up Google Translate's creek. I read, to the best of my abilities:

Where are signs to be seen in the day?
Where does the heart — speak aloud?
And when in life is it possible — that what
a word cannot name, when will what —
we mourn, what is banished to night, be
granted? —

I noted a possible pun here with the writer's name, Wunsch, meaning "wish" in English. I searched around among the foliage, roots, and branches and found additional language, here beginning with the phrase *AN MEINE GELIEBTE TOCHTER.*

To my dear daughter. Give me your eye if not your hand and believe. Elysia is real and these are the verses of your mother, encircled in the loving bands of my own art. There is no Elysia, but the stories I have told you are true.

I continued to scour the woods but could discover no further script. My eyes ached from the effort, were twin raisins stuck to the bottom of their sockets. So this was the paradise, here in the paradox of Wunsch's vow, that Elysia was "real," and that there was at the same time no Elysia. It reminded me a little of Paul Coral's division of his writings into "FACTS" and "LIES." Funny how categories like these had so little difficulty coexisting, particularly in the vicinity of a museum. Hennicott's and/or Brunhilda's fantastic tale had been pretty good for that, too, with its combination of two incompatible worlds.

I zoomed back out on the map. "Where is that blessed Elysia?" the large-scale poem still read. And now Brunhilda, if she had read her father's minuscule words, had a fairy — or should I say *star* for a mother: Étoile, that uncertain but beautiful figure, with her gauzes and maritime backdrop, with whom Wunsch had once sampled the joys of early American scamming. She sang; he sold bad advice. Then came the separation of mother and child, the disappearance of the mother; though Dad carried on without her. And so Brunhilda's mother had become a piece of magic lore, a spirit or idea. Just what every girl needs, as I myself knew, from not unpainful experience! Perhaps Caro, who might or might not have named me after a counterfeit etching (Étoile = star = Stella), would be willing someday to appear to me as a bobbing blue light and lead me away from whatever annoying picnic I was currently attending, into utopia.

As if on cue, my phone screen lit up and made some encouraging jingles, signaling that Caro herself was FaceTime-ing me.

"Speak of the devil," I muttered, before accepting the call.

An image of Caro's tetchy tortoiseshell, Poutine, appeared, along with Caro's own speckled hand. The hand was stroking the cat's tricolor head as it purred deafeningly into the iPad microphone.

"Hi, Mom!" I yelled.

Poutine screeched and departed.

"Goodness, dear, do you really have to do that to her? You know how she feels about trust!" The iPad was unceremoniously flipped to reveal Caro's face. She held the device out at arm's length, as if it were a mirror.

"I guess not," I said. "Do you mind looking at my ceiling?"

"What's that, dear?"

I put the phone well out of the way of my face. "I was saying, I hope you don't mind looking at my ceiling."

"Oh," said Caro. "I suppose that's a bit odd, but very well. Show me your ceiling!"

"You're already looking at it."

"Of course." Caro paused. "So, dear, I hope you are enjoying the weekend?"

"Yes. I've had just about enough of it."

"Oh, well, I'm sure you're doing many things. I'm sorry I couldn't make it to Paul's. It must have been very well attended."

"It was." I didn't feel I had the energy to go over the memorial with her, play by play.

"Yes. Well, I was calling because I wanted to discuss something with you. I know I mentioned your father's and my impending trip? And I wanted to see how you might feel if, well, I were to possibly take a longer sabbatical."

385

I wasn't sure where this was heading. I squirmed in bed, displacing the phone, which fell to the floor with a little slap.

"Hello?" Caro called, as if she had been abandoned in a well.

"Hi," I said, reaching over for the device. "I'm still here."

"Oh good. Wonderful. So, to make a long story short, I'm sure you would never dream of even thinking about this sort of thing, much less consider it as an actual option, but I want to make you an offer. I want to go away for a little bit. Nowhere exotic really, but I want to travel, and I'm not such a fool that I think that I can, as they say, take my business with me, but understandably I don't want to lose it."

You could have knocked me over with a feather, or maybe a molecule.

"I think you perceive what I am saying. You are, after all, my only child. You'll think it over and let me know what I should tell Charles." This was her assistant of many years.

I believe I nodded. She was offering me her business.

"No need to say anything!" Caro blithely maintained, possibly to cover her own discomfort at my present torpor and/or our technologically awkward situation. Only now did she see fit to announce, somewhat shrilly, "Your father and I are headed to the country this weekend, but don't forget that on Monday he will meet with you!"

"Yes," I managed. "Bye, Mom," I said, raising the phone again to face level, screwing my eyes shut, kissing the air.

■ ■ ■ ■

MONDAY

■ ■ ■ ■

29

It was Monday again. It was chilly and dry and the heavens seemed to be hollowing themselves out in preparation for the coming of spring, making room.

Now I was back in the workweek and on my way uptown early. I was meeting my father for breakfast so that we could go over some legal matters. (He does not do lunch.) I got out of the train and walked over to the Bageltopia he had selected, where he was already present, perusing a paper version of the *Times* and drinking a pulpy glass of juice. He lowered his spectacles and accepted a kiss.

My father is a little shaky. He grew up in a tough neighborhood and so has a tendency to speak quickly and, at times, in coded phrases. He is, in addition, not particularly emotionally reliable. "So what's up with you," he said in a not entirely kindly way, though that was not how he meant it. He is, by the way, seventy-seven.

I told him that I was doing all right. I ordered some coffee. I was debating about whether I should let him know about Whit's unwelcome appearances the week before. My father can become incredibly angry at mind-boggling speed, and I was sure that any emotional comfort I could hope to derive would be overwhelmed from the get-go by the solar death that would constitute my father's affective response. I'm saying, my father is sensitive. The coffee came and I put cream in it.

"Is that something your mother taught you?" My father was referring to my administration of dairy. He meant was I being a sissy.

I am a sissy, and so I said, "It tastes better this way."

"That's disgusting," my father said, though, again, not in a mean way. Or, he did say it in a mean way, but that was not how he meant it. At least, I prefer to believe that this is how he meant it.

"I like it," I told him. For my own benefit, I smiled.

My father had ordered some toast, and this came, and he began scraping various things onto it. He took a few bites, and while he was still chewing, revealing the food in his mouth, he said, "I have some good news for you."

"Really? That's unusual."

He was still dealing with partially chewed bread but went on anyway. "What, that I would have good news?"

"No," I said, "that anyone would have anything nice to tell me."

"Well, it's a good day, then." My father swallowed. He took a slug of juice. "Your soon-to-be former husband has signed."

I was stunned. All I could say was, "He signed the papers?"

"Didn't you hear what I said? Yes, he signed the papers." My father paused a moment to suck his teeth. "He has signed. There you go. *Les jeux sont faits.*" My father tore into the next piece of toast, and now with more bread impeding him he continued, "Though who knows what it's going to take in the courts. Be prepared to wait seven months." He chewed some more. "They can't do it any faster than that for some reason."

My father, may I reiterate, is, like Whit, a lawyer. However, here the similarity between the two of them ends. Whit was born to blue blood, my father to the proverbial collar, etc. And, unlike me, pace Sylvia from Stanford, my father is very good at math.

I was still staring into space.

"Hello?" said my dad.

"Oh," I said, "thank you. I just realized I'd been having a kind of a tough week last week."

"So?"

"So, I don't know."

"So, then, so what?"

I nodded. "Exactly."

Out on the street later I wasn't really sure what to do with myself. I had been champing at the bit, so eager to bypass this particular milestone that now that it was securely in my rearview I felt a little wobbly at the wheel, a little like I might just drive off the road, if that isn't too mixed a metaphor. I mean, I was going to be free. But what did that mean to me? I imagined myself toiling away at the museum, at last learning to correctly appease and satisfy Fred, so that I would not be banished to the running of a satellite CeMArt in one of WANSEE's smart cities; so that both of us could work on and behave as if nothing were wrong. Perhaps I would find another husband, and we would settle down and have children, and I could be confident in the security of my position, no matter how much time I needed to take off for the betterment of my spawn. Fred, who was soon to be anointed Emperor of Arts Administration on Planet Earth, would vouch for my value. I could still live the perfect life. Nothing was preventing me.

But thinking through this perfect life, during the course of which I would eventually switch from Barneys to Bergdorf's, in search of formal heels of a more modest height, the better to accommodate my sometimes ailing knees and back, and during the course of which I would continue to go in quest of ever more illustrious forms of servile prestige, some of which would be slightly out of reach, that is, until they were finally obtained by me, and during the course of which I would feel the minor twinge that accompanies doing what others have already done but which is mollified by the knowledge that you do it well, I felt like perhaps I might prefer to just go ahead and walk into traffic, get it over with. I mean, it was not that I really wanted to die, but that I saw quite clearly that it would be wise to take this option, rather than live through the fate that awaited me, if I let the combined dynamics of the laws of physics, plus history, plus society at large, plus Fred's genius for converting autonomous humans into chess pieces take their course.

I was on my way up the steps of the museum and there was a ding from my bag that I took for more flagpole noise until I realized, upon repetition, that it was coming from my phone. I dug it out, pausing in the shade of the façade. The text was from Caro, of all people, and all it said was, "Don't forget my offer." Because of my exhaustion and residual inebriation, it took me a minute to realize that she was referring to our conversation of the previous night. "Holy shit," I mumbled to myself, feeling fully drunk again, and went indoors.

I greeted Marco, "Yodel!" I saluted him. I stopped by.

"So what's new with you?" he wanted to know.

"Not much," I said. "How are you holding up?"

"It was a pretty pleasant weekend, actually." Marco was giving me the tiniest glance in, the tiniest sliver of view afforded by a door ever so slightly ajar. It looked nice in there.

"Wow," I told him.

"You?"

"Oh," I said, "you know, nothing. But actually I think I figured some things out."

"Is that so?"

I thought about this for a moment. "Well,

when does that ever really happen?" I didn't know what to say next. "Smell you later," I said.

The museum was quiet. It smelled all right. It was a pretty OK place to be.

Clutching my tote and finding it stiff I recalled that due to the massive influx of information reconfiguring my life at break-neck speed over the past seven days, I had not yet had a moment to crack the volume of *The Four Seasons* I'd been lucky enough to obtain, awkwardly but still, from Paul's apartment on Friday eve. I grinned and slid the item out.

I stopped midstride. This was not *The Four Seasons.* It was a slender 1971 catalog of the period rooms in the American Wing including, the title told me, "Special Emphasis on the Decorative Arts." I may have whimpered. The proof I'd believed I had in hand of Alice's vanished Elysia Club bequest was now unceremoniously lost again. In my defense, this 1971 thing was the exact same stupid size as the bound *Four Seasons* back issues, but, admittedly, I should have paid more attention to what I was carrying off with me, post Ella.

I frowned, examined the book. So this was what Paul had been looking at. How charming of him to review one of the department's more mediocre publications. Examining the spine and edges I noted a few dog-ears. At the base of the grand interior stair, I flipped to the first marked page. "Room 734: Virginia Salon, circa 1810–1840, with Games Table." I gulped. It was the number that did it, then the word "Games."

I was sprinting into the back of the museum like a freak. I saw who Paul was, what he had been doing over time. He had been, in a sense, working against the museum from within. And he had been hiding his works in plain sight.

I almost already knew what I would see. Or, as I had been gawking at these objects for several years without knowing what they were, I was aware of exactly what I was about to look at. In one of the hands of cards that sat as if abandoned by an invisible worthy on the green felt of the combination card and billiard table in room 734, there were not one but two queens of spades, and the face of one of these queens, who held a diminutive mallet made from cut glass in one fist and a yellow quill in the other, was the long-nosed face of Ella Voss; and in room 737, the Marble Parlor, so called for its trompe l'oeil limnings of a veiny approximation of this stone, in a corner of the elaborate if roughly executed mural that depicted a distant mountain pass, there hiked a drooping man who bore a ruddy fan of polished coral; and in room 740, the Pennsylvania Dutch nursery, the single false window with a view out onto painted conifers was hung with a mirrored prism in the shape of a daisy, which cast a daisy-shaped net of light over the finely joined cradle, an offering to the fictional Lorelei.

As I say, I did not need to gaze long. I had already seen all this. I already knew where and what each thing was. I had only to adjust my thinking regarding the provenance of these objects. But what I had not seen, I realized, was what Paul had secreted into room 743, which, if I am being candid, is perhaps my favorite out of all the period sector, but which, because of its remoteness, down a small stair at the northeastern edge of the wing, I had not visited in some months. This room was a narrow clerk's chamber, taken from a Wall Street turret long ago condemned. It was a favorite with children, who liked to run squealing into the slender, curved space, which was too small for many adults. As far as I could remember, the office contained nothing more than a folding desk built into the wall and a stool on a metal arm that swung out to permit the factotum a seat. And a lamp with a smutty glass chimney, for ambience, I presumed. My own minor stature made entering the spot a cinch, perhaps part of the reason for my liking of it. I descended the little stair.

At first, nothing seemed to have been altered. Deflated, I dropped onto the hard clerk's stool, an item the museum had long ago given up defending from contemporary buttocks. I gazed at the barren desk and dirty lamp, which, unlike the stool, were encased in a cube of Plexi. Here something pale to the right of the desk caught my eye: A metal pin held in place, to the desk's outer edge, a scrap of paper. I craned my head around and all but jammed my nose into the protective barrier. Foggily I could perceive that the scrap of paper was an image seemingly cut from some period print publication, a political cartoon, if I wasn't mistaken, probably of very early republican vintage. I got off the stool and squatted, pressing myself against the wall the better to look. There were two figures and a caption. Squinting, I made out the words: *Importing thee Curious LLASKA TUSKER.* I duly noted the parallel with my erstwhile article on "The Curious Zebra," which perhaps Paul had read, after all. "Jiminy

400

Cricket," I muttered, because maybe it was nonsense and maybe I just couldn't see. I breathed on the Plexi and wiped with my cuff. A minor shift toward clarity transpired. The two entities depicted in the cartoon were, I could now report, to the left, a diminutive human figure prancing along, gazing up to her left. This figure wore a slipper-shaped hat to which was affixed a star-shaped decoration. The hat wearer also held in her left hand a chain, and this chain was affixed to a collar at the neck of the figure on the right. And what a figure it was. It gazed boldly out of the print with a human face, a face nearly identical to the face of the woman who led it, containing large, almond-shaped eyes and a serene smile. It was roughly four times the height of the prancing hat wearer and stood on three pairs of legs, each of which appeared to have been derived from a different mammal, perhaps a goat, lion, and elk, though not necessarily in that order. Teats descended from the thing's impressive undercarriage and continued, plumply, in vaguely sexy pairs, up its chest all the way to its neck, indicating that it was capable of supporting quite a supply of younger versions of itself. The rest of the animal was cloaked in neatly organized feathers, like many rounded flags or leaves, and its shapely catlike body terminated in a tufted leopard's tail. Giant diaphanous moth wings patterned with illusory eyes sprouted at its shoulders; it had the soft, open ears of a deer, small tusks in its cheeks. Branching antlers hung with flowering garlands filled the top of the picture.

I stood, stiffly. "LLASKA TUSKER": I contemplated the familiar letters colluding in the strange creature's name. I recalled what I had told Cate about the invisible hand. The animal was similar. It was also mine, if I was its, if I were prepared to recognize that I was in no small part feral, i.e., *alive.*

I was letting myself into my own office now, arranging things and myself there. I was filled with an unusual glee even as I prepared for a mild day of ministering to everything I had neglected during the past week's adventures, which was really a lot.

What my mother does not realize, I reflected as I set the office to order, is that if I do what she proposes, and really I think I might, I will take her business and I will turn it into something else. Meaning possibly an actual gallery. Perhaps, in a final slight, she believes that I will not be *able* to transform it, and it is, paradoxically, to my weakness that she entrusts her life's work. But my mother does not know me. Her understanding of me takes a contradictory form. She both admits and ignores my capacity, and I mainly understand her largesse as an attempt to head off revenge. Because at some level my mother knows that I must be revenged on her if ever I am to become an adult, and she would rather that I take my revenge on her pseudonymous print dealership than on her pseudonymous self. She is a person who has a talent for being in more than one place at once, you see, and I imagine that this will still be true of her even after she is dead.

My mother does not entirely want to know me. In some ways this is a gift.

I was just about to turn on my computer when there came a sudden knock. I flinched. I continued to follow through with the initial gesture and hit the power button before I said, "Yes?"

But I already knew. I turned.

"Hello," said Fred. He was in the doorway, holding a large envelope.

"Good morning," I told him. "That was a nice service." I was referring to Sunday.

"Yes. It was." Fred paused. "May I come in?"

I lied. "I don't see why not."

Fred closed the door. He pulled the antique chair up to the side of my desk and sat down, setting the envelope between us. He smiled.

An unforeseen thought popped into my skull. *Paul wasn't the suspicious one.* I mean, in spite of his elaborate less-than-readymades. Paul had never been the suspicious one! All along *I* had been the one who was suspicious, who had felt there was something unsound here or there. Paul may have worked against the museum, but he had probably liked that there was something here to work against, to counterfeit, to de-authenticate; it was even necessary to him. My own feelings were a bit different. I wasn't sure how I should look at Fred right now, so I just looked at him like myself.

Fred eyed me, letting me know, even in the silence, that I should be impressed by the thing he had. He seemed fixated on his envelope and was eager for me to open it.

"Oh, I should open this?" I asked, mostly to be annoying.

"Yes. That would be great." Fred put his hands on top of his head, like he was twelve.

Gingerly, I unclasped the envelope. There was a single piece of paper inside. It was old, I could tell already. I drew it very carefully out in order to prevent tears or crumbling. In fact, part of it had already been torn away in the upper left-hand corner, as if a staple had been carelessly removed.

I knew quickly what it was and could feel Fred watching my face for new detail like he was going over it with his hands.

"Wow," I said.

"Pretty amazing, right?"

Something occurred to me and I said it before really having a chance to think it through. "I can't believe how many of these are in your show."

Fred was certainly wearing some sort of look of appreciation, although I was not observing his face. "I know, right? Paul was doing some very interesting research, *very* interesting, but he did not quite perceive its use."

Fred had Mabel Styke's letter, the document I had sought and been unable to find in the museum's archive. It included a list of all the paintings donated anonymously to the Central Museum of Art by Styke's employer, Alice Gaypoole Wynne, in August 1930. Many of these were portraits related to the Wunsch family, keys to the deep matrilineal history of the Wynnes. Others were classics of American modernism.

"So what happened to the later stuff? A

lot of that's privately owned now, no?" I asked. There was a Kuniyoshi, for example, and a few very early Stettheimers, all paintings, it now occurred to me, that were currently hanging in the limner show.

"Anything of any value was quietly deaccessioned after the war. The board felt anything too obviously associated with Alice Gaypoole Wynne was kryptonite. It all reeked of bohemia and loose morals, not to mention mediocre realism. Very scene-y stuff. Camp, kind of. Anyway, Alice was a total scandal because of what the tabloids said."

"And the older things?"

"I think the curator in charge, Jonah Durr Weiss, of whom you may have heard, had an affection for this material, if not for Mabel Styke, and he sort of half hid it in storage, whatever couldn't have sold at that time anyway. I came upon it by chance." Fred's voice grew warm, and he had to clear his throat. "Well, or almost by chance."

"You came upon it or Paul came upon it?"

Fred presented himself as completely unruffled. "Ha! It's a good question. I'm sure Paul knew about this for years! Paul kind of knew everything about everything, though of course, Stella, *you've* lately been becoming more and more aware of that."

He thought that he was threatening me.

I remained impassive. "Paul had a very impressive understanding of this collection," was what I said.

"And so," Fred told me, "do you, Stella. More and more, every day as things improve between us, I'm so glad that we can work together and admire one another's work. Which I do, so very much." He let out a deep breath. "And, as I imagine you also understand, my recovery of these paintings, that were within the collection but hidden, as it were, in plain sight all along, has certain additional interesting repercussions, because of the original donor."

He indicated the list in my hand.

"I've been having some incredibly rewarding conversations with Electra Wynne, who, as you know, is Alice Gaypoole Wynne's grandniece. She has been very gratified to learn more about this forgotten and truly fantastic piece of the history of her family, and as a way of supporting the careful work that is being done in our department, she would like to make it possible for us to offer a new endowed senior position to a member of staff who, in her words, best embodies the values of her grandaunt, and, Stella, I really can't think of anyone who better expresses those qualities than you."

Fred was beaming at me.

I stared down at the yellow typed page in my hands. For some reason, I really liked Mabel Styke's closing salutation, here deployed again: "Your friend." I liked how plain it was. I felt I knew what she meant by it.

It also occurred to me that I could now jump to my feet and tear this page up or even suddenly begin eating it, thus foiling Fred's plan, depriving him of proof. But if I knew Fred, he'd already photographed and scanned this thing a million times before sharing it with me. And even if he hadn't, and even if there were no other proof extant on this planet that those paintings hanging in his show were correctly labeled as he had labeled them, I could guarantee you that Fred was still going to get his way.

Carefully, I slid the letter back into its envelope. "We wouldn't want to damage that!" I said.

I started looking around my desk for a pen, because I had just remembered that Bonnie had said there were some forms related to insurance that I needed to print out and sign, and today was the deadline. I switched my printer on to let it warm up.

Fred was still sitting there. I turned to him. He didn't look angry or even frustrated

408

with me, rather, or by contrast, he appeared continuously amused. "What are you doing over there?" he said. I hope I may be allowed to observe that his suggestion of any significant distance between us was, at this point, farcical.

"Sorry," I said. "Just a few little chores!"

"Quite all right," he told me, taking the envelope back. In this process, I should mention, whether by chance or by design, his right index finger brushed gently against the side of my bare arm. It was electric. All I could think of was us holding each other.

Fred just kept sitting there, languidly tapping his long fingers against the surface of my desk.

I could feel him smiling. He said, "So I bet you might like a moment to take in this development. It's quite understandable. It's really a lot to consider, what with last week's tragic news, and I'm sure your feelings are all *over* the map. Makes sense to me." Fred stood. "So you'll think about it? And let me know when you're ready? This isn't something we'd announce for another few weeks, of course."

"Of course," I said.

"Great. Then I'll see you later on at the meeting?" he told me, preparing to slip out of my office before I had time to supply an ambiguous retort.

It had, anyway, by this moment become clear, as in crystalline, that I would not be staying, that I would not be accepting this wonderful new Wynne-afforded post, nor would I be contributing to the fulfillment of WANSEE's vision of a world of tens of tiny CeMArts, each enlivening its own exclusionary city. I had learned that I preferred the wilds, or as close as I could get to them, which might be by overhauling Basset's. And what I said, as Fred Lu left, was, "I will see you there," by which I meant, "I will see you *only* there," by which I meant, "My time is now limited." And then, strangest of things that are strange, I believe Frederick Lu heard my meaning. He heard something, I don't know what exactly, but he heard me saying "No," and to him, with the result that he became momentarily discombobulated, bereft of coordination and sense, and actually he fell pretty hard, even shrieking softly, as he collided with the hallway's ecru carpeting.

I sat in my chair, paging through insurance documents.

"I'm OK, I'm OK," Fred was insisting, somewhere.

In the event of, began the line I was reading.

APPENDIX: TIMELINE

1479–1458 B.C.: Reign of Hatshepsut, fifth pharaoh of the eighteenth dynasty of Egypt

A.D. 37: Emperor Caligula abruptly becomes insane after nearly dying of an unknown illness in the eighth month of his reign

1568: Art historian Giorgio Vasari describes Titian's 1509 *A Man with a Quilted Sleeve,* in his *Lives of the Most Excellent Painters, Sculptors, and Architects,* incorrectly maintaining that it is a portrait of the poet Ludovico Ariosto

1726: Publication of *Travels into Several Remote Nations of the World. In Four Parts. By Lemuel Gulliver, First a Surgeon, and then a Captain of Several Ships,* a.k.a. *Gulliver's Travels* by Jonathan Swift

1754: Columbia University founded

1782: Clemente Susini, renowned for sensual wax models depicting dissected fe-

411

male corpses, becomes chief modeler at the Florentine Natural History Museum

1792: Publication of Mary Wollstonecraft's *A Vindication of the Rights of Women*

1797: Étienne-Gaspard "Robertson" Robert, Belgian inventor, presents the first *fantasmagorie* at the Pavillon de l'Echiquier in postrevolutionary Paris

1799: New York State act freeing future children of slaves, and all slaves in 1827

1815–1850: Greek Revival in arts and architecture in the United States

1825: Settlement of Seneca Village, first Manhattan community of African American property owners, between West 82nd and West 89th Streets

1832: Amantine-Lucile-Aurore Dupin adopts the pen name "George Sand"

1836: Brunhilda Wunsch Gaypoole founds the Society of Refuge in Lower Manhattan

1837: Utopian philosopher and sometime correspondence clerk François Marie Charles Fourier purportedly coins the term *feminism*

1840–1860: Rococo revival in the United States

1841: Brook Farm Institute of Agriculture and Education founded

1843: Private publication of G. G. Hennicott's utopian novel *Lorelei of Millbury, or Impossible Views of the World, a Romance*

1847: Brook Farm closes

1852: Honoré Daumier lampoons the spectral "turning tables" of bourgeois sitting rooms

1857: Seneca Village torn down for the construction of Central Park

1860: Limner and photographer Erastus Salisbury Field produces *Betsey Dole Hubbard,* an oil painting made over an enlarged photographic print

1864: The Canal Company (later, WANSEE) awarded £3,800,000 by Napoleon III, for losses incurred through demands made by Isma'il Pasha, Wāli of Egypt and Sudan

1869: "Spirit photographer" William H. Mumler brought to trial for fraud

1875: Financial crisis forces Isma'il Pasha to sell all his shares in the Egyptian canal to the British government for £3,976,582

1892: George Eastman founds the Eastman Kodak Company

1895: Alice Marguerite Gaypoole, later Wynne, born

1907: Creation of the Department of American Objects at the Central Museum of Art

1917: *Fountain* by R. Mutt displayed at

Alfred Stieglitz's 291 Gallery
1918: Founding of the Elysia Club
1924: President Coolidge signs the Johnson-Reed Act, limiting annual immigration from any country to 2 percent of persons from that country living in the United States in 1890

Grand opening of the American period rooms section at the Central Museum of Art
1927: Poet John Ashbery born in Rochester, NY
1930: Dissolution of the Elysia Club

Artist Jasper Johns born in Augusta, GA
1932: George Eastman, aged seventy-seven, commits suicide, leaving behind a note that reads, "To my friends. My work is done. Why wait? G.E."
1938: British engineer Guy Stewart Callendar presents evidence that CO_2 levels in the earth's atmosphere have been rising for the preceding fifty years
1953: Helen Cooke receives patent for sock monkey dolls
1955: Death of Alice Marguerite Gaypoole Wynne at Wilmett Home, Hoboken, NJ
1957: WANSEE loses control of water hold-

ings in the Middle East due to armed conflict

1958: Paul Coral born in Rochester, NY

1963: Yukio Mishima publishes 午後の曳航 (literally, "Towing of the Afternoon"), translated in 1965 as *The Sailor Who Fell from Grace with the Sea*

1964: Mary Lynch (later, Carolyn Wedgewood Basset) declines dinner with Art Garfunkel

1968: Eleven-year-old Bonnie Mangold loses her left hand in a hunting accident in Granite County, MT

Xerox establishes its headquarters at Xerox Square in downtown Rochester, NY

1969: Calvin Klein appears on the cover of *Vogue*

1973–1974: Ethernet developed at Xerox PARC

1979: Publication of *Will to Beauty: The Untold Story of Alice Marguerite Gaypoole Wynne* by Rose Barthes

1981: Stella Krakus born in New York City

1984: *The Telephone,* by Paul Coral, published by Oberlin Press

1996: Internet Archive founded

1997: Frederick J. Lu places second in the U.S. National Target Championship for

WANSEE merges with Lyonnaise des Eaux, a leading French water company

2007: Electra Wynne places in Individual Freestyle Para Dressage at the FEI World Equestrian Games

2008: Jenna Lyons becomes creative director of J.Crew

2009: WANSEE begins negotiations with Clark County, NV, for purchase of its aquifer

2010: Governor David Paterson signs no-fault divorce into law in New York State

2012: Kodak files for Chapter 11 bankruptcy

Stella Krakus hired by the Central Museum of Art

2013: *Philip Crystal,* by Ella Voss, published

2014: Poet Paul Coral dies

"Land of the Limner" opens to rave reviews at the Central Museum of Art

Van Russel, longtime waiter at the beloved Orsay Restaurant in Manhattan, abruptly quits his job and moves to Quito, Ecuador, to pursue his writing

A NOTE

This book is for my friends, and that term is meant in an expansive sense. Nevertheless, there are certain individuals whose greatness and gentleness have made my life a better one and encouraged me to tell stories instead of jumping off a cliff.[1]

In particular, I would like to thank Claire Lehmann, an initial reader whose interest and delight let me know I should keep going. Megan Ewing has always been there; I hope that someday her daughter Elka may find her way to this implausible novel. I would also like to thank Matthew Shen Goodman for his kindness.

To beloved friends in and around *Triple Canopy:* Thank you for working with me. An early version of this novel was completed just as I became an editor in 2011 — and

1 As Sarah Resnick once told me, the things that happen in operas don't have to happen in real life.

417

your talents helped me to transform it, not to mention myself, for the (far) better.

To Cynthia Cannell, thank you for graciously teaming up with me. Every exchange we share is enlightening and heartening. And to Ed Park, an extraordinary writer and reader I feel lucky to have met: This book found its reluctant, neurotic heart via your ingenious attention. Indeed, there could have been no conversion of these views into a legible, shelf-size object without everyone at Penguin Press. To Ann Godoff, Scott Moyers, Juliana Kiyan, Danielle Gauthier, Matthew Boyd, and the fantastic Annie Badman: Thank you for hearing Stella out. She and I are deeply in your debt(s).

Lastly and most of all, I want to thank my mother, who took me to the museum.

ABOUT THE AUTHOR

Lucy Ives is the author of several books of poetry and short prose, including *The Hermit* and the novella *nineties.* Her writing has appeared in *Artforum, Lapham's Quarterly,* and at newyorker.com. For five years she was an editor with the online magazine Triple Canopy. A graduate of Harvard and the Iowa Writers' Workshop, she holds a Ph.D. in comparative literature from New York University. She teaches at the Pratt Institute and is currently editing a collection of writings by the artist Madeline Gins.